Jillian Kent's *Mystery of the Hea*

courage, romance, and faith. I w
when the heroine washes up on
half-drowned, only to be taken
Eden. This is a story to be savored and shared.

—Serena B. Miller
Author of *The Measure of Katie Calloway*,
2012 RITA award for best inspirational romance

Jillian Kent writes a sweeping romantic intrigue, brilliant with well-drawn characters and meticulous research of Regency England.

—Linda Windsor
Author of The Brides of Alba historical series:
Healer, *Thief*, and *Rebel*

Mystery of the Heart is a deliciously credible and moving account of a nineteenth-century woman pursuing her dream to become a doctor. From the elegant world of English royalty to the frightening venues of an insane asylum, author Jillian Kent presents a meticulously researched novel filled with suspense, mystery, and romance. I couldn't put this one down!

—Sue Harrison
Author of international best seller
Mother Earth Father Sky

A winning escape for the romantic imagination, *Mystery of the Heart* will keep readers on the edge of their seats! A sigh-worthy hero and an intelligent heroine make this Regency novel a pure pleasure for fans of the genre as well as anyone seeking a love story that's brightened by a healthy dose of adventure.

Fairer Than Morn

Jillian Kent

MYSTERY of the HEART

REALMS

Most Charisma House Book Group products are available at special quantity discounts for bulk purchase for sales promotions, premiums, fund-raising, and educational needs. For details, write Charisma House Book Group, 600 Rinehart Road, Lake Mary, Florida 32746, or telephone (407) 333-0600.

Mystery of the Heart by Jillian Kent
Published by Realms
Charisma Media/Charisma House Book Group
600 Rinehart Road
Lake Mary, Florida 32746
www.charismahouse.com

Unless otherwise noted, all Scripture quotations are from the King James Version of the Bible.

The characters portrayed in this book are fictitious unless they are historical figures explicitly named. Otherwise, any resemblance to actual people, whether living or dead, is coincidental.

AUTHOR NOTE: Bethlem Royal Hospital has a long and fascinating history. It is the oldest psychiatric hospital in the world. Today it functions as a modern psychiatric facility. It's been infamously known as Bedlam throughout history to denote chaos, confusion, and disorder. Bethlem in its early history was known for the cruel treatment of its patients at a time when little was known about what caused mental illness and how those patients should be treated.

Cover design by Rachel Lopez
Design Director: Bill Johnson

Visit the author's website at www.jilliankent.com.

Library of Congress Cataloging-in-Publication Data
Kent, Jillian.
Mystery of the heart / Jillian Kent. -- 1st ed.
p. cm.
ISBN 978-1-62136-015-5 (trade paper) -- ISBN 978-1-62136-016-2 (e-book)
1. Aristocracy (Social class)--England--19th century--Fiction. 2. Christian fiction. 3. Regency fiction. I. Title.
PS3611.E6737M97 2013
813'.6--dc23
2012034659

The opening of the wedding ceremony of Mercy and Vincent is taken from "The Form of Solemnization of Matrimony," in the *Anglican Book of Common Prayer.*

First edition

13 14 15 16 17 — 987654321
Printed in the United States of America

This novel is dedicated to Youth With A Mission and YWAMers everywhere, past, present, and future. And to my YWAM daughter Meghan Nutter, who chose the road less traveled and discovered her future.

"Now faith is the substance of things hoped for, the evidence of things not seen" (Hebrews 11:1).

Chapter 1

Appearances are often deceiving.
—Aesop

Northumberland, England, Spring 1819

Mercy Grayson gulped for air as another cold wave battered her, pulled her under, and scraped her along the coast floor. She propelled her way to the surface, kicking and climbing through the water. *God, help me get to shore. I have nothing left.*

Sand scraped through her fingers, and then she tumbled with another wave away from it. Again and again she stroked through the water, hoping to reach solid ground.

She gasped for air, silently prayed for courage, and choked as her mouth and throat filled with saltwater. The brightness of the sun inspired hope, and she pushed on, unwilling to let the sea win.

Sand from the coast floor squished between her toes. Her knees buckled when she tried to stand, and she splashed face-first back into the water. Finally she gained a wobbly stance and forced herself to put one foot in front of the other.

She'd made it. Looking heavenward, she simply whispered, "Thank You." Once onto the beach she fell to her knees. Tears stung her eyes as she vomited seawater. Coughing and sputtering, she dragged herself farther onto the sand.

Weary to the bone, she didn't care if anyone found her wearing trousers instead of a gown. She closed her eyes and vomited again. Vaguely it occurred to her that the trousers, her physician's attire, had saved her life, along with the prayers God had seen fit to answer. Lying limp, she had only enough energy to kiss the wet sand in gratitude before falling into an exhausted sleep.

An annoying brush of twigs drummed against her check.

Mercy opened her eyes to stare through several spindly branches.

She bolted upright when a crab pinched her cheek and then scuttled backward as if daring her to give chase and play. With the sound of her heart pounding in her ears, Mercy watched the creature dance diagonally away from her, but when she moved, the crab came closer. Mercy flicked some grains of sand. "Away with you, or I'll have you for dinner."

The crab seemed to consider her comment and then continued at a slower pace as if disappointed. Mercy drew in a ragged breath and focused on the now calm ocean that mere hours ago had nearly taken her life.

"Interesting little devils, aren't they?"

Mercy twisted around at the sound of a deep masculine voice tinged with humor. A large shadow fell across her, and she squinted against the bright sunshine as she tilted her face upward. His nearness caused her to push away.

"Wh–who are you?" Her voice trembled, much to her annoyance. Her arms supported her from behind, and her hands and fingers splayed across the sand. The breeze on her damp clothes caused a shiver to race up her spine.

"I'm not going to hurt you, if that's what you're thinking. You're safe enough, for now, but you must be half frozen if you were in the water for any length of time." He took off his coat and dropped it around her shoulders.

"Thank you. Where am I?" She took her eyes off him only long enough to glance around, her gaze shifting beyond him to the desolate sea. "Where did you come from? I see no ship. Are you a pirate?"

He grinned. "Do I look like a pirate?" At that moment a breeze lifted off the ocean, whipping a strand of dark blond hair across his tanned face. She cocked her head to the side. He had at least two days' worth of stubble and indeed sported that scraggy look of a pirate no matter what he said.

"All you need is an eye patch."

The man's grin widened. He took a step forward, and she drew farther back, fearful of his intentions. He loomed over her. His shirt blew open nearly to his waist. Grateful for the heat of the sun that scorched the beach, she hoped he hadn't seen her blush. She'd thought that kind of reaction well in control now after her work of the last six months.

"What do you want?" Thoughts of danger raced in her mind.

His gaze traveled the length of her, and she remembered her male garments. She could not imagine what he must be thinking, or then again maybe she could. Finally his look returned to her face. "I hate to disappoint, but I'm not a pirate. And the ship I'm on is in a nearby cove in hopes of evading real pirates." He sat down next to her. "I'm Lord Eden at your service. And whom do I have the pleasure of—?"

"You have the pleasure of nothing. Am I in Scotland or England?"

He blinked. "England, of course."

He leaned near and picked a piece of seaweed from her hair, and as his thumb brushed her cheek, a jolt of fear passed through her. "Don't."

He ignored her and picked more seaweed from her hair.

She glared at him. "I see you are incapable of following directions."

"Not incapable, just discriminating. Do you mind me asking how an English beauty ended up on this beach with no one to defend her? And wearing pants and a waistcoat?" He arched an inquisitive brow.

She considered recent events.

"I have no intention of telling you anything." She placed both palms on her forehead and leaned her elbows on her knees. "Did you tell me where we are?"

"The coast of Northumberland."

"I'm surprised it's this warm." She stood and brushed the grit from her trousers.

"I'm surprised you didn't freeze to death in the water. You're very fortunate."

She nodded. "May I go with you? I need to get to Yorkshire."

"I'm thinking the men won't take kindly to your boarding the ship, especially the captain, who believes in vodun and is more likely to sacrifice you than provide transportation."

"What's vodun?"

"A woman in pants.

"I was hoping for a quick swim to wash off, but I guess that will have to wait." He got up and walked in the direction of where he'd said the ship was anchored in the cove.

"Wait." The thought of relying on this man irritated her no end, but after surveying the area, she chose what she hoped was the wisest of decisions. "You will take me with you... won't you?"

"We'll soon find out." He nodded toward the cove and kept walking.

Seagulls walked the beach, and in the distance puffins dove into the ocean and returned to the sky with their catch. She watched Lord Eden striding away from her in black breeches, boots, and a white linen shirt hanging loose.

She took a deep breath and swallowed back panic, running to catch up with him. "Wait." He didn't stop.

"Please, wait." She trotted along beside him. "How do I know you can be trusted?"

He stopped and turned to look at her, quirking a brow. "You don't know if you can trust me or not, but I guarantee you that you can't trust them." He pointed down into the cove.

She sucked in a breath. Her heart hammered in her chest at the sight of nearly a dozen ebony-skinned men performing some kind of pagan dance with masks and movements that looked uncivilized indeed. Several small boats decorated the shore, and farther out she saw the ship.

"Is there no other way?"

"What's in Yorkshire?"

"Home."

"You can walk until you find a village. Perhaps someone will take pity on you and offer you a ride."

"But—"

"I'm going to London." He pointed out to the sea just beyond the cove. "On that ship. So make your decision now, for soon they will see you and then there will be no turning back."

"Surely you wouldn't leave me here without an escort?"

"I'm not in a position to take you anywhere. But if you wish to come with me, I'll do my best to keep you from harm."

"Your best? That is not very honorable for an Englishman. Is your best going to be good enough? Are you quite certain you are English?"

He sighed and pulled a knife from his boot.

She took several steps back. "What do you intend?"

"Are you coming with me or not? I'm offering you

transportation to London and only to London. The accommodations will be rough, and you will need to remain in my cabin at all times. Is that understood?"

"That depends on what you plan to do with that knife." She took several more steps away from him. She'd never get far if he really wanted to do harm.

"I'm going to disguise you as a lad. You're already dressed for the part. If you're willing, I have to cut your hair."

"My hair?" Her hands immediately felt for the long strands of hair that had come loose in the water. "No. You will not cut my hair."

"Then how do you propose to look like a lad? Did you not get a good look at the men I travel with?"

"There must be another way. Perhaps I could tie it up." But even as she said it, she knew it wouldn't work. Not in these circumstances. She had no hat to tuck her hair into and no other means to disguise her femininity.

She squeezed her eyes shut. *Lord, I do not think this wise, but running off on my own could be just as risky.* She opened her eyes. "All right. Cut it."

He drew near and grabbed a handful of her thick, dark hair. "This may hurt, for although the knife is sharp, it's sure to tug at your scalp. It will have to be short. Are you ready?"

"Do it."

"Stand very still." He sawed away at her hair. "I am sorry. You have the most beautiful hair." He continued his assault.

She bit her lip to keep from crying out. When she thought of all she'd endured in the past months, she considered crying over the loss of her hair absurd, but she still had to fight back insistent tears.

Finally he stopped. The ground was covered with what had once been her crowning glory. Gingerly she put a hand to her head. Her cropped hair felt shorter than his looked, which fell unfashionably below his ears and yet was not long enough to be pulled back in a queue.

Before she could say anything, he stuck the knife back in his boot. "There now. Pull your shirt out of your pants and cover your backside."

"Why?"

"Because it's obviously female, and if you are going to be my new—" He cleared his throat. "—valet, you must look like a man, albeit a young man, even a boy."

Her eyes grew round. "Your what?"

"Well, it's not like I'm asking you to be my mistress. I'm trying to help you without knowing the details of your family or your position. Do you want to tell me who you are now?"

She lifted her chin. "I don't believe so."

He looked at her and frowned. "Be clear that when we get to the ship that you don't open your mouth to speak. Your lips are far too tempting even without saying a word and—" He picked up a glob of mud and smeared it onto her cheeks and chin and over her lips.

"What are you doing?" That was a mistake. Now she had mud in her mouth as well. She tried to spit the mud off her lips and out of her mouth. "This is the most unladylike of situations."

"I'm making you presentable to a shipload of men who will not hesitate to take advantage of a woman. I suggest you follow my lead and my orders once we enter the cove and again onboard."

He started down the rocky trail.

Gritting her teeth, she followed him.

As they grew closer to the sailors, she realized they were naked from the waist up. The dancing and celebrating—if that's what it was—stopped the moment they saw her behind Eden.

A tall, lean black man wearing a necklace of ivory approached them. "Who this?"

"I found him, Fox."

"Share him." The man rubbed a hand through Mercy's newly cropped hair, grabbed a handful, and pulled her head back to study her face.

Eden smacked the man's hand away. "Not bloody likely. I'm taking him to the ship."

"Get in that boat, boy," Eden directed her. "Now!" he growled.

She scrambled into the small boat, and when she looked out over the ocean, she saw the ship's masts quivering in the wind. Mercy swallowed hard. She'd just been thrown overboard before daybreak from one ship, and now she was about to board another. When she looked back, the men onshore were already racing to get in the other boats.

"Are you all right?"

Mercy nodded.

"Take one oar and I'll take the other. Make it look good as we near the ship so you don't look as inexperienced as you are. The others are following to see what the captain does." He pushed the boat into the water and jumped in, picking up an oar and cutting through the waves with skilled strokes.

As they approached the ship, Mercy wondered if she shouldn't have just refused Lord Eden's hospitality, if one could call having her hair chopped off hospitality. She did her best to copy his movements with the oar and tried to appear as though she knew what she was doing.

"Don't say a word." Lord Eden pushed her ahead of him to the ladder she had to scale to gain access to the deck.

Mercy didn't dare cause trouble. She'd never heard of Lord Eden or vodun, but she desperately wanted to get home—not to London, for a number of reasons she didn't care to think about yet, but to York. She was grateful that she wore trousers since he climbed up behind her. When she reached the top and peered over the edge, her blood seemed to still in her veins, but her feet kept moving. She slid over the rail and fell to her knees on the deck looking up into the eyes of a half-naked white man squinting hard at her through bloodshot eyes. His crew surrounded him to see what would happen.

"What'd ya catch, Lord Eden?" Skinner asked. He grabbed her chin in his massive hand and studied her face. "Look me in the eye, boy."

Mercy raised her mud-caked lashes to his scrutinizing assessment and nearly choked with fear. She thought he must have seen through her disguise, but she prayed God would show him only courage reflected in her eyes. She gulped and waited for what would happen next.

Lord Eden grabbed her by the back of the shirt and away from Skinner. "He'll clean my cabin and serve as my personal valet. It's been a long journey."

"I imagine your cabin needs cleaning, Lord Eden." The man snickered, and the deckhands roared with laughter when he said something in a language she'd never heard.

Eden kept his hand firmly on her neck and guided her into the depths of the ship to his cabin. He opened the door into a room that held a narrow bed, a table and chair, and two trunks.

"This will be very close quarters. I'll leave you alone as much as possible."

Mercy looked at the tangled bed sheets. "Where will you sleep?" She looked up at him, and his eyes danced.

"With you, of course. I can't have Skinner presuming you have time on your hands. He can think whatever he wants, but I guarantee you his thoughts are from the devil."

She shivered.

"You're cold." He grabbed the dark wool blanket from his bunk. "I suggest you get out of your wet clothes and wrap yourself in this." He tossed the blanket to her.

She gaped at him as she caught it. Could he really be that dimwitted? "And what would I wear?"

"Your clothing after it dries." He grinned. "Lock the door behind me. I've got a key." He left and pulled the door shut.

"But—" Mercy let out a long, low sigh of irritation, locked the door, put her back against it, and sank to the floor of the cabin. The effects of her near drowning, as well as all that had led to her being aboard the other ship and then tossed overboard, crowded in on her. Lord Eden, Captain Skinner, and his ship of unusual sailors had opened a floodgate of panic and despair. She wanted her family, needed them more than ever.

She pulled his coat tight and realized if she didn't get out of her clothes soon, she was likely to get sick. Exhaustion taunted her, and she closed her eyes, wanting everything that had happened to go away. Common sense and the need for comfort drove her to her feet, and she shed her damp clothing. The salty wetness of the sea and… She breathed in the scent of the blanket while she wrapped herself in warmth. Cinnamon, clove, and the natural scent of…him.

She eyed the two trunks, looked toward the door, and wondered when Lord Eden might return. Guilt flashed through her. Need won out.

The aroma of sandalwood lifted with the lid of the first trunk. She gently searched through the first layer to find something to wear while she slept. Perhaps a shirt of Lord Eden's would do. She picked up several pairs of trousers, all too big for her to consider. A black silk shirt caught her eye. She pulled it from the trunk, and a box—light in color, oak, no, olive wood—fell to the floor, making so much noise that she glanced to the door, fully expecting Lord Eden to fill the doorway with a dark frown upon his face.

Mercy held her breath in fear of being caught snooping. When nothing happened, she let out the pent-up air. She was only looking for something to cover her under these extraordinary circumstances. She refused to sleep nude under a blanket with this man in close proximity. It was beyond the pale. She didn't ever sleep nude. No self-respecting English woman would dare to be so brazen.

Mercy picked up the box decorated with gold designs and symbols. It was heavier than it appeared. And then she reprimanded herself, thinking this was something her sister, Victoria—whom the family affectionately referred to as Snoop—would do, but not her. She respected others' privacy, and she expected others to respect hers. Perhaps she'd spent too much time in London last year with her sister. That memory brought a smile to her face.

Her hand followed the smooth grain of the box until her finger found a rough edge. *A lock of some sort?* She felt along the edges. Nothing. She pushed on the area with her thumb and gasped when the heavy head of what looked to be an ancient spear slid from the box and landed on the cabin floor with a thud.

Chapter 2

Adversity is the first path to truth.
—Lord Byron

Mercy studied the object in wonder. "What is this?" she whispered in awe. Perhaps Lord Eden was a collector of some sort. Could this be a rare antique? She prayed she hadn't damaged the piece. It might be worth a fortune, but she had no skill in determining its value. Antiques were not something she had studied unless it was in connection with the history of medicine.

The ancient spearhead lay on the floor of the room. Mercy sat cross-legged on the floor and gently lifted the relic. It was heavy and partially covered with a sheath of gold. She traced the tiny ridges and shape; a noticeable roughness caused by use or age or both tingled along her fingertips. The tip of the spear, although appearing dull, looked as though it could be sharpened to a deadly angle. She could imagine what the rest of the spear might have looked like in centuries long past before it splintered apart.

She pictured some soldier using it in battle, and sadness settled over her. This spear had probably killed someone, and perhaps many someones before it had finally splintered apart. Why were men always fighting and killing each other?

She examined both sides and then settled it back on the floor in order to study the box. A dark blue velvet lined the interior, and her fingers followed the indentation where the spearhead had lain. She fitted the antique back into the box and pushed until it clicked into place. Holding the box in both hands, she guessed it to be about a foot long and perhaps five inches thick. Mercy placed the box back into the trunk and covered the mystery with a pair of trousers. Curiosity couldn't force her to ask Lord Eden questions about the interesting object, for it would prove too embarrassing to admit that she'd been snooping.

She wanted nothing more than to soak in a huge tub of warm water and have a maid wash her newly cropped hair. What would she do with it when she reached London? The mud that had caked her face and neck cracked and dropped on the floor bit by bit, like a neglected sculpture. She refused to suffer this discomfort any longer. She surveyed the room, and her eyes locked on a pitcher and basin in one corner. Surely he didn't expect her to remain in this condition. It would only take another day, possibly two, to reach London, and then she would decide what must be done once they arrived. So what if she couldn't leave the cabin? She didn't want to see any of the men she'd met earlier. They were a frightening lot.

She studied the heap of discarded clothes. Perhaps Lord Eden would deign to wash them and bring them back to the cabin to dry. But that wouldn't work. They'd be expecting her to wash his clothes since she now served him as valet. She stood and wrapped the blanket tightly around her naked body and made her decision. The pitcher was half full of water. Mercy poured some into the basin and scooped it over her face and neck. Rivulets of mud sluiced down her arms and splashed over her legs.

Relief so sweet caused tears to pool, but she thanked God for the opportunity to rinse off. The water muddied, and she picked up the used cloth next to the basin to wipe the excess grime from her lashes. Exhaustion crept into her limbs. She donned the black shirt and huddled into a ball on the solitary mattress, pulling the blanket snug. Just before she slept, her thoughts dwelled on Lord Eden and she prayed if he returned to the cabin, he would indeed prove to be a gentleman.

The *Agwe* dipped and rolled with the waves of the sea. Lord Eden clutched the rail on the port side of the ship and heaved what must have been the very last remnants of his stomach contents. He didn't know what had come over him. He loved sailing. He wasn't prone to seasickness. He prayed for relief to whatever gods may have been listening to him. He was sorely tempted to seek out Fox for some vodun remedy but resisted for fear that he might be given some concoction that would bring on visions and cause him to throw himself into the sea. He wouldn't doubt for one moment that Fox could have very well cast a spell to cause the seasickness. He was probably jealous about the woman he thought a lad.

Blast it all! He just wanted peace, a calm stomach, and time to think about the woman in his cabin. Who was she? What had happened that a beautiful woman would wash up on shore with no ship in sight and no floating wreckage? He heaved over the rail again, but nothing came up. The last leg of this trip had nearly killed him, and it still might if—

A hand gripped his shoulder. "Want me to put you out of your misery, Eden? I can feed ye to the sharks or knock ye over the head. What's yer poison?" Skinner laughed and jostled him.

Eden grunted. "Leave me alone." A cold trickle of sweat ran down his back. "I'm going below. Don't be surprised if you don't see me till we dock." He took a deep breath and ignored Skinner's barrage of insults about no sea legs and a weak stomach as he stumbled away from the rail.

He lurched into his cabin after fumbling with his key to discover his new valet curled up on his bed. He groaned. Ordinarily he would not object if he'd found a woman in his bed, but this was different.

The woman's eyes blinked open, and she looked about for a moment, confused, the bewilderment of awakening in unfamiliar surroundings evident on her face. She gasped and sat up, pulling his blanket tight around her body.

"You could have knocked and announced yourself." Her emerald green eyes flashed him a warning. "Are you drunk?"

He steadied himself within the door frame. "I wish I were." He groaned again. "Sick. Seasick." Embarrassed by his condition, he wished only to be alone. "I never want to see a ship the rest of my days."

She laughed. The wicked woman laughed at him. She tried to hide her amusement but failed miserably. "How altogether fitting for cutting off my hair."

"And that's the gratitude I get for saving your life?" He swayed precariously in the doorway.

"You didn't save me. I saved myself. You simply offered me transport and enslaved me as your valet."

He watched her study him, not in the way he'd hoped a woman would study him when he wasn't sick, but as an object of interest.

"Have it your way. But be so kind as to remove yourself from my bed. I dislike throwing a woman out of my bed, but I find it necessary at the moment. I wish to die in peace." He heaved again, and again nothing came up.

She swiftly moved out of the way just in case. "Do you want me to make it stop?"

He gingerly sat on the mattress and caught a glimpse of a slender bare leg. "You look fetching in that blanket. Too bad I'm unable to entertain you, but I find myself hoping for a quick death."

"I asked if you wanted me to help you feel better—and not in the unholy way you are thinking. Do you want my help or not?"

He lay down and rolled onto his side. "If only you could." He buried his head in the pillow and caught the barest trace of her scent so different from his own. He grabbed the pillow from under his head and threw it on the floor. "Here. Take this and keep the blanket. I won't need either. If you want the bed, you must share it."

"Lie on your back, and I will help you feel better."

"Do with me as you like, but I think you'll find yourself disappointed." He followed her orders and shifted onto his back, not knowing what to expect and not really caring.

Her hands cupped both sides of his head, and he stilled. This was not what he'd expected. "What are you doing?"

"I'm going to apply pressure to certain parts of your head, neck, and arms. It is an ancient Chinese remedy that will help ease your dizziness. You may actually be able to fall asleep."

"That would be a miracle." Eden groaned again and thought he would do almost anything for relief. The cool tips of her fingers inched toward his temples and settled there. He sighed. His senses heightened as she applied pressure. Was it his imagination, or did he sense an inner shift?

Her fingers continued their ministrations and drifted down to his ear lobes and then to his jawbone. She rubbed the tension from his jaw in a slow rhythmic movement, and then her fingers slipped behind his head and she applied pressure at the base of his skull.

Eden considered himself worldly—a man who had experienced

much, including women, but this was the most intimate connection he'd ever felt with someone, and it made him wonder. "Who are you?"

She shushed him, and her fingers worked down his neck and arms to a place in the middle of each wrist where she applied more pressure. It wasn't unpleasant and it didn't hurt. Her hands were medicine to him. He could feel himself relax. Her hands slid under his back to below his shoulder blades, where they came to rest, and she applied more pressure. He no longer noticed the sway of the ship. Just the touch of her skin on his. A tingle of calmness melted over him and then the bliss of peaceful dreams.

Mercy huddled on the floor wrapped in the blanket and her thoughts. She loved the way the power of touch could soothe others; she'd always known she possessed a special gift from God. She loved being able to help others, even this man who'd so unnervingly burst in on her life. She supposed she owed him her thanks, for God knows where she would have ended up if he'd left her on the beach. Maybe she'd have made it safely to a village where she could have sought assistance, and maybe not. God seemed to have put him in her path, but when he'd cut her hair, her thoughts had taken a darker turn.

His breathing grew steady, and healthy color blushed his cheeks. She'd learned this technique from a Chinaman she'd met in Scotland, but she had none of the special needles with her that she'd been trained to use. So instead she followed the directions she'd been taught for such a situation. She applied the pressure points. And to her astonishment they had worked!

But what Lord Eden hadn't realized was that she also prayed

for him while she used her fingers. She prayed for his well-being, for a calm stomach, and for his soul.

Her thoughts drifted, and she couldn't help but wonder what her brother, Devlin, would think of such methods. She also couldn't help but cringe at the thought of what he would say when he found out what she'd been doing in Scotland, let alone how Lord Eden had found her and that she'd been alone with him onboard a ship full of dangerous men who practiced vodun, which she didn't even understand. All she knew was that vodun was not of God and that she might have been killed—or worse—if Eden hadn't been the one to discover her.

She stood and looked out the small window. The vastness of the sea made her feel so small, so vulnerable, but God was big enough for all her needs, and she clung to that promise.

A wind had picked up and was moving them quickly toward London. She'd have to make a plan, for it wouldn't be much longer until she'd have to face her family. Somehow she'd get to Victoria first. Her sister had been the catalyst for all that had happened in Scotland. Victoria would understand and Devlin should, but she wasn't so certain that would be the case, not when he found out what had transpired over the last few months.

Mercy curled up in her blanket on the floor. She watched Eden as the light from the sun dimmed in the small cabin. On the beach he'd appeared tall, in control, muscled, and tanned to a dark bronze unlike any Englishman she'd ever seen. Obviously he hadn't spent much time in England of late.

She considered the day, grateful she'd live to see another. That had been in doubt early this morning. Now her circumstances had completely changed, but she wasn't convinced she was any safer. She was just drier. The artifact, the spearhead, kept creeping into her thoughts. What was it? Why did it unnerve her? And what was Eden doing with it?

None of this was her business, she knew, but her thoughts would not be quenched. Maybe he was some kind of treasure hunter. Hadn't she read something in the papers about an expedition? She'd heard of such men. They never stayed long in one place. She remembered her brother mentioning some kind of club for such men, but she hadn't paid much attention, not having interest at the time. What did he call it? The Legend Seekers?

Lord Eden mumbled in his sleep and rolled onto his side. He did not appear distressed. Now that the nausea had subsided, he looked peaceful, almost like a small child. How could a grown man look like a young boy? The furrowed brow had disappeared, along with the hint of worry lines.

Mercy's eyelids grew heavy with fatigue, and darkness drew her into a profound sleep.

Chapter 3

Curiosity is lying in wait for every secret.
—Ralph Waldo Emerson

The London docks exploded in a cacophony of sound, which included some very intense profanity from sailors and dockworkers alike. Mercy followed Lord Eden after his footman had taken the trunks from the cabin. He'd confiscated a boy's hat with a brim that Mercy pulled low over her brow to disguise her feminine features. Eden also tossed a bag at her that wasn't as heavy as it looked.

"Remember, you're a valet. Don't say a word," he warned. "When we get to the coach I want you inside with me. Understood?"

Mercy nodded. She hadn't seen him for two days, not since she'd tried to help him. He appeared to be feeling much better. Still, he looked a bit pale. She watched two footmen come to attention as they left the gangplank and neared the waiting coach. The Eden crest, two black wolves and three gold stars, sparkled in the sunshine. One of the footmen dressed in fine livery of blue and gold immediately opened the coach door. Lord Eden entered, and when Mercy tried to follow him into the coach, the footman placed a hand on her shoulder. "You ride up top."

"Not this time, William. I need to speak to the lad."

The footman nodded and released her but not before giving her a disapproving frown.

Mercy settled into the seat of fine leather across from her benefactor. He looked bigger, broader, and grim.

"What am I to do with you?"

She studied him from under her cap. "I'd suggest you take me to Number 11 Berkeley Square."

He laughed. "The voyage must have addled your wits. You don't think for a moment that I believe you to be of noble birth? Who is it that you purport to be?"

Mercy removed the hat and shook her head, running her hand through the thick mass of short curls. What would she do now? Her freshly shorn hair wasn't in fashion in London. This cropped appearance probably wasn't in fashion anywhere in the world. She sighed.

"I am Lady Mercy Grayson of Ravensmoore. My brother is —"

"Devlin Grayson, Lord Ravensmoore. The doctor earl."

She nodded.

"Surely you jest. You must."

"You know him?"

"I only know of him. But if you tell the truth, he may demand a duel to salvage your honor. Why didn't you tell me who you were? Why this secrecy?"

"You made it clear that a woman of good character couldn't possibly wash up on a beach. I saw no point in arguing with you, for if I were in your place I wouldn't believe me either. However, I just happen to be telling the truth."

"It's not every day that I find a noblewoman—or any woman for that matter—half-drowned on the beach. It's highly questionable that you truly are noble born. Why didn't you try to explain yourself later?"

"You disappeared from the cabin after I treated you. There

wasn't opportunity to talk, and besides that, you cut off my hair! How am I going to explain this?" She rubbed her hand over her head, aware of the mess it must appear.

"I insist on being present when you do explain. First, I want to know for certain that you're not lying, and then I want to hear this story you've created. It should prove quite entertaining."

Mercy looked him first in one eye and then the other eye. She leaned forward. "You have a blue eye and a green eye. How fascinating."

He frowned, and his dark eyebrows nearly touched. "I am not an object to be studied."

"I'm sorry. It's just that I've never seen such an anomaly before. Is this common in your family?"

"No. I'm the only one." He shifted under her intense gaze.

She leaned closer.

"Unless you plan on kissing me, I suggest you restrain yourself."

Mercy gasped and sat back in a rush.

He smiled at that.

"I'm sorry. I've just never seen such interesting eyes." She tilted her head to the side and continued her study of him.

"It's rude to stare."

She blinked and looked away. "The left is blue and the right is green? Or is the right blue and the left green?" She risked another look.

"Uh-uh. No, you don't." He looked away from her. "Who is it that lives on Berkeley Square? Your brother?"

"Heavens no. He'd kill you. Of course my brother-in-law may kill you too, and at the very least he won't let you escape without a thorough interrogation. It's my sister's home. The Countess Witt."

"I have no intention of being interrogated by your brother-in-law or anyone else."

"You must help explain what happened, but then you cannot share this information with anyone. It will not only ruin my reputation, but my family will suffer, and I will not allow that to happen."

Lord Eden knocked on the driver door above his head. When it opened he said, "Number 11 Berkeley Square."

"If you tell the truth, then your secret is safe."

They rode in silence for several minutes. Mercy found herself looking forward to seeing her sister now that she was in London, and Lord Eden had proved to be more cooperative than she'd hoped when they'd disembarked. Excitement and relief grew as they turned onto the tree-lined street of Berkeley Square. A light breeze swirled through the open coach windows, and as she grew closer to her destination, she found her palms growing moist in anticipation.

They stopped in front of a red brick mansion. Mercy's heart hammered. She hadn't given enough thought to what she would say or do. This was not how she'd expected to return home. *Guide me, Lord. Let me be wise.*

The door opened. "Wait here," Lord Eden ordered the footman.

Mercy took a deep breath and pulled that ugly hat over her head. She didn't know which was worse, the hat or the hair—or the lack of hair. She wanted to run into the house, slam the door shut, and throw the bolt, successfully locking out Lord Eden along with the nightmare of the past few days. Instead she forced herself to remain calm and wondered how Victoria would react to this unexpected arrival. Her sister was now a Denning and no longer a Grayson. Married to Lord Witt, she was now also a countess. So much had changed, and Mercy had never even been to their new home.

Number 11 sat in magnificent isolation—a three-story, red brick behemoth trimmed in cream and surrounded by massive oak and willow trees with a fountain to the left of the house. It was an unusual home in the midst of elegant townhouses. It didn't surprise her, for both Victoria and Jonathon valued their privacy, and this particular home in chaotic London offered an atmosphere of serenity where that commodity was considered rare. She hurried past delicate and well-groomed gardens of tulips. And then, from within the house, she heard the familiar guttural welcome she loved.

The front door opened wide, and out bounded a great mastiff.

"Lazarus!" Mercy cried, holding out her arms. The dog rejoiced in his own special dance of welcome and stopped short of knocking her over. "You recognize me, don't you, old friend?" She ruffled the dog's ears.

"For the love of animals, what is that?" Eden asked, taking more than one step backward.

"Lord Eden, meet my sister's best friend, Lazarus, possibly the largest mastiff in all England. He's a bit extreme in his welcome, but he won't hurt you unless you give him reason to."

"How reassuring," Lord Eden said, eyeing the massive paws and drooling jowls. "He's a brute, isn't he? Rather like a small pony."

At that remark Lazarus barked and ran circles around Lord Eden.

"So sorry, old boy. I didn't mean to hurt your feelings," he said, laughing yet wary.

The Dennings' serious-looking young butler from India appeared. His gold and blue turban gave him a special exotic appearance. "And whom may I say is calling?" He stood straight and tall.

"Myron! Don't you recognize me?" She removed her cap and

combed through her hair with long slender fingers, hoping to look somewhat respectable and yet knowing that was impossible. "It's Lady Mercy."

He frowned and squinted at her. The shadow of a smile crossed his lips. "I don't think you are the Lady Mercy. I've met her, and you are not—"

"Shh. Not out here. We must go inside. I must see my sister at once."

Myron looked past her to Eden. "Sir, can you tell me what this is about?"

"Of course. It is rather complicated." He took a breath, keeping his eye on Lazarus as he addressed the servant. "My name is Vincent St. Lyons, Lord Eden. We've just had quite a journey, and I'd like to deliver this person to the countess and be on my way as I have urgent business with the prince regent." He handed the butler his card.

Mercy's ire moved her to action. "Come, Lazarus. You can take me to Victoria." She ran toward the house and then through the open door with Lazarus on her heels.

"Snoop! Where are you?" She looked about the large entry hall that opened into different rooms on both sides. "Victoria!"

"Mercy?" Victoria hurried into the entryway.

Mercy turned around when she heard her sister's voice and hurried steps.

"Who are you?"

"It's me—Mercy!" She threw herself into her sister's arms. "I'm so happy to see you. You have no idea. Oh, Snoop." She allowed herself a brief sniffle and quick tears.

Victoria held her back at arm's length, witnessed the tears, and hugged her tight. "What on earth has happened to you?"

Mercy swiped at the tears and tried to squelch her emotions. "I can't tell you all now, but—"

"I'm sorry, Countess." The butler entered the room. "This urchin insists that she is Lady Mercy."

"Look closer, Myron. She is Lady Mercy. It's just that she, she's not—"

"Not herself?" Lord Eden inquired.

"Exactly, sir. And you would be?"

"Lord Eden. I thought it best to explain—"

Mercy cast him an irritated glance, effectively cutting off his speech.

"I will explain." She turned her attention back to her sister. "I would like Lord Eden to remain long enough to answer any questions you might have, Victoria. And then I beg you for a long hot bath."

"Of course," Victoria said. "Myron, please bring some sandwiches and tea to the garden room."

"Yes, madam. And I beg your forgiveness, Lady Mercy." He placed both hands together and bowed. "You look so different."

"It's understandable, Myron. Do not worry."

Myron nodded and left the room.

"Please follow me." Victoria led them down a long hallway peppered with watercolors. And then Mercy stopped so quickly that Lord Eden nearly crashed into her.

"Oh, no." Mercy caught the very first glimpse of herself in a mirror since Eden had whacked off her hair. "It's no wonder Myron didn't recognize me. I hardly recognize myself." She watched her skin flush crimson and turned away. "I care not to tarry at this mirror a moment longer."

"This way, dear," Victoria encouraged her. After several more steps her sister opened a door on her right. The room flooded with late afternoon sunlight that poured through a large panel of French doors the width of the room that stood open leading into gardens behind the home. Several comfortable-looking chairs awaited them. Lazarus chose to lie in the doorway to the gardens where he could catch the late spring rose-scented breeze.

"This is a wonderful, Victoria. I can see why you love it." Mercy turned to see what Lord Eden was staring at on her right and then gasped. "It's incredible." She marveled at a huge golden-framed portrait of her sister sitting in a chair under an oak tree with Lazarus by her side.

"If I can be so bold, Countess," Lord Eden said, "it looks as though you and the dog could walk out of this painting at any moment."

"My husband insisted that Lazarus and I sit for this portrait so he could present it to me for my birthday. You can imagine just how difficult it was to get Lazarus to cooperate."

Mercy laughed. "I can imagine how difficult it was for the artist to get you to cooperate as well. You've never been one to sit still."

Victoria smiled mischievously. "Touché."

Mercy walked over to the portrait to study it up close. "It's at least twice my height in both directions. Who painted it?"

"The gifted Richard Westall. The man possesses the patience of Job. I understand that Thomas Lawrence is much the same and such a wonderful artist as well, but he's in Rome painting the pope at Prinny's request. He won't return to London until later this year. I understand there are many awaiting the skills of his brush stroke. Well, enough of art for now. Please sit down, both of you. We have so much to discuss."

Mercy sat next to her sister in an identical wing-backed chair covered in dark green damask. Lord Eden took a seat in a straight-backed chair with elaborate wood carvings and claw feet.

When they were settled, Victoria leaned toward her sister. "Tell me what happened, Mercy."

Mercy rarely found it difficult to put her thoughts into words, but now she struggled with how to begin. "Lord Eden found me washed up on the shores of Northumberland two days ago."

Color drained from Victoria's face. "You were at sea? I thought you were in Scotland. He found you washed up on the shore? How?"

Mercy thought she'd never felt so horrid. She didn't want to cause her family worry. "I realize this is shocking, but there's more. Lord Eden was onboard called the *Agwe*. Mostly Africans sailed with him. And so to protect me he–he cut my hair in order to disguise me. My clothes were soaked, and he found me in the trousers and waistcoat I'm wearing now."

Victoria gasped. "You can't be serious."

"You've been known to ride in pants," Mercy said in her own defense.

"I'm not talking about the pants. I'm still thinking about how easily you could have been lost. You could have been killed. Praise God you are safe!"

"Praise God, indeed," she said, still amazed she'd survived.

"But how did you end up on the beach?"

Lord Eden leaned forward. "She wouldn't tell me what took place. There were no signs of a shipwreck. I too was hoping to find out what happened."

Mercy sent her far too curious sister a look that clearly said *not now*. "I still don't wish to discuss it."

She breathed a sigh of relief when Myron arrived with refreshments. He carried hot tea and sandwiches upon a silver tray along with plates and cups.

Victoria said, "Thank you, Myron."

He nodded and then settled the tray on a side table near Victoria. He stole another glance at Mercy and then blatantly stared hard at her, seemingly unable to accept that it was her.

Mercy straightened in her chair, trying to look very regal. "Myron, it's not polite to stare."

This flustered him. "My apologies, Lady Mercy. Will there be anything else, Countess?"

"No, Myron. We'll be fine. Thank you."

The butler left the room with one more backward glance.

"Please, Lord Eden. Eat. You must be hungry."

Victoria poured tea, and Mercy watched Eden bite into cold beef and cucumber sandwiches. Her own hunger dissipated in the presence of increased anxiety over her situation.

"And, Mercy, I know just how you like your tea." Victoria scooped two teaspoons of sugar into a cup followed by a liberal dollop of cream and then the tea.

Mercy couldn't help but smile watching Lord Eden bite into another sandwich. "You must be feeling much improved if you can eat again with such gusto."

Lord Eden swallowed and said, "Countess, your sister saved me from a most unpleasant bout of seasickness." He picked up his cup. "I don't think I've thanked you for your efforts, Lady Mercy. I am in your debt."

"You most certainly are not. You helped me, and I am most grateful to have been of help to you. I believe we could say we are even."

Lord Eden turned his attention back to Victoria after gulping down a second cup of tea. "Most importantly, Countess Witt, I want you to know that your sister was kept safe. Although she was disguised and no one discovered her secret, I regret that I impulsively cut her hair. I could think of no other way to protect her from the men on the ship. I truly never thought her to be a noblewoman. Still, there was little else to be done unless I left her to her own devices to wander off by herself to the nearest village."

Victoria clasped her hands together. "Thank God you did what you had to do, Lord Eden. Should you ever need anything at all, please know that I am very grateful for my sister's safe return. You are a most honorable gentleman."

"Thank you, Countess. I'm glad all has turned out well. I must be on my way, however. My driver waits, and I must reach Windsor yet tonight." He turned to Mercy. "Lady Mercy, it has been a memorable experience. I wish you well."

"And you, Lord Eden."

"Forgive me for rushing off. I'm sure you understand. Thank you again, Countess." He left the room.

Mercy heard Myron showing him out the front door.

Victoria turned curious eyes on her then. "What have you been doing?"

Chapter 4

If you do not expect the unexpected
you will not find it, for it is not to
be reached by search or trail.

—Heraclitus

Eden studied the darkening sky. Dusk would be upon them soon. He'd like nothing better than to go home and sleep for a couple of days. Instead he sank into the cushioned seat of the coach and let out a long pent-up breath. "Cursed nightfall." The coach lurched forward, and his thoughts tumbled along with each turn of the wheels.

The journey from London to Austria had been uneventful aboard the *Destiny*, but he'd been forced to pay Skinner to travel by means of the African *Agwe* upon his return when the *Destiny* had been rammed in port by a drunken fool, thus disabling the ship for the trip home. It appeared that from that time forward he'd met with one disaster after another.

He'd rarely taken seasick when he traveled, but the rolling of the *Agwe* had made him ill more than once. Fox had concocted some remedy for him the first time. He'd thought it simply a strong drink at the time, but it proved far more potent, possibly connected to herbs used within the practice of vodun.

A vision or hallucination had overpowered him, but he couldn't quite recall the details after the darkness lifted. Then he'd felt as though he wanted to jump out of his own skin. It was a most unpleasant experience that he didn't care to repeat, and he suspected Fox could be a formidable enemy.

He didn't know how long he'd been dozing when he heard the driver Mac shout "Riders!" and pound on the coach hatch above, startling him awake. The team bolted forward in an effort to outrun whoever pursued them.

He stood unsteadily and braced himself, then lifted the hatch. "How many?" he yelled.

"Too bloody many, sir, from the sounds of it. Can't tell for sure even with the moonlight."

"Blast them! How far to the palace?"

"Too far. We're smack in the middle of the route, sir," one of the footmen shouted against the wind.

He let the hatch slam shut. *Perhaps they won't find it.* The relic remained safe in one of the trunks secured on the roof. The coach hit a huge rut and slammed him against one side. If he didn't make a decision soon, they might lose the horses at this outrageous pace.

Hoofbeats like vodun drums pounded out behind them and grew closer. He opened the hatch again. "Slow the horses, Mac. There's no sense in crippling the animals."

"But, sir."

"Slow them now, Mac!"

Mac eased the horses down. The riders overtook them in moments, and the coach soon rocked to a stop. Someone with a proper English accent drew his attention.

"Come out, Lord Eden, so we can greet you properly," called one of the thieves. "Cooperate, and we might let you live."

The moment he heard his name he knew they were not typical highwaymen. They knew who he was, and they wanted the relic. Several expletives escaped under whispered breath, and he punched the seat cushion.

"Nice and slow, yer lordship. Don't think too much. We want no bloodshed. But we're not afraid to use our pistols if necessary."

Eden opened the door and climbed out, assessing the situation with caution. Bright moonlight had made it easy for the thieves. However, he was not prepared for their numbers. There were at least a dozen. All armed. All masked.

He saw his driver and the two footmen on their knees. Mac appeared ready to fight, while the servants looked scared out of their collective wits. He pinned the leader with a lethal glare. "I see my reputation precedes me," Eden said dryly. "Even I can't manage to fend you all off. What is it you want?"

"I believe you know what we want." The leader and his sweat-soaked horse moved forward. He dismounted and tossed the reins to another rider. "I warn you, Eden, don't play games with me. You won't win. Get on your knees now."

Eden weighed his alternatives. He could take this man, but what of the others? He couldn't fight them all off, and there were Mac and the footmen to consider.

"I can tell you are thinking. Let me make it easy for you. If you try anything, if you fight back, one of your men will be shot for each punch you throw or any tricks you try. Now, hand over the relic."

"I don't have it. One of the regent's guards came for it in London."

He looked up into unreadable eyes, and then his assailant's boot smashed into the right side of his face. Pain pierced his skull, and he hit the ground hard.

"Search the trunks," ordered the leader.

Through a haze of blurred vision he watched his trunks tossed off the coach and ripped open. Clothes, packages, and other valuables were thrown onto the ground until one of the men held the rectangular wooden box high in the air.

"So you gave it to one of Prinny's guards, did you? It's not a good idea to lie to me." The man's booted leg struck out at him again.

This time Eden reacted by grabbing the man's ankle and turning it viciously, throwing the leader off balance, who tumbled to the ground. Eden leveraged himself upright and his boot came to rest heavily on the robber's throat. "You were saying?"

Four pistols appeared at his head. They cocked one at a time.

He grudgingly removed his foot from the throat he wished to crush.

The leader righted himself, dark mask still in place. He breathed heavily and wiped the sweat from his forehead. "You nearly broke my foot. You're a fool. A bloody fool." The butt of his gun came down hard against Eden's left temple.

Eden's knees buckled. He collapsed in a heap.

"I'm not playing games." He turned toward his men holding pistols on the servants. "Shoot one of them."

Eden squinted, his own warm blood trickling into his eyes as he tried to focus on the others. "No. If you are going to shoot anyone, shoot me."

"I warned you."

A shot rang out, and one of the footmen, Thomas, fell forward.

"You—"

A hard boot connected with his ribs. Vicious kicks created wave after wave of pain that rolled through him until he could bear no more. Blessed unconsciousness brought relief.

"Lord Eden. Lord Eden. Do ye breathe, man?" Mac asked, worry evident in his tone.

Mac's voice. He could hear, but he wasn't able to respond or open his eyes. His tongue, thick and still within his mouth, forbade him to form the words he wanted to say. For a moment he thought it might be easier to die than suffer the effort to move.

He tried again to speak. A deep rasping groan was his only reward. An arm snaked underneath his shoulders, lifted him up a bit, and supported him. Pain sliced down his body.

"Try some water."

A splash of water trickled into his mouth.

"Can ye open yer eyes?"

He choked and sputtered.

"Ye scared the devil out of me, yer lordship. Can ye speak?"

"Is Thomas dead?"

"He's breathing. A nasty flesh wound, but he'll make it."

Those words allowed a bit of mental relief, though he realized his reaction to protect himself resulted in Thomas's injury. He'd not thought. He'd just reacted. "The relic?" he asked. A blur of features appeared and he reached out to touch Mac's face, but squeezed his eyes shut again. "Did they—?"

"Afraid so, sir. The blackguard nearly killed you."

Eden groaned, not for himself this time but for the loss. "No."

He could feel Mac's rough, calloused fingers on his face, wiping the blood from his eyes.

"Try that now."

He blinked. A hundred colors swirled in front of him, a blur of shadows and lights. "Ouch." Several blinks later Mac came into view, his worried expression hovering. Eden tried to push himself up but had no strength.

"Not so fast. Let me see where yer bleeding from." Mac poked and prodded for broken bones and the like.

Eden winced. "Enough. Help me up, Mac."

"I will if you just sit for a while."

He nodded and only followed Mac's orders because he felt about to be sick. He could smell his own blood and felt a trickle of it in his ears.

"A nasty bit of work." Mac brought him up to a full sitting position.

He vomited. Several minutes passed before he could recover himself. "What direction did they take?"

"Every direction but west. Guess they were leaving that just for you. Since this relic was for the regent, they weren't foolhardy enough to head in that direction. Their good-for-nothing leader rode east, but my guess is he switched off in another direction later just to confuse."

"A nice plan they had. Prinny will have my head."

"'Tis not France, Lord Eden, and the last I knew of there were no guillotines in England."

"Do you forget the chopping block, Mac?"

"I doubt His Majesty will have your head on a platter. But he may put your neck in a noose if you're not careful."

"I need you to take me back to Countess Witt's home in London. She and Lady Mercy will help. I need a physician, but I think maybe she'll do."

"But don't you need to go on to Windsor? The regent will be expecting you, won't he?" Mac asked. "He may allow you the use of his personal physician."

"Give me your arm. I must get on my feet." He clung to Mac and Donald, the uninjured footman. "I doubt that Prinny will be very accommodating when he learns I've lost what's taken me almost a year to bring home."

"Thomas is inside the coach," Mac said. "I think it best that Donald ride inside with both of you. Those cowards won't be back."

Mercy soaked in a claw-foot tub of warm water scented with orange blossoms in her sister's magnificent bathing room. Her muscles relaxed along with her mind's swirling thoughts.

"Victoria, you shouldn't be doing this. Where is Nora?"

"Nora has gone up to Cumbria to care for her sister who is ailing, nothing serious. I miss her dreadfully though, but I couldn't deny her this request. She's waited on me for years."

"You make her sound ancient. I'll be surprised if she doesn't get some sense into that pretty head of hers and find herself a handsome husband while she's home."

"If she does, she better bring him back here with her." Victoria laughed. "You played nursemaid to me most of your life. Why not allow me the pleasure of helping you? It's really quite enjoyable to wash someone else's hair. I've never washed anyone's other than my husband's, and my own of course."

Mercy imagined her sister washing Jonathon's hair and smiled. "You are happy, aren't you? I can hear it in your voice."

"I am exquisitely happy. I believe I am as happy as our brother and Maddie. I pray someday you will find such joy."

"Ah. That feels so wonderful." Mercy kept her eyes shut and sighed. "I am in no rush to marry."

"That's only because the right gentleman has not yet come into your life. Although I have to say that Lord Eden is quite handsome with his sculpted good looks."

Mercy sat up and splashed water over the tub. "I've no desire to see Lord Eden again."

"Mercy, be careful. You just soaked my gown."

"Sorry. But you brought up a subject that I'm not fond of. He helped me out of a difficult situation, and that is all there is. Thank God that no one on that ship knew I was a woman. It was a frightening situation, but because I was in his cabin the entire time—"

Her sister gasped. "You were in his cabin?"

Mercy sank below the water, but Victoria pulled her above the surface with an ungentle hand around the hair she had left. "Ouch! Be careful," she sputtered, slapping Victoria's hand away. She dared not turn to look at her sister. She knew the look well enough from memory.

"Mercy?" Victoria asked with that edge in her voice that expressed both curiosity and that you-better-tell-me-right-now tone.

Her body stiffened in the water and her thoughts raced. What should she say and what should she not say now that she'd said entirely too much? She chewed on her lower lip for a moment, wanting to delay her response as long as possible.

"I know your nature, Snoop. Your curiosity must be wreaking havoc with your thoughts by now. Am I right?"

"That would be an understatement of significant proportion," Victoria said, slipping both hands around her sister's slick neck and pretending to strangle her if she didn't capitulate.

Mercy laughed and sensed the smile on Victoria's face. She loved using the pet name Snoop that the family had bestowed on her sister as a child for her ceaseless questioning of everything and everyone. It had been difficult for Victoria being ill and homebound most of the time.

"I must know what's happened to you. Every little detail. Not only for my own sanity, but because I want to help. How often does an English noblewoman appear in London with her hair practically shorn from her head, dressed as a lad, and escorted by a handsome stranger? Why, it's the stuff of novels."

Mercy finally turned in the tub to see the huge grin and tell-me-right-now expression on Victoria's face. "All right. Dump that pitcher of water over my head to rinse out the rest of this soap and then hand me a robe, dear sister. We have much to discuss."

Within several minutes Victoria and Mercy were comfortably ensconced in the massive bedroom that Victoria shared with her husband. Mercy thought the room attested to the love her sister and brother-in-law shared since they refused to keep separate rooms as was the custom.

Tea and scones had been delivered to the room while she bathed and made a very enticing treat upon the silver tray. "Mmm. That smells delicious. And I love wood burning in the fireplace." She grinned. "Can't do that on a ship."

She lay upon a plush golden damask chaise in front of the pleasant fire in one of Victoria's green wrappers, which was several inches too long. Though her sister had been ill most of her life, it had not impeded her growth. Darkness had fallen, but her sister's bedroom glowed from candlelight and the flames dancing in the hearth.

"Where to start," Mercy wondered. She studied her sister, who wore a beautiful indigo wrapper designed with swirls of white orchids that made her appear exotic and worldly, stretched out on her side on the massive marriage bed, one hand propping her head and blue eyes wide with curiosity and impatience.

"I must know every detail if I'm going to be able to help you out of this mess you've gotten yourself into. So start at the beginning and tell me what's happened."

Mercy took a long deep breath. "It's not easy."

"Of course it's not easy," Victoria agreed. "The truth rarely is. But out with it nonetheless. I can no longer bear the suspense."

Mercy thought her sister would break into giggles of excitement as she did when she was very young and waiting for Devlin to read her a story. She steepled her fingers and bounced the tips against each other as if making a very important decision that required great thought. "Remember when I visited last year, when you and Lord Witt were trying to decipher who was attacking the lords of Parliament?"

"I'll never forget that time. But what does that have to do with what's happening to you?"

"Patience, dear sister. It is a virtue."

Victoria harrumphed. "Out with it."

"I told you I wanted to practice medicine, that I wanted to be able to do everything Devlin does."

Lazarus yawned and let out a long, deep sigh.

Mercy reached over and patted his enormous head.

"Do you still want to do this impossible thing? If so, I hope you didn't share that information with Aunt Kenna and Uncle Gordon while you visited in Scotland. They'd be horrified."

"On the contrary. They aided me in my endeavor. In fact," she bounced the tips of her fingers together again, "I have been attending classes at Edinburgh College of Medicine this past year." There, she'd said it. The cat was indeed out of the bag.

Victoria sat straight up on the bed in one fluid movement, her long legs hanging over the side. "You've been what? How? It's not possible. Heavens—it's not permitted. For all I know it may be against the law."

Mercy stuck out her chin. "I vow that women will be allowed and even encouraged to practice medicine right alongside men someday. But until then we must find ways of doing so if we're called by God."

"Called by God? How do you know you've been called by God?" Victoria got up and started to pace the room, much as their brother Devlin did when he was thinking about a serious matter. "And I don't care what you vow, you cannot—"

"Please, don't. Don't tell me I can't do something I want to do." She sat up. "I thought you would understand, Snoop, you who know no fear. I'm good at healing. I really am."

Victoria stopped in front of her sister, opened her mouth to say something, and then changed her mind. "You *are* good at healing. You always were. Scoot over." She sat next to Mercy, reached up and smoothed a stray piece of hair from her sister's face, and then clasped her hand over her sister's hands.

"Explain something to me. You said you've been attending classes. How is that possible?"

"I was disguised as a man when I attended class. And I used the name Mr. Edward Nichols. No one knew I was a woman until several days ago. Someone discovered my secret and is pursuing me, Snoop. I could be in a great deal of trouble. And by coming here I could cause you trouble as well."

"Do not be concerned, dearest. We are family, and we will help you through this–this difficulty." Victoria gently squeezed Mercy's hands. "Do you have any idea who might be following you and what he wants?"

Mercy pulled her hands away from her sister and picked up a nearby hairbrush from a small end table. She pulled the brush through her short locks, missing the old length. "The man chasing me is dangerous. He's angry because I outwitted him a number of times in the amphitheater. But it goes beyond that. I received a letter—a blackmail letter threatening to destroy my reputation and my family's reputation if a ghastly amount of money was not received. I was afraid of putting Aunt Kenna and Uncle Gordon in danger, so I knew I had to leave."

"This is serious, very serious. We will need to tell Devlin and Jonathon immediately."

"Perhaps not immediately, Snoop. I just need a bit of time to settle my nerves and my mind. So much has happened to me in such a brief time. Please, don't send for Devlin yet. Please." She was stalling for time. The last thing she wanted to do, the thing she hoped to avoid for as long as possible, was facing her big brother. Even with all he had endured to become a physician, she still feared he would not understand or accept her dream.

"A couple of days at the most, Mercy. I don't feel right not letting him know you're here. And if someone has been pursuing you, it could be too dangerous to wait even that long. But you do need rest, and then perhaps you will have the strength to put into words what you need to explain to Dev. He will be overprotective, and that will mean you'll have a fight on your hands."

"I know." She set the brush down on the table and focused her attention.

"Now tell me what happened the night you left Scotland."

"The night I was thrown from the ship, a dark-skinned man with a live serpent around his neck who called himself *Agbe* slipped a necklace over my head. His amber-colored eyes seemed to glow, though I'm sure it was just a trick of the moonlight. He said, 'You must never part with this until *Sakpata* asks you for it. When he does ask you, and he will, be certain that it is on your person, or harm may come to you and your family.'"

"How fascinating!" Victoria's eyes widened. "I can say that because you are safe and sitting here. And what do the words *Agbe* and *Sakpata* mean?"

"I have no idea if they mean anything, but we'll delve into that another time. They may simply be names."

"And then this Agbe threw you overboard?"

"I don't even remember him touching me, everything

happened so fast. But just before I went over the side, I thought I heard someone shout at him. It sounded like the man who I thought might be following me, the blackmailer, John Marks."

"How very odd. It almost seems that Mr. Agbe may have saved you from this wretched man."

"It was probably my imagination. I thought I'd quit breathing forever the moment I plunged into the water. It was cold, and I'd heard the sailors talking about sharks earlier. I don't think I've ever been so terrified. When I surfaced, the ship was very near. The sensation of being in the sea as opposed to being on the ship was surreal, the thing of nightmares. But then it got worse when I could no longer see the lights from the ship and all was dark. I understood at that moment why some people go mad. Fortunately I couldn't have been that far from the shore and daylight or I would have died."

"And where is this necklace?" Victoria asked.

Mercy padded in her bare feet to a small drawer in her sister's dresser. "I slipped it in here for safekeeping." She pulled out the black and gold amulet of pure onyx hanging from a gold cord.

Victoria hurried to see it. "It's incredibly fascinating, Mercy. It must be very rare. I've never seen anything like it."

"I never have either, but then we haven't traveled much, and this may have come from as far away as Africa."

"Why do you say that?"

"Only because the man who put it around my neck reminded me of a primitive but noble black man, not much different from the freed slaves we see in England. But there was something mysterious about him, even powerful. I can't explain it. If I didn't have the amulet, I'd think I dreamed the whole thing."

A loud knocking on the front door and voices broke the spell of the story. "Whoever can that be at this time of night?" asked Victoria.

Mercy jumped to her feet, every nerve on edge. She couldn't help but wonder if John Marks had found her. "Don't go. It could be him."

"Who? The man following you?" Victoria handed the amulet to Mercy, who returned it to the drawer.

Mercy nodded and then jumped when someone knocked on the bedroom door.

"Countess?"

"Myron, what is happening?" She asked from the other side of the door. "Who is here?"

"The gentleman who brought Lady Mercy, Lord Eden. He and one of his servants are injured and asking for help."

Chapter 5

Bear ye one another's burdens, and
so fulfil the law of Christ.
—Galatians 6:2

"Lord Eden! What has happened?" Mercy asked, having quickly dressed in a muslin gown the color of the sea. She and Victoria hurried into the drawing room, where the driver and footman had carried him to a settee.

When the men stepped away, Mercy gasped. "He looks as though he's been trampled by horses."

"How awful," Victoria said.

Mercy knelt next to him and carefully began an assessment of his wounds. "Lord Eden, can you hear me?"

"Excuse me, yer ladyship. I'm Mac, the driver." He nodded and removed his cap. "Lord Eden lost consciousness about an hour past, according to Donald here. Thomas, the other footman, is in the coach with a flesh wound. He'll need tending to as well."

"Of course." She looked from one to the other. "What happened?"

"We were overtaken by highwaymen. His lordship explained they were looking for something of value he was to deliver to the regent."

Mercy recognized the driver's loyalty to Eden the moment he

did not reveal exactly what the "something of value" was that had to be delivered to the regent.

"Their leader nearly beat him to death," he continued, "with the aid of his ruffians. If the cowards hadn't been holding guns to our heads, me and the footmen, I swear his lordship would have done them a great deal of damage. He's quite—"

"How long ago did this attack take place, Mr. Mac?"

"Beg pardon, yer ladyship. It's Mac. No need for Mr. in front of it. Me last name is MacDougal, but everyone calls me Mac."

"Mr. MacDougal."

The driver sighed. "Yes, ma'am. We was about an hour away from Windsor when the thieves struck. But Lord Eden asked us to bring him back here, to you. Said he couldn't go to the palace empty-handed or His Majesty would finish him."

"I think I understand, Mr. MacDougal." She turned her attention to Victoria. "I'll need to move him to a comfortable bed and gather whatever herbs are available to make a poultice for his eye. Then I'll assess him for other injuries."

Victoria took command. "Gentlemen, please take Lord Eden to the room that our butler will direct you to, and bring your servant in so he can be attended to as well. Then go to the kitchen, and Cook will make you something to eat. You must be exhausted."

"That we are, yer ladyship," Mac said. "We'll get his lordship and Thomas settled and then tend to the horses. Victuals will be most welcome. Thank you for your kindness."

She nodded. "The stable is at your disposal. Now, let's get Lord Eden upstairs."

Mercy placed her hand on her sister's arm. "I think I can care for him, but I'm not taking any chances. We must send for Devlin."

Victoria nodded. "I'll take care of that, and I'll have Myron bring you warm water and whatever healing herbs we have available after he shows the men what room will be best. I'm sorry, Mercy. You may not get any rest for a while, but I'll help you, and so will Dev."

"Thank you." She embraced her sister. "I'm so glad you are here and not in the country with your husband."

The men carried Lord Eden up the stairs as Myron led the way. Mercy followed. When they entered the room she scooted in front of them. "Wait." She pulled down the coverlet and sheets. "I need you to strip him out of his clothes and cover him up. I will treat his upper extremities. My brother, who is a physician, will be sent for and will help determine if there is any internal bleeding."

"Yes, yer ladyship," Mac said. "You want all his clothes off?"

"Yes. My brother will make a thorough evaluation of any wounds that may complicate matters of healing, but I think for the moment his loss of consciousness is of the most concern."

The men went to their task with gentle fingers. It amazed her how rough-looking men could apply a gentle hand when the situation warranted it. She smiled and turned to Myron. "Do hurry with the water and clean cloths. Ask one of the maids to help you settle the footman in and attend to his wound if you are certain it is only a flesh wound. I will see to him as soon as I can."

Mercy left the room while Mac undressed his master. She returned to the first floor to find Victoria dispatching a footman to their brother's home only a mile away. She prayed he was at home.

When the door closed, she asked her sister, "Do you have nothing shorter than this gown? I'm going to fall if I'm not careful."

"That is one problem that is easily remedied. Follow me." She led the way to a room that was clearly meant for a seamstress.

"This should help." Victoria picked up a pair of shears and knelt on the floor.

"What are you doing? You'll ruin the gown."

"This is an emergency, and we don't need another one by having you trip and break a bone." She used the scissors deftly to cut away the hem. The material fell, revealing indigo slippers and bare ankles.

"Perfect." She hurried to the door unencumbered and then turned. "Come with me, Victoria. I may need your help."

When they quietly entered Eden's room, Mercy was pleased to see that he'd been neatly tucked in. His bare shoulders, one dark with bruising, showed above the sea green coverlet. Mr. MacDougal stood over Lord Eden mumbling something.

He looked up when he realized he was no longer alone. "Thank you for taking care of him. I'm a mite fond of his lordship. Do you wish me to stay?"

"You've already had a difficult night," Mercy said. "I'm sure he will appreciate your continued prayers."

"Those he's got," MacDougal said.

"I will send word to you," Victoria said, "when he is awake and feeling stronger. Go eat in the kitchen, and Cook will show you to a comfortable bed after you've finished."

"Thank you, yer ladyship. That's most kind."

He was leaving the room as Myron entered with a pitcher and basin of warmed water and several clean, white cloths, along with ointments, the makings for a poultice, and a bottle of brandy in a crystal decanter. "The footman, Thomas, fairs well. The man Donald sits with him."

"Good," Mac said. "I'll go check in on him."

Mercy immediately soaked a cloth in the water, wrung out the excess, and propped her hips on the bed. She gently wiped the dirt and grime from Lord Eden's face, wincing as she wondered how his head survived the blows. She dipped the cloth in the water again and squeezed. The water turned a muddy brown. She could see now where his cheek had been sliced open, and as she removed the caked-on blood, the wound began to ooze.

"Lord Eden, can you hear me?" she asked. No response. She continued to bathe his face and arms and shoulders. His muscled body wasn't anything a woman of her years was privileged to see, and it caused her pause. She tugged the coverlet down a bit and laid her hand on his chest. The steady rise and fall comforted her and let her know he wasn't at this moment in serious danger. The human body created by God was a truly mysterious design. She prayed silently while she continued her ministrations.

Mercy sighed. "At least he's still breathing." She continued to work gently at the smudges and cuts on his face and the severe and worsening bruising around his left eye. A deep gash narrowly missing the eye needed stitching. "Myron, can you bring some ice? Do you have some available?"

"Yes, my lady. We've a bit."

Mercy nodded and smiled. "A bit will be enough."

Victoria sat in a comfortable chair upholstered with blue silk in the corner of the large guest room. "You have a special touch, Mercy. Much like our brother."

She looked up at Victoria. "I wish I had our brother's skill. I'll see if I can get this swelling down overnight. Perhaps I can stitch it tomorrow." She gently touched the puffy area near the gash. "Unfortunately it will leave a scar."

"Come close, will you, Snoop? I want to take a good look at his ribs. Since you're married, Devlin will be less likely to have a fit should he arrive while I'm examining a naked man."

Victoria leaned forward. "He's not really naked, is he?"

Mercy turned down the coverlet and sheets to expose his torso. "Good heavens. If he doesn't have a broken rib or two it will be a miracle. He's taken a terrible beating." Her eyes roamed his injuries and then studied all the discolorations and swellings based on all she had learned in Scotland. Her fingers traced the outer edges of the substantial bruising. "I'm concerned that he might have an injury to his liver, perhaps Devlin will know for certain."

Victoria squeezed Mercy's shoulder. "He will get better?"

"He'll need rest. Men don't like to sit still. It's one of their biggest faults, don't you think?"

"I couldn't agree more."

"I'll rest easier when he wakes up." Mercy pressed her lips together, thinking. "The longer he remains unconscious, the longer it will be until we know how seriously his thinking and memory have been affected."

"Perhaps it's best that he sleep. When he wakes he will be in pain." Victoria returned to her seat. "Are you going to place an awful-smelling poultice on his ribs?"

"It's the only thing I can think to do that may help him."

"Do they have to smell that bad to work?"

Mercy placed a hand on Lord Eden's cheek. "I haven't yet found a way to make them smell pleasant."

A knock on the door announced Myron's arrival. Mercy recognized the items he carried upon a large wooden tray: multiple herbs for the makings of the necessary pungent poultices, the pestle and mortar, a large crystal decanter of brandy, and next to the brandy a smaller container she knew to be tincture of opium.

"Thank you, Myron," Victoria said. "Please set the tray on this side table and then clear the dresser. We'll make our own small apothecary and surgery if need be."

Mercy got to work immediately and picked and chose herbs to crush. "It is because of you, Victoria, that I know so many of the uses of a poultice." Victoria's childhood illness had often been treated with many a smelly poultice. She smiled as she crushed willow bark, pennywort, and yellow root.

She gripped the pestle, enjoying the familiarity of the smooth object in her hand. She'd had much experience with these tools. Although some physicians didn't believe in training others in the way of the apothecary, Mercy's uncle Gordon knew an apothecary who agreed to teach her all he knew. Though her time with him had been cut short, she'd learned much.

Victoria wrinkled her nose. "I still dread the odor of those awful things."

"I'm afraid not much has changed over the years, dear sister." Mercy grimaced. "But I can assure you that I will not bleed the man or burn him with the rim of glasses as they've tortured so many others, including our poor, sick king."

"That's such a horrid thing to do to anyone. I know firsthand that bleeding doesn't work, and God help the doctor who would have ever taken a hot-rimmed glass to me. Devlin would have surely killed him."

The three of them made an efficient line along the dresser. Mercy chose, crushed, and mixed the ingredients. Victoria allowed Myron the honor of pulling the poultice together within the fabric, and Victoria quickly tied off the pouch with a look of great disgust.

"I forgot what a difficult patient you could be," Mercy sighed. "I'm so glad you are well. But I wager Lord Eden won't be as difficult as you were."

"In all fairness," Victoria said, "he hasn't been sick for a long period of time. I wish God would just wipe out death and disease. It would make living that much more enjoyable."

"I think that's called heaven." Mercy smiled. "While I was in Scotland, I met a man, a surgeon, named John Bell. He told me the only way to understand and learn the anatomy of the human body was to dissect the body."

Victoria gasped and quit tying the second poultice together. She looked at her sister with wide eyes. "Tell me you never..."

Mercy remembered that conversation after she had participated in her first anatomy lesson with Dr. Bell. She knew she must be following the right path into medicine when she didn't vomit as some of the men surrounding the cadaver had when the first incision had been made into the chest cavity.

"Well, I certainly hope Lord Eden didn't hear that. He may think you have plans for him should he not recover."

"Snoop! How dreadful. I can't imagine." She turned and looked over her shoulder at her patient whom she'd come to know just a bit since the awful night she was thrown off the ship. She didn't want anything bad to happen to anyone, but there was something about Lord Eden. She mentally shook herself. The image of someone she knew undergoing an autopsy or being used for study made her stomach churn.

The front door knocker sent an echo of alarm throughout the house.

"I hope that's Devlin," Mercy said, putting her hand on Victoria's arm.

Victoria turned to Myron. "Bring my brother upstairs immediately."

But before anyone could move, a quick knock on the bedroom door startled Mercy. A thousand thoughts filled her mind. What would her brother say? More importantly, what would she say to her brother?

Victoria opened the door.

"Beg pardon, Countess. A message has arrived."

Mercy could see the footman through the crack in the door opening. He handed her sister an envelope.

"Thank you." She closed the door, looked at Mercy, and then ripped open the letter. She scanned the contents and looked up.

"What does it say? Where is he?"

"He's not at home. His butler, Henry, reports that he's been called away to assist with a patient at Bethlem Hospital. It's not known when he will return."

Mercy swallowed hard. "Then we'll have to do the best we can without him." Her mind wandered to the walls of Bethlem and occurrences of the past year. She couldn't help but think of Lady Phoebe and of the toll it had taken on Snoop. Then she forced her thoughts away from the past and focused on the need of the moment.

A deep groan brought her quickly out of her reverie.

"Lord Eden." Mercy hurried to his bedside. "Lord Eden. Can you hear me?"

No response.

She placed her hand on his forehead. "He's warm but not fevered. Let's place a poultice over his eye and along the darkening bruising on his ribs. Myron, I'll need your help to bandage the poultice in place by wrapping it around his torso."

The three of them worked to position the poultice. "There," Mercy said. She laid the remaining poultice over his eye and secured it with a bandage. "That should work. I'll alternate icing his eye and using the poultice." She stepped away from the bed. "I'll sit with him the rest of the evening. I can doze in the chair, and if he awakens I'll be here."

"Mercy, I know you're exhausted from your journey and all you've been through. Allow me to—"

"I must stay. I know it seems odd, but after caring for him on the ship with his seasickness, I feel I should. I'll come get you if needed. Agreed?"

"Agreed. I, for one, am going to bed." Victoria kissed Mercy on the cheek. "Good night, little sister. I'm so glad you're here."

"I'm glad to be here. I don't know what I'd do without you." Mercy looked from her sister to Lord Eden. "Perhaps he'll sleep through the night."

Mercy watched her sister and Myron leave the room. She cuddled under a blanket in the chair near the bed and fell asleep saying her prayers.

But uninterrupted sleep was not to be. Lord Eden's screams woke her a few hours later.

Chapter 6

Thou shalt not be afraid for the
terror by night; nor for the arrow that
flieth by day; nor for the pestilence
that walketh in darkness; nor for the
destruction that wasteth at noonday.
—Psalm 91:5–6

"No! Don't!" He heard the cry of anguish escape from his own throat before he could smother it. Lord Eden jerked awake.

Someone's voice said, "You're safe, Lord Eden."

He thrashed upon the bed, aware of battling the fog that prevented him from becoming fully conscious. Then the pain brought him up from the depths with a gasp. "Where am I?" His heart thudded so hard he thought it might burst through his ribs, which burned like fire. Rivulets of sweat slid down his back. "Who are you?"

"It's Lady Mercy. You are safe. You're at my sister's home in London. Do you remember what happened to you?"

"No." Memory fought to surface. "Wait. Light a candle, will you? I can't see."

"Of course. Your left eye is covered."

His fingers probed the bandage. He watched the silhouette of her lithe form move from the side of the bed to the dresser. She lit three candles and then held the taper near her face to blow it out. Her features were delicate, softly sculpted. She reminded him of someone that Blake would want to paint or write about for her ethereal quality. But with the illumination of the room came a restless growing knowledge.

"Lady Mercy." He reached out his hand to touch her, to be certain she was flesh and blood and not an illusion. He hungered for reassurance.

"You are safe, sir," she repeated and allowed him to grasp her hand in his.

"Safe," he muttered. Her small, soft hand in his was reassuring indeed. "My eye. What happened?" His hand again swiped over the bandage. "The odor in this room is most unpleasant."

"It's a simple poultice we made. The herbs will help ease the swelling and bruising."

He labored for breath. "My ribs. Broken?"

"I'm not certain."

He dared not touch them. "They feel broken. How did I…?" Memory flooded his thoughts. "The relic! That bloody, rotten son of a serpent. He took the relic." Eden swung his legs over the side of the bed.

"Don't!" Mercy caught him but tumbled to the floor with him.

Pain splintered his side, paralyzing his movement. A curse caught in his throat. He took shallow breaths until he gained control. "Are you—?"

"I'm crushed beneath you. I see quite clearly now that your right eye is blue. So it's your green eye that has been injured. Your left eye is green."

"Sorry," he ground out. He gathered all his strength, what little he had left, and rolled to the side.

He watched her take a deep breath and then release it almost as if it were a prayer. Perhaps it was. He wasn't sure.

"That was unwise," she said, lying still and looking at the ceiling. "Don't move." Sitting up, she kept her eyes averted from him.

He wondered for a moment if he was so unsightly that she couldn't bear to look at him any longer. Something was wrong. Then he heard the sound of hurried steps.

The door to the room crashed open. "What's happened?" Victoria asked, her eyes wide with concern. "I was just coming to relieve you—"

"Stop where you are, Snoop, and call Myron. Lord Eden is not decent. We need to get him back in bed. But first throw me that blanket."

Victoria grabbed the blanket Mercy had slept under, tossed it to her, and swiftly exited the room.

Mercy turned away while holding the blanket out to him. "Cover yourself, sir."

It wasn't until that moment that Lord Eden looked down and realized he was naked. He couldn't have cared less. His pain overrode any sense of modesty. But he glanced up at Mercy, who had quickly scrambled to her feet, to see that she kept her eyes glued to the opposite wall. Despite the dim room he could tell her cheeks flamed. If he hadn't felt as though he'd just survived a stampede he would have laughed. Instead he whispered, "Thank you. I had not realized."

Myron hurried into the room. "My lord, let me help you back into bed." He rescued Lord Eden and tucked him under the blankets. "There you go, sir. I will bring you some hot tea and breakfast if you are up to eating."

"Thank you for your help. Myron, is it?"

"Yes, sir. I'll bring a bell and have a footman sit outside your room. If you have any needs, just ring for assistance if neither Lady Mercy nor Lady Victoria are available."

"I'll do that."

Myron bowed to him and Lady Mercy and left the room, closing the door behind him.

"Forgive me. My emotions took control of what I mentally keep under lock and key... most of the time."

"Count your blessings, Lord Eden. That rotten son of a serpent did not kill you. You live."

"For the moment." He scrubbed a hand over the uninjured part of his face.

"Be grateful." Mercy wrung out a cloth in a basin next to the bed. "You're not dead, and that's a good thing. Now lie back and keep still. You have a bit of blood seeping from under the bandage on your eye."

"I'm afraid Prinny won't be understanding or rational. In fact, he may very well have me hanged when I don't deliver the relic."

Mercy gently removed the bandage.

"How dreadful is it?"

"Not so very dreadful, sir," she lied. "But I'm afraid infection may be setting in. However, with your cooperation and plenty of rest, the correct herbs, and constant attention, you will not lose your vision."

He sighed. "How reassuring. And by the bye, you are not so accomplished at hiding your thoughts. You'd make a terrible spy."

"I don't have to worry about spying. I have my sister. She loves to play the detective." Mercy dabbed at the blood seeping from the gashes below and next to his eye. "You were fortunate, sir. Very fortunate."

"Ouch! I don't feel very fortunate."

"I'm sorry. Your skin will be very tender for several days. I thought it would be best to apply the poultice first, but I think you need ice to further reduce the swelling. In fact, I planned to rotate both for a while." She opened the door to the room and asked the footman to bring more ice.

"Thank you for helping me. I didn't dare show my face, bruised or otherwise, at Windsor."

"But why? What is so important about this relic you found?"

"I'm not at liberty to discuss it."

"I see. You lose an object of some value because a highwayman and his thugs take it from you on a dark road after a lengthy trip at sea."

"Excuse me, but—"

"Ah, but you didn't allow me to finish." She stood back from him a moment and allowed him to squint at her with his one good eye, the blue one. "They beat you so severely that I thought for a while you might not wake up at all."

He waited and wondered why she seemed so angry. "May I—"

"No. Not yet." She took a deep breath and returned to caring for his eye. "And in addition to all you've been through and all I've been through these last few days, you now reveal that His Majesty is somehow involved—"

"Ouch. I beg you not to take your frustration out on my already injured eye."

"Forgive me. Now, where was I? Oh yes. And for all I know he may summon me to Windsor to account for why I am harboring a lord of the realm who may now be considered a fugitive. And all you can say for yourself is that you are not at liberty to discuss it? I think not."

Eden again scrubbed the uninjured side of his face with his hand and moaned. Despite his pain he couldn't suppress a smile. "You do have opinions, don't you, Lady Mercy?"

"Most assuredly. Now, will you please explain what you've drawn me and my family into, sir?"

He clamped his jaw together in an attempt at defiance but also to keep from groaning aloud from the gentle pressure she was applying near his eye to stop the bleeding. It hurt like the devil, reminding him of the time a childhood friend, some friend he turned out to be, threw a rock and hit his very same eye that was now injured. He was forever being taunted for having eyes of differing colors. He determined to keep his dignity intact, and instead of staring past her he focused on her. She had the most amazing green eyes, a mesmerizing swirl of darker greens within a pale green set off by flecks of gold. His attention must have quelled her ministrations, for she stopped and stared back at him.

"Well, what do you have to say? What is all this talk of relics and the regent that has brought you to this end?"

Her eyes did sparkle with golden flecks, even more than he'd first distinguished. This produced a decidedly disturbing sensation within him, as though she were trying to climb inside his brain and deduce what he was thinking. He hoped that wasn't the case. He prided himself on his ability to have withstood a month of torture at the hands of the French, so to be undone by a slip of a girl would be most embarrassing.

"I am not at liberty to discuss it."

Mercy put both hands on her hips and paced the room. "And what if these thieves track you here and put all of us in danger? Will you discuss it then?" She stopped and pinned him with a green tempest glare.

At that, Eden put both hands to his temples and closed his eye, the other one having already been closed for him. "Are you always this brutal? I think you could be used as a weapon to force secrets from those who spy on England."

She burst out laughing. "You've got me confused with my sister, who, as I mentioned before, would like nothing better than to be a spy."

"That's nice." He breathed through the pain thundering in his side.

"What's nice?"

"The sound of your laugh."

The silence forced him to peek. "Could it be that I've shocked you into silence?"

She arched a brow. "Ah, a compliment. I won't be receiving any of those again after I'm found out." She pointed to her shorn hair. "Thank you very much."

A quick rap on the door drove her thoughts away from her appearance. "Enter."

A tall, kindly faced footman carried a large bowl of ice and settled it on the dresser. "Will there be anything else, my lady?"

"No. Thank you, Robert."

The servant left the room, and Eden studied her for a moment as she wrapped some of the chipped ice in a cloth. "This may be uncomfortable for a couple of minutes, but the cold may numb it enough that you will find relief for a bit."

When she placed the ice on his eye, he sucked in his breath and then refocused his thoughts in hopes of distracting himself from the pain. "You could take advantage of the time you've been away. How long were you in Scotland?"

She immediately went on guard. "I never told you I'd been in Scotland."

"Actually, you did. When I found you on the beach you asked me if you were in Scotland or England. Don't you remember?"

She shook her head, looking thoughtful, as if trying to capture the memory.

"So how long have you been away?"

She pressed her lips together, looked toward the ceiling, and then sighed in exasperation. "Long enough. And what do you mean by 'take advantage of the time I've been away'?"

She turned and pulled open the dark blue velvet drapes to his left, an action done so quickly he wondered if she'd chosen the drapes to thrash instead of him. He could see the sun beginning its ascent in the east. The sky, streaked with purple and pink, promised a pleasant day.

He cleared his throat. "Don't some women wear wigs? You could adorn yourself in any hair fashion and color that appeal to you."

"I did not know you were an expert on women's fashion, sir. Beau Brummel would be more suited to provide such advice." She fluffed her hair with both hands. "Still, you may have hit upon something I hadn't yet considered. It seems so false."

He decided not to say anything about the clothes he'd found her wearing. He sensed she wasn't naïve about the power of deception. However, he didn't think this was the time, and his head ached. He thought it would be nice to sleep if only his body would allow him the privilege.

"The ton is often false, is it not? I don't mean to imply that you would be false. You would be justified in your need to do so, and no one would suspect anything was amiss."

"I appreciate your thoughts on the matter, sir, and will discuss it with my sister."

"I need your help. A favor, Lady Mercy." He clenched his jaw to disguise another wave of pain that bit into his side. What was he going to do? He needed help, but he didn't want to pull her into this mess. "Think twice before you agree. It will be dangerous."

Victoria sent a message to Bow Street, and then Mercy gratefully fell into bed at her sister's insistence. She slept like the dead, as the medical students in Scotland were fond of saying when kept up too late and too long caring for the sick and dying on their medical rounds. She came awake in darkness, and her belly growled when she smelled the aroma of food cooking. What was that? She sniffed. Onions and beef? Whatever cooked in the oven could not be ignored. She could eat a heaping plate of anything.

Then she heard voices raised in argument downstairs, and one of them was clearly her brother's. She desperately needed to talk to Devlin, yet she was anxious about what he would have to say. Well, she had a good idea what he would say, but after he calmed down, he would help her find a way to do what must be done. She quickly lit a candle, pinched her cheeks to usher forth some color in the pale face reflected in the mirror, and then donned her slippers.

When she opened the bedroom door, the voices were not muffled but loud and of differing opinions. She imagined those opinions were all about her unannounced arrival and the man who now occupied another bedchamber not so very far from her own.

The first clear sentence she heard while descending the large, ornate staircase was, "Why don't we ask Mercy that question when she's awake?" Victoria's voice held a distinct edge of frustration.

She could see Devlin in his black waistcoat, white shirtsleeves, and black cravat. His hair was mussed and cut short, and his expression was as dark as his clothing.

"I'm awake, brother. One could hardly sleep with the two of you engaged in battle."

"Make that three, my lady." Simon Cox of Bow Street strutted into her line of vision. His dwarfism did not minimize his wide grin. He bowed with a quick jerk and looked oh so regal in the blue and scarlet of the horse brigade. Lazarus barked and romped around the foyer.

"Simon! You are looking fit and ready for duty. Thank you for coming. You'll have to forgive my appearance. It's been a trying week."

"Mercy!" Devlin took several long strides to where she stood, two steps up on the staircase. He whisked her into his arms and held her close as he turned her in circles within the expansive foyer. "I've missed you."

His green eyes sparkled. Those orbs were twins to her own. She possessed the same ability to put someone in place with authority that emanated seemingly from soul to eyes.

"What happened to your hair? What have you gotten yourself involved in?"

Mercy frowned into his shoulder. "So much for the social pleasantries. I thought we might at least relax and have some family time together before we got into... details."

He gave her one last squeeze and whispered in her ear, "I worry about you." He then set her on her feet and inspected her to such a degree that her eyes narrowed and she huffed, "Haven't you ever seen a woman with short hair?"

"Not you. Not most."

Victoria stepped next to her and linked her arm with her sister's. "Let's go into the dining room. I have Cook whipping up something hot and filling. I know you all neglect your stomachs when you're working, and I don't think Mercy's eaten much of anything since she arrived. We can talk about all these things at the table."

Simon's stomach rumbled. "Excuse me. I've been riding all day. Haven't had more than a quick bowl of soup at the Growling Bear Inn on the edge of Southwark." He wrinkled his nose. "Wasn't very good, I admit. Be afraid to guess what was in it. Said it was chicken. Not sure about that."

"You're always welcome at our table, Simon," Victoria said.

Devlin arched a black brow. "That's a matter of opinion."

"The two of you are like small children," Victoria laughed. "Although you are most different in height, you seem to share similarity of thought. Or maybe it's some of your memories from Ashcroft Asylum."

"Safe Haven, Victoria," Devlin said. "I changed the name when I changed the treatment of the patients there."

Mercy interrupted. "Don't say it, Devlin. She set you up admirably, and I can see by the set of your jaw that you are prepared for battle. I ask that you and Simon make a truce for the rest of the evening. You know you like each other, but I think you enjoy your teasing too much. Agreed?"

Devlin stared Simon down and Simon stared right back. Both looked at the women and then back at each other. Grudgingly the two nodded.

Victoria directed Mercy to sit at her left and Devlin at her right. Simon chose a seat next to Mercy.

"Cook has prepared a delicious stew, and I promise you, Simon, that it will far surpass the soup you had earlier today."

"I'm looking forward to it, Countess."

A footman brought in a fresh loaf of warm bread. Its mouth-watering aroma filled the air. Butter had already been set in small bowls upon the table along with glasses filled with lemonade, and Victoria poured hot tea from a white pitcher decorated with blue dragons. When she'd finished serving tea, she bowed her head and the others followed her lead. She said grace ending with, "And thank You, God, for bringing Mercy safely home to us, and please heal Lord Eden of his brutal injuries. Amen."

Devlin's head snapped up. "Lord Eden has returned?"

Mercy's palms grew moist. "You know him?"

"I know of a plan by the regent that sent Eden to Vienna. It was a foolish, desperate plan that will bring no good."

CHAPTER 7

But one of the soldiers with a spear
pierced his side, and forthwith came
there out blood and water.

—JOHN 19:34

"DEVLIN?" MERCY FROWNED at him. "What are you talking about?"

He studied each of them. "Why did you send for Simon, Victoria?"

"I think we will need help, and Simon can be trusted. Is that not correct, Simon?"

Simon nodded, his mouth full of food he was chewing in earnest.

"And Simon has a special relationship with Bow Street. He's more of a consultant than an actual runner. Is that not correct, Simon?"

Simon swallowed. "That's one way of putting it, my lady."

Mercy explained, "Lord Eden forbids me to contact anyone else of an official capacity about the theft."

Devlin dropped his fork. "Don't tell me that Lord Eden is here?" He looked at Mercy and then at Victoria.

She nodded. "That is why we sent for you."

"I thought—" He pushed back from the table. "—that you sent for me because Mercy is here." He stood. "At first I thought you were ill, Snoop," he said, looking at Victoria. "But when you told me Mercy had come home, I thought... What's happened? Someone explain and explain quickly." Devlin started to pace, which was his habit when dealing with difficulties. "Where is he?"

"Upstairs," Victoria said. "He's been seriously injured. That is why we sent for you. But he's resting at last, and Mercy has done an admirable job of caring for him."

A chill of dread settled in the back of Mercy's neck as she forced out her confession. "Lord Eden found me washed up on the beach near Northumberland."

"Washed up on the beach?" He stopped in his tracks as he walked toward her. "In the name of good medicine, how did that happen? Tell me who is responsible. I'll have Simon arrest him just as soon as I finish with the—"

"Fiend." Mercy finished his sentence, nervous that her very levelheaded brother was about to let go a stream of invectives worse than one heard on the docks. That would have gone against his very nature as a godly gentleman, but she didn't care to take chances when any member of her family could be in harm's way. She thought of John Marks and his pursuit of her. Even godly gentlemen suffered lapses in judgment at times.

"Tell me the rest of this misadventure. If I were hearing this tale from someone else and not looking into your eyes as you speak, I would be undone with worry." His jaw tightened, and she saw the familiar fire in his eye that suggested he was struggling with difficult emotions.

"It's been a very long day." Victoria poured another cup of tea and handed it to her sister. "Perhaps the rest of this conversation should wait till tomorrow after everyone has received adequate rest. You must examine Lord Eden, Devlin. I'm quite concerned, but he refused to seek aid elsewhere."

"The rest of it, Mercy. Please." He tightly gripped the back of his chair with both hands and stood at the head of the table.

She revealed most of her story with a few exceptions. She thought it best not to tell him yet about studying medicine in Scotland, or how she dressed in disguise, or how her aunt and uncle were aware of and even in league with her desire to become a physician. And she did not disclose any information about the relic, though her brother seemed to know a bit more than she regarding that mystery.

"He kept me quite safe on the ship after he cut off my hair."

Devlin's eyes widened. "He cut off your hair? The man is obviously a candidate for Bedlam. And if not him, than I certainly am. I wonder if they've ever admitted any physicians for treatment. Surely I can't be the first who's had a sister drive him to insanity." He loosened his grip on the chair, pulled it away from the table, and dropped back into it. "I certainly will be a raving lunatic by morning."

"'Tis already morning," Simon said. He grabbed a piece of bread, smothered it with butter, dipped it into the stew, and then popped the morsel into his mouth as if indulging a particularly scrumptious delicacy.

Devlin turned an icy look on Simon.

Simon simply raised his bushy blond brows.

"Mercy." Devlin turned his attention back to his sister. "I cannot believe you survived this ordeal, and I don't even know all that has happened. You sustained no injuries?"

"Just a few scrapes and bruises. I'm fine."

"Thank God for that." Devlin's shoulders noticeably relaxed.

"I do thank God for that," Mercy said, trying to gain control of her rising temple. "However, I'm not so certain Lord Eden is going to have an easy time of recovery. He's taken quite a beating, and his left eye is so swollen and black that I'm afraid he might lose his vision."

Devlin frowned. "I find that hard to believe. Eden has a reputation for being one of the most skilled pugilists in all of England. He's also said to possess some rare fighting skills he learned in the Orient."

"His driver," Victoria added, "Mac, who sits with him now, explained that if Lord Eden had resisted, the footmen and the driver would have been shot—one by one—with every punch Eden might throw. They were brutal men he came face-to-face with, and to his detriment. He took the beating because he had no choice. The driver explained that at one point when he tried to protect himself and merely reacted, they did follow through on the threat and shot one of his servants, who is now faring well in another of the guestrooms."

Devlin walked to a heavily draped window, pushed back the burgundy colored fabric, and stared outside. "Blast the cowards!" He hit the frame with his hand. "You are lucky to be alive, Mercy. These men could have attacked anywhere at any time." He turned from the window. "I insist you take no more risks. This situation is far too dangerous. I think there's more to this than we are yet aware of, and it's not good."

"If I may ask, Lady Victoria—" Simon sat very straight in his chair, his long blond hair pulled back with a dark blue ribbon in a tight queue. "—why have you sent for me?"

"I thought perhaps you could be hired to work on this without everyone at Bow Street knowing. You're discreet and know the city well now. You have resources that others don't and can get in and out of places without being easily seen because of your small stature. You're perfect for this, Simon. Wouldn't you agree?" Victoria arched a slim brow.

Simon's brilliant blue eyes sparked. "A private case? I'd be honored to provide my excellent detecting skills for such a purpose."

Devlin held up both hands. "Wait. I want to examine and speak to Lord Eden before anything is decided. But there is also the urgency of locating the relic."

Mercy took a sip of her lemonade and glanced at Victoria, who only nodded. "Devlin, what is this relic? Why is it so important that Lord Eden would risk his life to bring it to England and nearly get killed transporting it to Windsor?"

"It's complicated," Devlin said, taking his seat again at the table. He clasped both his hands in front of him on top of the table. "What I'm about to say must stay among us. The relic is known to some as the Spear of Destiny, the Holy Lance. This is said to be the Roman spear that pierced Christ's side after He died on the cross."

"What?" Simon bellowed. "Such a thing exists?"

CHAPTER 8

And without controversy great is the
mystery of godliness: God was manifest
in the flesh, justified in the Spirit, seen of
angels, preached unto the Gentiles, believed
on in the world, received up into glory.
—1 TIMOTHY 3:16

MERCY GASPED. "No wonder Lord Eden was so angry." Could she have touched the spearhead that had actually pierced the side of Christ? It was beyond comprehension and surely beyond possibility, wasn't it?

"A mystery, to be sure," Victoria said. "And absolutely fascinating."

"I do not put much stock in relics," Devlin said, "other than for the historical significance they have. When people become engrossed by the influence of myth and legend, reality is sometimes lost. The power of our Creator is not to be confused with the fantastical abilities that some would bestow upon ancient artifacts. Do not allow yourselves to be tempted to believe in the power of something that is legend and legend alone."

"But think of it, Devlin," Mercy said, still in awe of what she'd just heard. "What if it's true? What if this is the spear that pierced Christ's side? Could it not somehow have the power of Christ available to it? His blood would be on it. And the blood of Christ is what saves us all from sin. I would like to learn more about this."

"Do not be duped, Mercy. There is no way to know if it is real, and the unlikelihood far outweighs the possibility. I think I should go check on Lord Eden, and when he is able to talk further about this unholy situation, we will decide what must be done."

"May I come with you?" Mercy asked. "I can tell you about his wounds, what I've done so far, and—"

"Help me!" It was the driver, Mac, running down the stairs. "Where are ye, Lady Mercy?"

Devlin and Mercy hurried into the hallway.

"He's vomiting blood!" Mac said, out of breath. Blood spattered his shirt and face. A look of pure fear filled his eyes. "What can be done?"

"Where is he?" Devlin asked, already taking the stairs two at a time.

Mercy followed on his heels. "He's in the blue chamber." She suddenly stopped. Mac and the others nearly fell over her. She turned around. "Victoria, would you keep these gentlemen downstairs and find Myron to help us? This will not be manageable with so many in the room."

Victoria took a deep breath. "You're right, of course. Tell us as soon as you know something, though, because we will worry. We shall look in on our other patient."

Mercy nodded and rushed up the stairs and through the doorway where Lord Eden battled a spasm of uncontrollable coughing. Her brother stood over his new patient, and to her horror she realized that Devlin's shirt was now bloody as well.

"Light some candles, Mercy, and don't stay unless you have a strong stomach. Then get plenty of clean cloths and ice."

While lighting the candles she glanced at Lord Eden, who

looked horribly pale. He vomited over the side of the bed, but it was the amount of blood that made her mind reel. "He has severe bruising on the left side of his body. Mostly in the area of his ribs. I don't think a rib broke, but if it did, his lung might be punctured." She knew there were different reasons people vomited blood. Her brother would know what they were dealing with soon.

"Lord Eden, I'm Ravensmoore, Mercy's brother. I'm going to help you. I need you to sit up if you can." Devlin helped him into a sitting position and the severity of the cough improved. "Can you talk?"

Eden shook his head, groaned, and coughed again.

Mercy grabbed two pillows that had fallen to the floor and propped them behind Lord Eden's back. She listened to him gasp for breath, and finally the coughing subsided.

"What's wrong with me?"

"I'm not sure yet. Have you been sleeping, or were you awake and talking to your driver when the coughing started?"

"I didn't even know Mac was here until I heard him say he would get help. What's going on? Have the thieves killed me after all?"

"I don't think so, but I want to make sure. My sister explained that you've taken quite a beating. I know your ribs are sore, but I must examine the area to be certain one hasn't broken and possibly punctured a lung. It will hurt like the devil."

"It already hurts like the devil."

"Mercy, help me get his shirt off."

They quickly slipped off the once-clean nightshirt he'd been given after the earlier incident. Mercy wondered if she'd missed something important. "He took a tumble out of bed earlier, but I think I broke his fall. I hope he didn't injure something then and I missed it."

"Now don't move," Devlin said. "I'll do this as quickly as possible."

Mercy reached for Eden's right hand. "Squeeze my hand. I'm quite strong."

She watched her brother examine each rib. Lord Eden looked as though he was being tortured, and indeed in a way he was. He squeezed her hand hard. Some of the things doctors were forced to do to uncover the nature of a problem were simply horrific.

"Nothing is broken. The bleeding isn't from the rib injuries."

"Now you tell me." Eden tried to laugh, but it sounded more like a groan.

Blood suddenly gushed from Eden's nose.

Mercy grabbed the already bloodied nightshirt. "Hold this against your nose. Don't lie down; the blood will run down your throat." She held her hand over his.

Myron entered the room. "How may I help?"

"Lots of ice and plenty of clean cloths. He's got one awful nosebleed," Devlin explained.

Myron nodded and left the room.

Devlin poked and prodded and asked questions of both Lord Eden and Mercy. "It's all from the nosebleed," he announced wiping his hands on one of the clean cloths Myron had just returned with, along with mountains of ice.

"Lord Eden?" Devlin asked. He stood at the head of the bed. "I've heard of your skills as a pugilist. You've been in fights before. Does this blood feel as though it's from swallowing blood while you slept?"

"Perhaps," he rasped out.

She glanced at the clock on the mantel. It had only been half an hour yet seemed much longer.

Devlin continued with his assessment. "I think during the beating your nose was more seriously injured than it appears—not broken, but the inside suffered. Mercy rightly attended to you. The shadow of what is certain to be two black eyes is coming up now just beneath the skin. Your nose bled profusely and caused the formation of a clot. When the clot dislodged, it caused you to cough. Swallowing the blood made you nauseous, and the vomiting cycle continued."

"I'm so very sorry, Lord Eden, for not having the foresight to consider the possibility. I hope you will forgive me." Mercy blushed in embarrassment and was grateful that the dimness of the lights did not give her away.

"Don't fret, Lady Mercy," he said hoarsely.

"My diagnosis is a beast of a nosebleed," Devlin said. "Thank God it was not more serious. You have much healing to do as it is, and you need nothing further to impede that process."

Mercy's heart slowed its hammering as she breathed a sigh of relief. She thought she might have unintentionally killed him with her lack of perception. She had much to learn about the science of medicine.

Lord Eden's shoulders noticeably relaxed, and he nodded. "My throat hurts."

"Your throat has been greatly irritated," Devlin explained, "but that will resolve within a couple of days if not sooner. You will notice that the strength of your voice may come and go. Some rest and warm tea should help." He turned to Mercy. "You'll see that's taken care of, Mercy?"

"Of course," she said, thinking she was capable of so much more.

Devlin directed his attention back to his patient. "Now, I want you to remain propped up while you rest and allow my sister and Myron to apply ice to both eyes and across your nose."

Eden nodded. He looked exhausted.

"The ice will help reduce the swelling, and hopefully we've

seen the end of the bleed. Your nasal passages will also be irritated, but I think you'll heal nicely. Time will tell."

Mercy and Myron went to either side of the head of Lord Eden's bed. "This is going to be very cold, but you will gain relief. We are going to hold this in place for as long as you can tolerate it."

Devlin added, "I'm going to keep close watch on you and on that eye. It's a nasty bruise."

"Thank you," Eden said.

Mercy and Myron then placed the ice-filled cloths gently over his eyes and across the bridge of their patient's nose, allowing him to get accustomed to the chill.

"Dev," Mercy said, "thank you. Thank you for coming when you did. Please go finish eating and get some rest. I'll call you if you're needed." She smiled. "You are the best of brothers."

"And what of your need for rest and your unfinished meal?" He took a breath. "And our unfinished conversation?"

"You should go," Eden said. "You must be tired too."

She squeezed his hand. "I will soon, but I believe I'll sit with you awhile. I'll have Mac come up again later." She turned to her brother. "Just till he sleeps, Dev. You'll tell the others he is out of danger?"

Devlin studied her with curious eyes. "You've changed, little sister, and you've been away too long. I fear I was wrong not to visit you in Edinburgh."

"We'll speak later." She wrapped her arms around his neck and hugged him. "Thank you."

"You're far too independent," he whispered.

She smiled against his neck. "I know. It's a family trait."

He held her back at arms' length. "I know how indulgent your aunt and uncle can be. Indeed, I must hear all about your adventures." He turned to leave. "Especially this latest adventure. I'd wager there is much you have yet to disclose."

She nodded. "We shall catch up soon," she said. In truth, she was glad to have time to think before she shared more details. She was evading the inevitable.

Devlin squeezed her shoulder and left the room. Mercy stared at the closed door. So much was changing so quickly. She turned back to her patient and adjusted the cloth. "Are you comfortable?"

He smiled. "I'm not sure I would call it comfortable, but better."

"Good." She fluffed the pillows behind him and added another.

She had opened her heart and mind to God in a way she never had before when she was in Scotland. God seemed to guide her and encourage her in all kinds of ways. His invisible presence was evident in Scotland and in the words from Philippians 4:13: "I can do all things through Christ which strengtheneth me." She'd earnestly prayed for His direction and wisdom. But now, with all that had happened, she wondered if she was following that direction or if she'd somehow lost her footing and stumbled onto a different path that was leading her astray.

Mercy kept one hand on the ice-filled cloth and the other drifted to the top of Lord Eden's head. "Rest now," she murmured softly and hummed a gentle tune from childhood to help him relax. It was from a song that she'd hummed often when Victoria was so very sick.

Later when she and Myron removed the packs of ice and placed a poultice over the injured eye, Eden slept. The rise and fall of his chest indicated no distress.

"Myron," she whispered, "I believe we've done all we can for now. Please take these used cloths and the bloodied shirt to the laundry. The ice is melting, and I don't want frigid water running down his neck."

"Of course, my lady."

"And wake his driver. Ask him to sit with his lordship and to tell the footman to send for my brother should there be a need."

"Yes, my lady." He collected all that needed to be laundered and left the room.

She didn't know why, but she gently stroked Lord Eden's forehead and then kissed the top of his head. "Godspeed, Lord Eden," she said. "Lord Jesus, please heal him completely."

He felt her lips brush the top of his head, and a sense of peace settled over him. She had prayed for him. She prayed to a God he wasn't even sure existed. How could one know, really know, that God did exist? He guessed that was what faith was all about. But he'd always had confidence in his own abilities. He was six and twenty, strong of body and mind—well, maybe not at the moment, but most of the time—and he had an overdeveloped need for adventure.

He heard someone settle into the chair near the bed with a heavy sigh.

"Mac?"

"I'm here, sir," Mac muttered.

Eden grunted. His head must have taken more of a beating than he'd realized. Of course he hadn't yet looked in a mirror. He'd postpone that as long as possible. Not that he was a vain man, not at all. But he'd watched Lady Mercy closely as she assessed his damaged eye, and her reaction told him much. It was ugly and serious. She'd covered her response quickly, to her credit, but he'd seen the shadow in her eyes and the brief expression of concern.

He'd seen excessive bruising to the eye on occasion when he practiced his pugilistic skills at Jackson's Club on Bond Street.

Although some would describe him as a member of "the Fancy," he did not. Nor did he consider himself a dandy or a rake, but he did enjoy his horses, a good sparring match, and adventure. Unfortunately his latest adventure was quickly turning from success to the worst of disasters.

He coughed and suddenly rolled to his side. "Mac," he croaked and opened his eye to see his driver staring at him in concern, holding a basin at the ready just in case. The strong taste of blood filled his mouth, forcing him to spit into the basin. Blood trickled down his throat.

"Are ye going to be sick again?"

"I don't know."

"Ye had me scared there for a moment." Mac sat back in his chair.

"Mac?"

"Yes, sir?"

"Find him."

A week passed before Eden could admit that he felt almost human again. He'd experienced no further nosebleeds, and the pain radiating from his ribs had subsided enough that he could dress himself with a little help from Myron. It was his vision that worried him most.

He entered the breakfast room. "Good morning, Countess, Lady Mercy, Lord Ravensmoore. How do I look this morning?"

"Like a one-eyed colonial raccoon," Devlin said. "Have a seat."

Mercy glared at her brother. "Is that a nice thing to say to someone who is healing?"

"Thank you for coming to my defense, Lady Mercy, but he's right. I looked in the mirror. Frightening, really, and not nearly as charming as those rascal raccoons, I dare say. I'm glad the species does not abide in England."

"Pay my brother no heed, sir," Victoria said, and then nodded to the stone-faced footman near the buffet.

Eden chose a seat across the table from Mercy. "You look remarkable in that green gown, Lady Mercy. And I believe your black wig appears so natural that no one will be the wiser. It's most becoming."

The footman delivered a blue Wedgewood plate loaded with eggs, bacon, tomato, and fresh warm bread. "Will there be anything else, sir?"

"No. This is excellent." He inhaled deeply and studied the food with appreciation. "The aroma of this fine meal helped pull me from my bed this morning."

Victoria dismissed the footman with a nod.

"You are very mistaken, Lord Eden, if you believe you are going to get away with having—" Mercy waited till the footman had left the room before continuing. "—chopped off my hair and then pay me empty compliments as way of restitution. Only I will decide when the debt is paid for such an inconvenience and embarrassment."

"Is there any chance, then, of gaining your sympathy and convincing you to walk with me in the garden this day? Your brother has given me permission to venture outside." He glanced at Devlin with a raised brow.

"You've permission to go outside. However, I don't know if I should allow my sister to accompany you." The corners of his mouth twitched. "You may try to cut up her wig this time."

Mercy's eyes grew wide.

"Devlin!" Victoria halted with the teapot in her hand ready to pour. "Is that any way to treat a guest?"

"He's not my guest. He's your guest. He's my patient. I

apologize, Lord Eden. You'd think after all these years my mischievous sisters would know when I'm trying to have a bit of fun at their expense."

Both Victoria and Mercy rolled their eyes.

"You have a kind and generous family, Ravensmoore. And because I have two sisters of my own, I recognize sibling teasing and appreciate when it is not recognized by those on the receiving end."

"You tread in dangerous territory, Lord Eden," Victoria warned with a glint of humor in her sparkling blue eyes.

"I was lucky indeed to have been the one who discovered Lady Mercy on that beach. If I hadn't, we both might be dead. I rescued her, and because of her you all rescued me. Then again," he shrugged his shoulders, "who knows?"

Victoria passed him a cup of tea.

"I don't believe in luck or coincidence." Devlin picked up a piece of crispy bacon and devoured it. "I do believe in the power of good and evil, however."

"Belief is an interesting word," Eden mused. "I've seen my share of differing beliefs in my travels from the west coast of Africa to my most recent expedition to Austria. What exactly have you discovered while I've been incapacitated?"

"What I've discovered is the ship you returned on with my sister was filled with men from West Africa, yet you said you've been to Austria on a mission I'm aware of and very concerned about."

Eden slowed his fork heavy with eggs he was about to eat, then changed his mind, settling the fork to his plate, the eggs ignored. "Perhaps you should share what you know. My mission was quite secret. I find it unlikely that you would be aware of the particulars."

Devlin clasped his hands in front of him on the table. "The

regent called me to Windsor a month ago. The king grows worse, and I'm afraid he will not live much longer—weeks, maybe months. It's impossible to predict of course."

"I don't know if it's wise," Eden said, "to share this information with the ladies. It's sensitive, and though I have no doubt they can be trusted, it may put them in danger if they are aware of details."

"We already know some of the details, Lord Eden," Mercy said. "You talk in your sleep, and your driver and footmen have been anxious about your health. Bit by bit some of the pieces to a very mysterious puzzle are falling into place. You hold the key."

A knock on the door to the room squelched the discussion. Myron stood in the doorway with a silver tray in his hand. "A messenger has just delivered two notes, Countess. One for Lord Ravensmoore and one addressed to Lord Eden."

"Are they of an urgent nature, Myron? Can they not wait until we've finished breakfast?" Victoria asked.

"I'm afraid not, madam. They were delivered by royal messenger. He awaits their replies."

Chapter 9

Wherefore, my dearly beloved,
flee from idolatry.
—1 Corinthians 10:14

John Marks stood in the elegant townhome drawing room of his cunning business partner, Jasper Kane. Burgundy drapery at the windows provided a deep richness to the large room that made it feel extravagant yet comfortable at the same time, a richness that he envied.

"I swear it grows hot with its power, Kane. I don't know if the legends surrounding it are true or not, but I do know that if the prince regent awaits its arrival, then it's worth a fortune, and I, for one, plan on making it my fortune. Are you interested in presenting it to the Legend Seekers?" He knew the value of the spearhead he cradled in his hands—and the potential danger.

"Perhaps. Is Fox with you?"

"I met up with Fox on the docks after the passengers and crew of the *Agwe* had disembarked. I sent Fox after them so he'd know exactly where they went and who they spoke with. I also wanted assurance that the relic never exchanged hands."

Fate had dealt him a surprise in Scotland and then another surprise aboard the ship the girl was on. He'd barely made it onboard when they'd set sail. He'd waited till they were close to England and almost had her cornered when Agbe had secured the amulet about her neck and thrown her over the side. He'd never seen Agbe on the ship after that moment. The power of vodun eluded him even though he'd grown up in the middle of a practicing tribe in Dahomey. And he had no intention of telling Kane about the amulet. That would be his secret and another source of power for him alone.

Kane swirled a snifter of brandy in his hand while sitting at the large, highly polished ebony table. "I'm pleased that you stayed away for the week to avoid throwing suspicion in my direction. I must keep up appearances and don't want anyone knowing we possess such a treasure, especially since Prinny wants to get his hands on the piece."

"Ah, but I'm the one in possession of the spearhead. We haven't yet conducted business, and this certainly isn't business as usual. I want half."

"Half?" Kane said. "I'm the one taking the risks here in London. This isn't Scotland. It was my men who rode with us the night we claimed the relic, while I thrashed Eden. That I enjoyed."

"You have to keep your pretty face free of bruising or you wouldn't have the women swooning over you so often. You're fairly popular amongst the ton, thanks to my adventuring. You wouldn't have much to keep you in high fashion if it weren't for me and Fox and all the risks we take on the sea and abroad."

"Wasn't Eden commissioned by the regent to go after the relic? You were in Scotland playing at the doctoring trade. Still trying to emulate your missionary father?"

"Enough! That part of my life is none of your concern."

"I wonder what he would say if he knew you were trying to put a price on the Holy Lance. Wouldn't he believe he'd failed at raising a good Christian man? Someone to follow in his footsteps? Thou shalt not steal?" Kane snorted. "Blasphemy."

Marks took two long strides and grabbed Kane around the neck with one hand and pressed the spearhead into his cheek with the other. "You wouldn't want me to mar your handsome face, now, would you? How far would your blond good looks get you then?"

"Let go, Marks, before I have you sent to Newgate. One more prisoner to dangle from the gibbet should entertain the crowds."

"And what makes you think I'd be hanging there without you?" Marks watched Kane struggle with emotions to mask his anger. He was like two men fighting within the same body. One, the well-respected archaeologist that members of the ton loved to listen to during the special lectures he gave at the now popular Legend Seekers Club. And the other was a manipulative devil capable of anything if threatened with exposure that would prohibit him from living the lifestyle he valued. They were very much alike, but Marks knew he was physically stronger than Kane and didn't have much to lose in the face of English society.

"Half," Marks insisted.

Kane's eyes narrowed to slits. "All right, half." He cursed. "Now get your hands off me."

Marks backed off. "Don't try to cheat me—I'll know. And I have the power of vodun on my side." He returned the relic to its box. "You have a safe place for this, I assume?"

Kane straightened his cravat and ran a finger over his cheek where the ancient spear had pressed into his face.

Marks watched as Kane discovered that a red smear appeared on his finger. "You drew blood. You take much for granted. I hope you know what you're doing, because I will not be made the fool." Brown eyes glittered rage.

"I take nothing for granted. Now what do you plan?"

"I'm presenting a brief, private, and, I trust, lucrative session about archaeology and some of its mysteries to members of the ton on Wednesday evening at Egyptian Hall. I want you there, but remain in the shadows."

"I don't socialize with the upper crust, and we know there is reason to lurk."

"Lurk then. But I want you to hear and see what might appeal to these lords of the realm. Perhaps we can take advantage of their adventurous spirits."

"You're up to something, Kane. What is it?"

"An archaeological expedition that will impress even you."

Carlton House loomed ahead of them. Eden's mouth was dry and his thoughts anxious. Prinny was going to be in the foulest of foul moods, he knew. But why was Ravensmoore summoned to accompany him?

The carriage stopped in front of the six Corinthian columns. A footman let down the steps, and Eden and Ravensmoore quit the conveyance and climbed the stairs to the entryway.

"I'm not looking forward to this," Eden said as the guards opened the doors into the elaborately decorated foyer. He pulled at his cravat, which suddenly seemed too tight, and took a deep breath.

"I've been in a similar situation myself," Ravensmoore said. "It's quite unnerving when he's in a mood. Fortunately for me he needed my services."

They were met by a young page dressed in royal livery who bowed. "His Royal Highness awaits you both in the music room. Follow me."

Ravensmoore whispered, "You on the other hand—" He stopped for a moment. "—may need my continued services."

"Not very funny. Everything that happened was out of my control. What can he make of that?"

"Prinny can do whatever he wants. And well you know what a tirade he can throw. Just like a child at times."

They continued to follow the page past anterooms and through hallways filled with the paintings of Rubens and the contemporary portraits of Gainsborough and into an octagonal room with a huge chandelier. They passed the grand staircase on the right, and, despite the seriousness of the situation, Eden found himself wanting to run up the steps and away from his current course to inspect and explore the interesting floor that lay above. He was far too inquisitive, and he knew that others did not always understand his need to roam. Sitting still was almost impossible.

The page halted in front of two large doors, nodded to the footmen, and bowed away from Eden and Ravensmoore. A pianoforte could be heard on the other side.

The doors were opened, and the footmen indicated with a nod that they should enter. Ahead of them sat the prince lounging on a large, well-cushioned settee contentedly listening to a piece of music from Mozart.

He dismissed the musicians with a flick of the wrist and then turned his head toward Eden. With a barely perceptible movement of his index finger, he called them to him. His cheeks were flushed, his hair beyond unruly, and he wore a brown cravat, black coat, and buff trousers.

"Your Majesty," the two of them said in unison and bowed.

"Eden, what do you have to say for yourself?"

"I'm sorry to have failed in the delivery of the relic, sir. I would have come sooner, but the man who took it from me on my way to Windsor—"

"Beat the stuffing out of you, I heard. Too bad." He continued to lie comfortably against purple, gold, and amber cushions that appeared more appropriate for his palace in Brighton than here in London.

Eden noticed that he did not offer either of them a seat. "Yes, sir. If it weren't for the kindness of Countess Witt and her sister, Lady Mercy, and Lord Ravensmoore, I don't know if I would have survived the ordeal."

"I thought you were a combatant, a pugilist, and an expert shot. Why did you not defend yourself and my relic?"

"I was not the only one who was attacked, sir. I had a driver and two footmen who were threatened if I defended myself. I couldn't take the risk. We were outnumbered. One of my men was injured because I tried to defend myself. He could have been killed."

"Sad, indeed. Still, I'm distraught. I have it in my head that if this is indeed the Holy Lance that is said to have healed the failing vision of the legendary soldier Longinus after he pierced the side of Christ and was spattered with our Lord's blood and water, then it may also have the power to heal my incapacitated and growing-madder-by-the-day father."

"Sir," Ravensmoore said, "I have cared for Eden's wounds, which were extensive. As you can see, he must wear a patch over his left eye, as it is still healing. I think he did all he could do to bring you the relic."

"You defend him?"

"Yes, sir, I do. And I encourage you not to put your faith and hope in this spearhead. It is not the spear that has the power to heal. That comes through God's ability alone. I—"

"It is not for you to tell me what you believe about the power of God, Ravensmoore. I only called you here along with Lord Eden to gain your knowledge of his injuries and to ask you to see my father."

Ravensmoore did not speak for a moment, obviously taken by

surprise at the request. "I know your father suffers greatly from madness, and I would do all I can. But from what I understand, sir, he is close to death. I don't know what I can do that your other physicians have not already done."

"That is what I want to find out. As long as you continue to play the physician and function as a lord in this country, I would take advantage of anything you may know that the others have missed. Not that I truly believe they have missed anything, but I don't want my father to die if there is anything else that can be done to save him. That includes your knowledge and that spear-head from Austria. Is that understood?"

"Of course, sir. When would you like me to examine your father? I know he is at Windsor. I will have to make arrange-ments to travel."

"I will send a coach to your house tomorrow morning at eight o'clock. Is your wife in residence?"

"No, sir. She's in the country."

"Then I suggest that you, Lord Eden, accompany the lord doctor to Windsor. It will give you the opportunity to discuss how you will find and recapture the spear. I understand the country that possesses this relic cannot lose in war. You under-stand now my personal interest in it. When I am satisfied that all has been done to restore the health of my unfortunate father, then I will take possession of the relic until I know the full mea-sure of its power."

The beginning of a migraine hammered away at the back of Eden's skull. "We will do what can be done, sir, and ready our-selves for travel. But you cannot keep the spearhead. It belongs to Austria. You gave your word. I informed them of your trust-worthiness and that you would return the spear to Vienna. This would cause another war, Your Majesty. Surely you—"

"Hold your tongue, Eden. You cannot tell me what I can

and cannot do." He stood and puffed out his chest over his big belly. "I am the regent, soon to become King George IV! Do not forget it."

Eden could not understand what had come over Prinny. He forced the words out of his mouth. "I understand, sir."

"I hope you do. I hope you both do. This is no parlor game. I hope my father can be saved, but I know it is unlikely. I want to begin my rule as king with every strategy available, and that includes keeping this Holy Lance or Spear of Destiny, whatever you want to call it. Now go and do what is commanded of you—or suffer the consequences of disobedience."

"Did you find out if the club is open to women?" Mercy asked Victoria as she joined her in the garden. "I'm desperate to attend and see what can be gained. Perhaps someone there knows something about this relic." She basked in the sun, holding back the brim of the hat Victoria had insisted she wear to protect her from the rays as they walked through the maze of hedgerows.

"Your skin will dry up and get horribly tanned if you continue to raise your face to the sun." Victoria pulled the brim of Mercy's hat down and laughed. "It's fun giving you orders after all those commands you gave me when I was sick."

"Enough of that. Tell me what you've learned."

"Let's sit here." Victoria nodded to an iron bench in the shade. "It is a beautiful day." She sighed. "Well, I stopped in to see if my new gowns are finished. I'm so excited. Jonathon should be returning to town soon and I want to surprise him. He has some business to attend when he arrives, and then I will have him all to myself for awhile."

"The man dotes on you constantly, Snoop. You're a fortunate

woman who is spoiled with so many gowns. I'd think you had more than enough. But tell me what Madame Thompson said. She always seems to know of everything that happens within miles of London, doesn't she?"

"Indeed. She explained that the Legend Seekers Club is only open to men."

Mercy groaned in dismay. "That ruins all our plans."

"Not yet, it doesn't. Listen. The man who runs this club, Jasper Kane, is an archaeologist of sorts and has decided to open the club exclusively to members of the ton for some kind of special lecture and announcement at Egyptian Hall."

Mercy frowned. "And how does that help us?"

"He's opening it up to the women of the ton as well for this particular event."

"This is marvelous," Mercy said. "What an excellent opportunity to do what you do best."

"Me?" Victoria asked unassumingly.

"We call you Snoop for a reason, dear sister. And I, for one, am going to test your skills."

"You'd best hope this happens before my husband returns to town, or it may not happen at all. He's overly cautious when it comes to me. I'm very concerned that he will lock me up and throw away the key."

"I doubt he would lock you up because of that or for buying more gowns you don't need."

"But I do need the gowns, sister. I have a waistline that will be increasing in the not-too-distant future."

Mercy's eyes widened. "What? You're... saying what?"

Victoria's hand covered her sister's, and she squeezed. "For someone who wants to be a doctor, you are having a difficult time understanding the most rudimentary processes of the human body. I'm going to have a baby," Victoria said proudly, rubbing her flat stomach. "And you're the first to know."

"I've never seen Prinny so adamant about something he was entirely wrong to even consider. Something is amiss," Ravensmoore said thoughtfully. "Perhaps grief regarding his father's illness and the responsibility that comes with that loss has affected his mind. Perhaps he too is going insane. He lost his mother this November past, and his brothers are a constant embarrassment."

Eden stared out the window of the carriage as he listened to Ravensmoore's words mix with the sounds of the street. He watched people of all classes as the carriage rolled past them on their way to wherever life was leading them.

"What can we do to stop him? He's got advisors aplenty. Perhaps this is someone else's idea." Eden turned from the window. "Or perhaps, as you say, he also is losing his mind."

"Whatever is going on, I think the journey to Windsor may be Prinny's best suggestion yet. A discussion with those caring for the king may shed some light on this odd situation. I've been curious about the king's condition for a long time. It may help us see what is possible, or not."

"What of the relic? I must recover it. That is my solemn responsibility, and then I must find a way to return it to Vienna and not get myself hanged in the process." Eden wondered what Mac had been able to discover, if anything. Why hadn't he heard from the man in more than a week?

Chapter 10

Boldness be my friend.
—William Shakespeare

Lazarus barked, alerting Mercy and Victoria to the arrival of their brother and Lord Eden. "Not a word about my condition," Victoria whispered.

Mercy nodded, her thoughts filled with the fact that her sister was going to change all their lives with the birth of a child. Amazing what one little baby could do to a family. If Victoria had a boy, Witt would have an heir, and if she had a girl, the child would wrap her father around her little finger—as she would the rest of the family.

"Come and join us," Victoria said, "and tell us everything that has happened. Spare no details."

Myron stood behind the other men, awaiting his orders from his mistress.

"Tea and sandwiches, Myron. And a pitcher of cider, please."

"And I wouldn't mind it, Myron," Lord Eden said, "if you were to strengthen the tea, a bit." Eden winked.

Myron glanced at Victoria for approval.

She nodded. "Medicinal strengthening, Myron."

The servant left as the men took their seats. A dark pink tablecloth covered the mahogany table, and a vase of fresh flowers brightened the room and perfumed the air.

"What's happened?" Mercy asked insistently. "You both look glum-faced." She could see that their pleasant facades were quickly disintegrating into seriousness. "What did Prinny say?"

Devlin rubbed the back of his neck to ease the tension that must have settled there. "He's not thinking clearly. Eden and I are both to travel to Windsor tomorrow, where I am to assess the king's current state of unbalance."

"But why?" Victoria asked. "What could you possibly do at this point in time, Dev, to help the king? Is his condition changed?"

"I don't think so. But Prinny wants me to evaluate him nonetheless. I believe he wants me to assess his father's current condition so that when the relic is found, I will be able to attest to its power to heal the king's mind."

Mercy glanced from her brother to Lord Eden and then to Victoria. "He must be losing his own sanity."

Myron settled a silver tray loaded with sandwiches, a teapot, a pitcher of cider, and fresh berries on the table. He delivered a prepared cup of tea to Lord Eden. "My lord, I believe this cup of *strengthened* tea will meet with your approval."

Eden picked it up and carefully sipped the hot brew. "Perfection. Thank you, Myron."

Victoria noted that Myron departed with a smile hovering on his lips.

"Lord Eden, perhaps you should explain exactly what it is that this relic represents and why it's so important to Prinny," Victoria asked.

"I went to Vienna with an understanding that Austria would lend the prince regent the Holy Lance to try to validate the claims about it that had been passed down through the centuries. It is said the relic can heal and can also protect the country in which it lies and possibly even empower that country to rule the world."

"But why would Austria part with the spearhead, then?" Mercy asked. "What has Prinny bargained with that would convince them to part with what they believe to be such a powerful object? Even though that power couldn't exist. It's myth and legend, is it not?"

"The power of thought is very strong," Devlin explained, "and can distort one's imaginings. If one wants to believe something is true, then in order to make that something happen, one will do whatever one thinks one must. And have no doubt that our regent is desperate for his leadership not to be seen as weak and useless."

"But he's going to such great extremes," Victoria said.

"He's drowning in grief," Devlin continued, "and he's turned to the spear for hope instead of to God. The regent doesn't want to lose his father. He's only recently lost his mother, the queen, and not two years ago, his daughter, Princess Charlotte. He complicates and twists the matter, believing this lance must have power due to the blood of Christ that once covered the object."

Mercy said, "It makes an illogical sort of sense, does it not?"

"It's really very sad." Victoria poured tea and passed it to her brother and sister. "Quite a fascinating mystery. The Bible does say that a Roman soldier pierced the side of Jesus to confirm that He was dead, a prophecy from the Old Testament revealing its truth in the Book of John."

"What do you mean?" Eden asked.

"The other soldiers," Victoria continued, "broke the legs of the men crucified on either side of Jesus, which was a brutal process to hurry death. The person hanging on the cross actually suffocated because he could no longer push himself up to breathe. So horribly sad."

"And," Mercy continued for her sister, whose eyes had filled with tears, "in the Book of Isaiah and in the Psalms it mentions that the Messiah's legs will not be broken. Then, in the Book of John it tells us that the Lord's legs never were broken because He was already dead when the Roman soldier pierced the side of Christ with his spear. It fulfills prophecy."

"You seem to know your Bible, Countess," Eden said and then gulped down the remainder of his tea. "I've never read the Bible."

"When you do," Ravensmoore said, "you will see that nothing else is mentioned about this spear. It's highly unlikely that it exists."

"Even though I have not studied the Bible, I do know of Bible stories," Eden continued. "What of the spear the giant Goliath carried? Maybe this is that spear. Too much history and too many tales make this impossible. And know this. The spearhead I brought back from Vienna had a nail enclosed in a section carefully concealed within the spear, a nail, according to the Habsburgs, that had pierced the flesh of Jesus on the cross."

"I saw no such nail." The words tumbled from her mouth before she could stop them.

All eyes turned on Mercy. Her face grew hot, and she immediately recognized what she had revealed. "I mean. I'm sorry." She looked at Lord Eden. "I didn't intentionally spy. I was looking for a shirt or something to cover myself in—"

"Cover yourself?" Devlin looked at her in horror. "Why would you need something to cover yourself? Please tell me that you—" He glanced at Eden. "—and he did not—"

"Of course not! Devlin, how could you think such a thing? I'd been in the ocean, remember? I was on a ship full of men. There was nothing to change into. I was simply searching through Lord Eden's trunks for a shirt so I could sleep while my clothes dried."

"Now that we have cleared up the fact that no improprieties took place in my cabin," Eden said, glaring at Mercy, "I suggest we return to the conversation of the relic. Simply because you handled it—that is, I assume you handled it, Lady Mercy—you would not necessarily have discovered the compartment that stored the nail."

"I didn't. I noticed it was quite heavy. The beautifully decorated box it was kept in slipped from the shirt I pulled from your trunk. I admit I was mesmerized by it and could not help but see if I could open the box."

"You are my sister and know my wicked ways of snooping, Mercy. I must share in the responsibility of your downfall." Victoria smiled. "Beware. Such curiosity grows on one after a while. You've heard of Pandora's box?"

Mercy frowned. "Hmmm." She noticed that Devlin studied Lord Eden and was not paying a bit of attention to what was being said. "Devlin? Is something wrong?"

His eyes narrowed. "You were in his cabin? I thought you had your own cabin. You'd better hope that information never gets to the ton's ears, or your reputation will be shredded—and with good reason."

Mercy struggled to control her temper. "Nothing happened. The only time we were in the cabin together was when I helped Lord Eden's seasickness subside. He was quite ill."

"I don't believe what I'm hearing, and you act as if what happened is an everyday occurrence. And how did you quell his seasickness? Since, to my knowledge—which seems to be very limited where you are concerned—you did not possess skills related to this ability when you left England, the only possibility that remains is that you learned something about it while in Scotland."

The sting of acute disappointment burned with a fierce, unexpected force. She thought her brother, of all people, would understand. She refused to cry or show any weakness. "Actually I possessed none of the required needles, so I used my fingers to apply pressure inside the wrists where the needles would have been inserted. Really, brother, you make far too much of the situation."

Devlin sat back in his chair, closed his eyes, and took a deep breath.

"Devlin?" Mercy asked. "What is it?"

"I'm praying for the patience I will need to refrain from doing or saying something I will regret. Please give me a moment." He kept his eyes closed and his hands clasped together with both index fingers tapping against his forehead.

"Then I will do likewise."

They all remained quiet for several moments while the two siblings offered silent supplication. When Mercy looked up, her brother was glaring at her in the way only a brother can when he is blind to the fact that little sisters eventually grow up.

"Let's continue the conversation about the spear for now," Devlin said, "and we'll talk about other matters later."

Mercy nodded and searched her memory to get the topic back on course and off her actions while onboard the ship. "I think the regent's preoccupation with the Holy Lance will eventually prove fruitless. People cannot harness the power of God except through prayer, of course. Only God possesses miraculous powers. I'm afraid this obsession with the relic will lead to nothing but heartbreak. Anything truly of God is not of superstition and magic; it is miraculous. People are so easily deluded when they want to be."

"Have no doubt that there is an element of evil at work here," Devlin added. "I think it goes beyond the regent's fixation. I just can't grasp what is happening. I think, Lord Eden, you may know things we do not. For instance, who is this man or group of men who stole the relic? Why did they want it? How did they even know about it? There are far too many unanswered questions."

"It's important that we all get some rest tonight," Victoria said. "I am feeling very tired."

Devlin picked up a sandwich and bit into it, easily demolishing the morsel. "I forgot how hungry I was. I will return to my home tonight and pack for tomorrow. I fear you may have a difficult go of it, Eden. All the jostling of a coach will not help you gain strength or maintain comfort."

"I'm not looking forward to it," Eden said, "but I'll manage." He reached for a sandwich, and the countess poured him a glass of cider. "I'll sleep well."

"Dev? I would like to go with you." Mercy prepared for battle.

"Why? You will have nothing to do."

"Have you thought about speaking to Princess Sophia? She was her mother's constant companion and must be at least forty years old now. I believe she still resides at Windsor. I might be able to discover some information as a woman, where you two may only succeed in frightening her."

Lazarus raised his head off the floor and looked around the room, sensing something before the humans did. Then he barked and ran toward the front of the house. A moment later the knocker announced the arrival of a visitor.

Myron entered. "My Lord Eden," he said, bowing, "your driver awaits you in the foyer. Should I show him in?"

"Of course. I've been wondering what happened to him." He wiped his mouth with a napkin.

A moment later voices could be heard. Simon Cox entered the room, his small stature in sharp contrast to Mac, who stood directly behind him.

"Simon?" Victoria said in surprise.

"Mac." Eden stood and came around the table. "It's about time. I expected you days ago."

Mercy studied the faces of the two who filled the doorway.

If any two ever wore conspiratorial grins, it is these two, she thought. *They definitely have something to say.*

"Lord Ravensmoore," the butler said, hustling in front of Mac, "Mr. Simon Cox of Bow Street has also arrived." He shot Simon a glare of indignation.

"How did the two of you come to be here together?" Devlin narrowed his eyes.

Mercy arched a brow. "You don't even know each other."

"We do now." Simon strutted into the room. "We have much in common."

Lord Eden laughed. "I find that hard to believe, Mr. Cox."

Mac nodded. "It's true, though. More than one would think, given our differences. Including a local pub." He followed Simon. "We have news."

"Lots of news." Simon pulled up a chair. "Forgive me, Countess, but may we join you?"

"I thought you already had." Devlin indulged in another sandwich.

Victoria poured more tea. "Simon, you are family to us. Please, both of you, sit down and share this news."

Chapter 11

The will to do, the soul to dare.
—Sir Walter Scott

The morning sparkled with sunshine and unexpected warmth as they readied for the trip to Windsor. Mercy looked forward to this journey. There was something exhilarating about a trip with her brother and Lord Eden together in the same coach. She felt protected and able to enjoy herself without the need to hide her femininity as she did when in Scotland and attending medical classes.

Why did society demand that women not pursue the things men did if they so desired? Even if women were just as capable or possibly more so? It was ridiculous and unfair, not that that would make any difference.

The four huge chestnut horses stomped in anticipation. The beauties looked as though they could move mountains without difficulty. The regent had indeed provided a handsome coach and four. The sun bouncing off the royal crest nearly blinded her. She turned and bumped into her brother.

"Careful," Devlin said, catching her by the arm. "Are you all right?"

"Fine. It's just the sun. I long for it most days, and then when it makes an appearance, I'm nearly blinded."

"It's powerful today." He looked down at her. "You look so

grown up. I still think of you as a little girl, but you're not, are you?"

Mercy watched a flicker of sadness shadow Devlin's green eyes. "I'm all grown up, Dev, but I'll always be your little sister." A strange tug of emotion overwhelmed her. She stood on her toes and pulled the sleeve of his jacket so he would come down to her, and she kissed him on the cheek. Guilt mixed with the need to protect her brother from her activities in Scotland, and yet she wanted to share her secrets and tell him about her desire to practice medicine and to follow in his footsteps. She wanted to ask him questions, share the knowledge she had acquired, and compare it with his experiences.

This web of deceit hurt her heart and soul. She wanted to trust him with her secrets, but he had so much weighing on his mind with the delicate balance he struggled to maintain within society as a lord who practiced medicine. And now with the regent's request to evaluate the king, this was not the time for her to unburden herself. If it was so difficult for her brother, how dare she imagine she could succeed? Her status as a woman would always prohibit such actions. Still, she knew she wanted to be a doctor. But did wanting it make it right?

She shook off the thought, which was immediately replaced by a whisper of Scripture: *I can do all things through Christ which strengtheneth me.* Once again she wondered if she'd truly heard the call of God in her spirit to pursue medicine, or had she merely nurtured her own selfish desire?

A footman opened the door of the coach, and Devlin handed her inside. She sank against the well-cushioned banquette and sighed. "This is heaven."

"Nothing is too good for the regent. His coffers know no bounds, unfortunately," Devlin said, following her and sitting directly across from her. He continued his study of her. "Your hair looks entirely lovely. I'd never know it's not your own."

Lord Eden entered the coach and sat down next to her. "Does that mean you hold no grudge?"

"I hold no grudge. I simply question your actions."

"Dev," Mercy interrupted, "it's all well. I wish you two could just start over again and realize that no serious harm has been done. Please?" She glanced from her brother to Lord Eden, who still wore his eye patch, and back to her brother again.

Devlin nodded. "Agreed. Let's enjoy this trip to Windsor and plot a strategy that will make the best use of our time."

"Does your eye bother you over much today?" Mercy asked.

"Irritating and itchy. I can't wait to be rid of this patch. It's a nuisance, yet I can't tolerate the sunlight and the discomfort without it." Eden removed his hat and set it on the seat across from him next to Devlin. He ran a hand through his hair and adjusted the patch.

"I think it wise to keep the eye covered for at least another week, maybe two," Devlin said.

"Is the patch too tight?" Mercy asked.

"I find myself in constant battle with the thing. Too tight, too loose. Still, I'm grateful I didn't lose my eye altogether."

"A blessing to be sure," Mercy said. "May I be of assistance?"

"Please. I find it too snug this morning. I believe that's Myron's way of conveying his concern since he helped with the adjustment."

She reached behind his head and adjusted the strap. "There. How's that?"

"Ah, a woman's touch." He smiled. "Thank you. That's much better."

Mercy caught Devlin scowling and decided to take advantage of the declared truce between them before war broke out anew.

"So tell me what is happening at home. We've had little time to discuss these things."

"Mother's returned to her love of digging in dirt." Devlin couldn't contain a grin.

"Dirt?" Lord Eden asked. "Your mother digs in dirt?"

Mercy laughed. "Gardening, Lord Eden. Our mother is an avid gardener. She irritated Ravensmoore's gardener no end when she told him what to plant where and introduced him to some new ideas of color and structure within the mazes and hedgerows."

"I thought that is what a groundskeeper is for."

"You can't tell our mother that," Devlin said. "You should see the conservatory. She's ordered plants from all over the world. She has a wonderful touch and quite the green thumb. And now she has Maddie doing the same thing. I swear the place will be eclipsed by flowers when we return."

"An unusual household," Mercy teased.

"You haven't heard this yet, Mercy. I thought the groundskeeper might give notice," Devlin said, "but my wife and Mother have his full cooperation now."

"What did they do?" she asked with wide eyes.

"Not them, me. I gave him an extra afternoon off so they could dig and plant all they wanted without interference. Problem solved."

She laughed. "I look forward to visiting. I miss everyone so much."

"She misses you, dreadfully. You've stayed away far too long."

"I know. I didn't mean to. It's just that Scotland captured my heart. And Edinburgh. I can't explain it, but I felt at home there too."

"Probably Aunt Kenna's cooking and Uncle Gordon's constant experiments."

"What do you mean?" Eden asked.

"Our uncle Gordon believes himself the family apothecary," Devlin explained. "When I was a child and visiting my mother's sister, her Scottish husband was forever experimenting on me with one herb or another."

Devlin turned his attention back to Mercy. "He didn't try to experiment on you, did he?"

"Whatever do you mean by 'experimenting'?" An image of her uncle testing herbs and such in the kitchen suddenly forced unexpected laughter to bubble up, and she clamped her hand over her mouth to keep from snorting.

"He did. Didn't he?"

"No, not really. What did he do to you? I don't believe you've shared this story."

"He thought there must be some way to keep me from roaming around in the middle of the night. Nightmares and sleep-walking I'm told. He's too much of a modern thinker."

"Look who calls the kettle black."

"Indeed," Eden said. "Perhaps that's one reason you champion medicine."

Arching a black brow, Devlin directed an annoyed glance at Eden.

"I believe Uncle Gordon's a scientist of sorts," Mercy added. "You need to spend some time with him yourself, Dev. He thinks you're the greatest of all men now that you've become a physician. 'Ravensmoore is a man much like me,' he says."

"By the bye." Devlin looked hard at Mercy.

She wanted nothing more than to escape the coach at that moment, but after a quick assessment of the speed at which they traveled, she knew that would not be possible. That kind of look from her brother created emotional upheaval that usually resulted in disagreement and hurtful words. Then, deciding to confront the "look"—as she and Victoria had come to call it—she calmed her nerves and stared directly back into his deep, searching, and curious stare with a look of her own.

"He is staying out of mischief, isn't he? He hasn't pulled you into some dark plot of his? He was forever conjuring up stories. I don't think any of them were true. With him, however, it's difficult to really know, isn't it? He should have been a novelist."

Mercy nodded, thinking if Devlin only knew how much their uncle had contributed to her disguising herself as a man to attend medical school, he'd have an apoplectic fit worthy of commitment to Bedlam.

Expertly dodging the subject she said, "No more than you would expect."

Swiftly changing course, she asked, "And why isn't Maddie here in town? I expected to see her with you."

"My Maddie is quite well. She will be joining us later in the week, in fact. I've promised to accompany her to the theater, the modiste, and she again desires to visit the patients in Bethlem."

Mercy leaned across the short distance between them, resting both hands on her brother's knees. "She's coming in a few days? And you didn't tell me? Brothers are wretched creatures when they keep such secrets to themselves."

"Be prepared for a scolding." Devlin took both her hands in his. "She's quite upset that you've stayed away so long."

Devlin released her hands, and she settled back against the cushions again.

Lord Eden asked, "What and where is this Safe Haven?"

"It's the old Ashcroft Asylum in Yorkshire. I purchased the hospital a couple of years ago because of patient cruelty," Devlin said. "It's a far better place now."

"I want to accompany you when you go to Bethlem," Mercy said. "I wasn't able to the last time, if you recall. But I wish to see what these patients are dealing with and how Bethlem differs from Safe Haven. Perhaps I can help you at some time in the future back at home."

"I had no idea you wished to be involved with the sick, Mercy. You dedicated most of your life to Victoria through the many years of her illness. Even when you were very small I can remember you bringing her a doll or a cup of tea, or climbing into bed with her to keep her company. I thought you'd want to get as far away from illness as possible."

"Not at all. In fact, I feel called to help heal the sick."

Devlin's body tensed. She could tell by the rigidity of his jaw. She wondered if she'd been unwise to bring up the subject.

"Called in what way?"

"Called by God, of course. How else is one called?"

Lord Eden caught her glance as she looked away from her brother, and suddenly she felt trapped and not protected at all.

"How is one called by God?" he asked. "And by which god?"

"I can't really explain it. It's the nudging of the Holy Spirit within me. Perhaps we should discuss this at another time, Lord Eden."

"How do you know it's not your conscience or your own desire?"

"Because I seek His will. Have you never felt…led?"

"I attribute any yearnings as my own and not as God's call, as you describe it. You don't then believe there are other ways to God? Such as the practice of vodun?"

"Vodun?" Devlin blurted. "Where in the blazes of the pit did you hear about vodun?"

"Like the men on the ship?" Mercy purposely ignored her brother's remark. "There was one you thought put a curse on you."

"A curse!" Devlin stood and smacked his head on the ceiling of the coach. Struggling to regain his dignity, he quickly collected himself and glared daggers at Eden. "You have subjected my sister to the practice of vodun and men who pretend to curse others and spread fear by such means? Have you lost your bloody wits, Eden?"

"Your sister has a gift. And my wits are well intact, sir."

"I doubt you possess any wits at all if you've subjected my sister to vodun," Devlin said, breathing hard.

"Stop. Stop this arguing right now," Mercy said. "You don't know anything about me anymore. And you certainly don't know what occurred on the ship. Now let Lord Eden explain."

Devlin crossed his arms, took a deep breath, and looked from his sister to Eden. "Explain."

Mercy interrupted. "And you must promise to listen, Devlin. Promise?"

His face darkened, but he nodded. "I'm listening."

"As I was saying, your sister has a gift. Seasickness overtook me on the journey to London after I had found Lady Mercy on the beach. I'm rarely seasick, and I enjoy sea travel for the most part, but that particular day—" He looked at Mercy. "—I became quite ill. She touched me in a way that eased the tempest in my stomach. Her skill was near miraculous. I believe she may be as good a physician as she says you are if she were given the chance. But the closed-mindedness of society today will not allow that to happen. More's the pity."

Mercy listened intently as she stared out the window at the landscape. She desperately fought for control of her emotions and the tears that threatened to betray those emotions. Here was a man she barely knew, yet he understood. Her brother, on the other hand, only wanted to protect her. He'd always taken care of both her and Victoria after their father and brother had been lost at sea and after their mother had disappeared.

Her gaze wandered back to her brother. "Do you understand now?"

His features had softened. "I understand that once again you have proven to be more like me than is good for you. I'm proud of you, Mercy. Forgive me for acting less than brotherly. You know I only want you safe, and you were anything but safe aboard that ship."

He turned his attention once again to Eden. "However, I do appreciate your efforts, Lord Eden, in keeping my sister out of danger and bringing her back to London and her family. Especially under those very unusual circumstances that I hope to discuss further with you at another time."

"It was indeed my pleasure," Eden said.

Devlin frowned at Eden and then turned his attention back to Mercy. "Now, little sister, I'd love to hear about this gift of yours."

"I met a man from China while I was visiting in Scotland, a friend of Uncle Gordon." Mercy swallowed the lump in her throat and pulled her thoughts together. *Give me strength, Lord, to find the right words.* "He taught me about healing in the Far East. Not everything, of course, but enough that I was able to help Lord Eden feel better. It's as though God allowed me to experience what you must often experience, Dev, and what Jesus Himself experienced on a much higher level, the power to heal." She held her breath and waited for what she feared.

"That's fascinating," Devlin said. "Tell me how it works and what you know. Teach me something." He leaned toward her, his eyes bright and curious.

She was delighted and surprised by his response. "All right. Stay just where you are so I can reach you. I know you've been having your headaches again. I can always tell by the way you rub the back of your neck." She placed both index fingers on his forehead and drew them across until each came to the slight dip on both sides. Then she applied pressure in an upward motion for several minutes.

When she stopped, Devlin opened his eyes. "It's better. Not gone, but improved. That's amazing, but I'm afraid you've nearly put me to sleep. We will talk of this further." He leaned back against the cushioned seat and closed his eyes.

"I think I'm getting a headache," Eden said.

"Don't *think*, Eden," Devlin said, keeping his eyes closed.

Mercy glanced at Eden, smiled, and then closed her eyes.

They rode in companionable silence for several miles. Mercy wondered how she would ever be able to tell Devlin of her dream to become a doctor. She knew her dream would always lead her into dangerous situations. As her big brother he would have difficulty seeing past that, but then what of her desire and God-given gift? Could he let her go into the world as it was with God's blessing, understanding that she had to do what she felt called to do, just as he had done? She knew it was impossible to resume her education now. Scotland was too dangerous, and it appeared that London was even more so. And even if she'd been able to complete her training, society would not permit her the freedom to practice.

They stopped briefly at an inn, took refreshment, and stretched their legs as the horses were given a chance to drink and rest. They were settled back in the coach and on their way to Windsor within the hour.

"We should discuss what will happen when we arrive," Mercy suggested. "We've not much longer now, and I find myself growing nervous and excited at the same time." She reached out and put her hand over her brother's. "Allow me to speak to Princess Sophia if she is in residence and if it can be arranged."

"Very well. I don't know what you hope to discover, but it may be worth the effort. And as you said last evening, she's more likely to open up to another woman than to either of us. The more I think on it, the more prudent it sounds. You are wiser than your years, Mercy."

"Thank you, Dev. I'll do my best to help in this matter. While I am with the princess, will you and Lord Eden see the king together?"

"Two heads are better than one," Devlin said. "I believe another set of ears and eyes can only help. Eden, I'd like you to pay careful attention to what happens when we enter the palace. All my efforts will be focused on the king when we are with him. But if you focus on everyone else and their conversations, we may be able to learn a bit more about the regent's request for this visit. I can't help but think he's not told us everything."

"I'll do my best. I'm just glad to still have my head after losing the relic to those thieves. The regent won't tolerate much more delay in finding and presenting him with the Spear of Destiny."

The remainder of the trip Mercy turned her thoughts to questions she might ask Princess Sophia, and hoping the woman would be willing to talk. Mercy knew the chance of meeting with the princess was not great, but still she wanted to try.

Later Devlin gently shook her. "We've arrived."

Chapter 12

Can I see another's woe, and not be
in sorrow too? Can I see another's
grief, and not seek for kind relief?
—William Blake

Mercy blinked and opened her eyes. "I must have dozed off." Then she came awake in a rush, no longer captured by the remnants of sleep. "Windsor," she breathed, looking out the window. The huge castle walls loomed ahead of them as they quickly covered the last mile. "Isn't it magnificent?"

Eden nodded. "I think we could get lost in there for days. William the Conqueror did not lack for imagination. Imposing… defiant…and 'I dare you' fairly screams from its stones."

The moment the horses came to a stop in front of the castle, several footmen appeared in the blue and red uniform that the Hanovers required to be worn at Windsor. The carriage doors opened and the steps were lowered. Mercy was the first to be handed out by Lord Eden. He followed and then Devlin.

"Welcome to Windsor." A burly man with a wide smile approached. Footmen surrounded them like ants at a picnic. "We've been expecting you, Lord Ravensmoore. My name is Symes."

He bowed low in front of Devlin, and Mercy wondered how

he knew who her brother was as opposed to Lord Eden. That mystery was quickly resolved.

"Lord Eden. Can't forget you. The prince is vexed. Vexed indeed. You'll be hard put to remedy this mess you've created."

Eden cleared his throat. "It was an unexpected and incalculable attack, Symes, and I hope to put it to rights now that I can stand again."

"Ah, yes. You can stand, but can you see?"

Mercy's ire got the best of her. "His vision should improve soon, sir. The attack and theft of the relic was not his fault."

"My apologies, my lady," Symes said. "I was not expecting a woman to accompany you, Ravensmoore."

"My sister, Lady Mercy. She's recently arrived home from Scotland, and I didn't want to leave her behind since I haven't seen her for quite some time."

"I understand. You are most welcome, Lady Mercy. Now if you will all follow me, I will show you where you can refresh yourselves."

Mercy couldn't help but be awed by the vast opulence that was Windsor. She felt like a small child lost in a great forest. "It's just as you said," she whispered into Lord Eden's ear. "We may never find our way back without leaving a trail of bread crumbs."

"Never fear, young damsel. I will protect you," he teased.

Mercy felt a blush crawl up her neck and into her face and thanked God when Symes showed them into a massive drawing room with several crystal chandeliers gracing the ceiling. A sideboard held an assortment of food fit for a ballroom of guests.

"You will also find rooms well staffed with servants to accommodate your every need just across the hallway. Please make yourselves comfortable, and I will take you to the king within the hour. Should Lady Mercy want to walk about the castle, I will see that an escort is provided."

"That's very kind of you, Symes. We shall discuss it," Devlin said.

"Very well. If you have any needs, you have only to ask the footmen. I will attend you shortly."

"Gentlemen," Mercy said, "if you will excuse me, I will freshen up across the hall."

"I should be happy to escort you, Lady Mercy." Symes held out his arm. "You must be exhausted after your journey."

"Thank you."

What awaited Mercy inside the suite of rooms where Symes left her was exquisite. Servants stood by not only to assist her with the delicate fastenings of her gown but to wash her feet. She almost declined but had to admit she couldn't resist. To think that Jesus did this for others. She wished she could have done it for Him.

A young serving woman soothed Mercy's clean feet with an array of oils. She chose one that smelled of juniper, and then she rejoined her brother and Lord Eden.

"What took you so long?" Devlin asked.

"We were about to come looking for you." Eden smiled. "Symes will return soon, and you haven't yet had anything to eat." He was enjoying a leg of pheasant and large mug of ale.

"First of all, brother, that is not a polite question to ask a woman. And second, Lord Eden, I have no intention of allowing Symes to prevent me from eating. But I must say it's not every day someone offers to wash my feet."

"Wash your feet!" The men said in unison.

"I found it exquisite and very humbling. Far different from a maid helping with a bath. So refreshing as to be better than Gunter's ices."

"Sacrilege." Devlin bit into a raw carrot.

Eden gulped his ale. "No one offered to wash my feet," he said in dismay.

"You obviously didn't enter the correct room." Mercy sat next to her brother. "May I accompany you when you evaluate the king?"

He speared a piece of ham. "I thought you wanted to seek out Princess Sophia."

"I still do, but I also want to see the king. I think it may be important for me to gain an idea of what his life is like now before I visit with Princess Sophia, if she is in residence."

A footman delivered a cup of tea to her. "Beg pardon, your ladyship, I could not help but overhear. Princess Sophia is indeed in residence."

Mercy looked into the kind eyes of the elderly footman. "Thank you, sir. That is most helpful."

He smiled and nodded. "May I fill a plate for you?"

Mercy's thoughts danced. "I think I'll come explore the sideboard."

"Very well." He returned to his post.

"I have developed a voracious appetite." She excused herself and went to the sideboard. So many choices. Far too much food for just the three of them. But if the regent had anything to do with it, then she should not be surprised. He went overboard in most things, especially his updating of Carlton House in London and the pavilion in Brighton.

"I think this will do nicely," she said when she'd returned to the table. The footman set the plate of food she'd chosen in front of her.

Lord Eden laughed. "Are you going to eat all that?"

"Of course." She picked up her fork and indulged her appetite, first tasting the ham, then roasted rosemary potatoes, and then the fresh raspberries. "I've been blessed all my life to eat whatever I want and not gain weight." She then tasted the roast beef, a mushroom pie, and sherry glazed carrots.

"I fear the man who marries Mercy will spend much of his money on food," Devlin teased. "You make me full just watching you eat. Would you like my piece of cake?"

She shot him a threatening glare. "Not yet."

Twenty minutes later Symes returned. "You may now visit the king. I trust your refreshment has been satisfying."

"Wonderful." Mercy dabbed at her mouth with a napkin. "I feel as though I could walk the entirety of this castle and still never wear off the meal I've just enjoyed."

"If you will follow me, I will take you to the king." He guided the three through long corridors filled with magnificent tapestries, glowing chandeliers, and sculpted artwork. He directed them up several different stairways to the entrance of the king's royal chamber, where they were met by two guards.

Symes nodded to the guards, who then opened the heavy paneled doors.

"How lovely." Mercy examined the room that was decorated with portraits of the king's immediate family members. This included his now-deceased wife and portraits of each family member from infancy to adulthood. They all seemed to be looking at her, beginning with the king and queen through all fifteen of their royally dressed children, ending with Princess Amelia.

"A most impressive arrangement of portraits," Mercy said, thinking it was all a bit much to absorb.

"The queen wanted His Majesty surrounded by his family at all times whether or not they were actually here at Windsor, alive or deceased," Symes explained. "Unfortunately the king has not been able to enjoy the portraits since he lost his vision some time ago."

At that moment a door opened off the far end of the room, and a man dressed in a dark gray coat, trousers, and white cravat entered wearing a sour demeanor. He closed the door behind him with an authority that implied they should not go farther. "The king is resting. I suggest he not be disturbed."

Symes sniffed. "I'm sorry, that will not be possible, Dr. Halford. Lord Ravensmoore has arrived to see the king at the regent's request. Allow me to introduce his lordship Ravensmoore, his sister Lady Mercy, and Lord Eden."

Dr. Halford sized up her brother and then spared both Mercy and Lord Eden a cursory glance. "Lord Ravensmoore." He nodded. "I do hope you understand that no ancient relic will heal the king. I don't expect him to survive the year, and this bizarre idea the regent has concocted is nothing more than hopeful superstition from a distraught son."

"My faith in God precludes that argument. I myself see no value in a spiritual relic. However, the regent has asked for another opinion, and, though I expect to agree with you, I'm here to carry out that request," Devlin said, towering over the doctor.

"Then, by all means, assess His Majesty and put an end to this delusional thinking. I will remain and watch."

"Symes," Devlin said, ignoring Dr. Halford for the moment, "let's get on with this. I'm feeling the need to finish here as soon as possible."

"Follow me. I see Dr. Halford has rattled you," he whispered.

Devlin walked with Symes, while Mercy fell back with Lord Eden and Dr. Halford.

"The doctor does not rattle me, but the reason I'm here certainly does. I hold no belief in miracles from relics. Miracles come from God, and He does not need help from a broken spear, no matter the significance, even if it did survive all these years, which is doubtful."

Symes opened the door, allowing Mercy to go first.

Her eyes settled on the king. She gasped and took a step back.

Chapter 13

A prudent question is one-half of wisdom.
—Francis Bacon

Mercy turned on Dr. Halford like a protective mother. "Why is he shackled to his chair like an animal?" The king looked nothing as he had prior to the end of his public appearances ten years ago. His hair and beard were long and unkempt, giving him the air of an ancient troll. She thought this was what King Nebuchadnezzar must have looked like when God drove him away from his people and he lived as a wild animal. But even Nebuchadnezzar could see and hear.

"Why, indeed?" Devlin said, walking toward the king with Halford at his heels. "He cannot see or hear, and no one sits with him? A king deserves better treatment than those restrained at Bedlam. And God knows they deserve better as well."

The king, Mercy noticed, had been resting his head on his hand as though bored, but as Devlin approached, the king seemed to know he was no longer alone.

"Who is it?" the king asked. His words slurred due to his deafness.

"He knows we're here," Devlin said to Symes.

"He knows someone is here. He feels the vibration from the door that opens and closes and the vibration made when we walk across the floor."

Symes puffed out his chest and raised his head high. "He is well cared for. The restraints are for his protection. Since he cannot see or hear, he can easily hurt himself if he is allowed to roam around unescorted. Don't forget he's quite mad."

"So you keep him tied to a chair. Does he ever get outside?"

"No, never," Dr. Halford said. "Such outings are prohibited. The king is too difficult to manage."

"Rubbish," Devlin said. "How much trouble can an elderly man give you who also happens to be deaf and blind?"

"But—"

"Dr. Halford, I am the one who was ordered by the regent to make this assessment. You can choose to help me if you stay. Otherwise, leave now." Devlin turned to Symes. "I want you to remove the king's restraints at this moment, and then I want you to escort Lord Eden about the grounds."

"That is not possible." Symes puffed out his chest again.

Mercy couldn't help but wonder if Prinny had left no one with any sense at Windsor to care for their ailing king other than this pompous incompetent who seemed to be in charge and Dr. Halford, who wanted the king constantly restrained.

"Is that what you want me to tell the regent when I return to London with my report?"

"It makes no difference to me what you tell him."

Symes rummaged through his pockets and pulled out a solitary key on a silver chain. He walked up to the king and grabbed the chains that bound him.

The king threw back his head in fear and moaned unintelligible syllables. He waved his arms in front of him to feel who had come near. Symes grabbed one of the king's hands and seemed to squeeze it. The king immediately calmed.

"What did you just do?" Mercy asked. "You took the king's

hand, and he calmed after you nearly frightened him out of his wits."

"He's no wits left, your ladyship. 'Tis simply a signal we've developed so he knows who is about. I squeeze his hand twice, and he knows it's me. Princess Sophia came up with the idea before he'd gone completely blind and deaf. Seems to work."

She turned to Dr. Halford. "Do you have a signal as well, sir?"

"Of course. I put my hand to his forehead." He turned to leave.

"Wait. Please, wait a moment," she said. "The king doesn't know us, so I would suggest that Dr. Halford introduce the three of us. No, wait. Lord Eden, would you be greatly put out if you were not to be introduced?"

"Not at all. It may overwhelm His Majesty."

"Then go with Symes and meet us back at the coach within the hour." She turned to her brother for his approval.

"That should be fine."

"And, Dr. Halford," she continued, "if you would be so kind as to use whatever means you know to introduce my brother first and then me, it would be helpful."

"For what little benefit it will provide," he sighed as if greatly put out, "I will do so. Come forward, Lord Ravensmoore, and give me your hand."

The doctor placed his hand on the king's forehead, and then he took Devlin's hand. "Place your index and middle fingers on his neck after I run my hand from his forehead to his neck."

Devlin did so, and the king nodded. He understood that this was a different person, and because of the typical way a doctor may check for a pulse in the neck, it made sense in a strange way that he would understand. When Devlin removed his fingers from the king's neck, Dr. Halford motioned Mercy forward.

"How will he know I'm a woman?"

"With your permission, may I lift the hem of your dress into his hand when I introduce you?"

"Yes. Of course."

Mercy watched as Dr. Halford once again laid his hand on the king's forehead and then ran his hand down the king's right arm. He stopped and nodded to Mercy. She raised the edge of her blue gown, Halford took it, and he gently rubbed the material against the king's hand. Then Dr. Halford let go and said, "Now you must take his hand, allow him to feel the size of your palm and fingers for some moments, and then make a signal he will recognize as yours."

She lifted her hand and laid it gently against the king's cheek.

He smiled. "Ahh, woman." When he nodded, she went to pull her hand away, but he brought it back to his cheek and held it there. He smelled her hand, and she was glad she had used her sister's jasmine perfume that morning. He gently let go.

"Thank you, Dr. Halford."

His features softened, and he bowed and left the room, closing the door behind him.

"How very sad," she said, looking at the king. "He must be a very lonely man."

Devlin put his hands on his sister's shoulders. "Please sit down while I conduct my examination. When I'm finished, we will depart."

Mercy watched Devlin reintroduce himself to the king. She noticed that the king had not moved from his chair and perhaps didn't even recognize that his restraints no longer kept him there. Devlin, however, did remember.

"Huh, 'nother doctor." The corners of the king's mouth turned down in disappointment.

"Mercy," Devlin said, while keeping his hand in contact with the king's shoulder, "I want to see if he is able to walk. I expect no trouble, but if he should act out in some way, get the guards just outside the door. Now, come here and we will see if our king can move about with assistance."

Mercy approached the left side of the king, and Devlin waited until she had reintroduced herself. She held the king's hand then, and together they encouraged him to stand.

"He's very weak," Devlin said. "My guess is he doesn't go farther than this chair and to his sleeping chamber."

"He's very thin as well. He should have someone with him at all times."

A woman's voice interrupted from the rear of the room. "Someone is always with him. It's usually me. I see my foolish brother has wasted your time in bringing you to Windsor. I'm sorry for your trouble." She walked to them, accompanied by her maid.

"Forgive me for spying, but I couldn't help myself. I've heard much about the lord doctor. You've quite a reputation, Lord Ravensmoore. I am Princess Sophia."

"Princess Sophia." Devlin bowed deeply while he supported the king.

She held out her hand, which was covered in a glove that matched her emerald green gown. Devlin bowed again and kissed her gloved fingers.

"I'd heard you'd arrived," the princess said. "And who is this?"

He stood. "My younger sister, Lady Mercy."

Mercy curtsied and brought her eyes up to lock on the youngest of the king's surviving daughters. *So this is the one who was the queen's constant companion. I wonder why?*

"A pleasure to meet you both. Though I must agree with Dr. Halford. I don't know what my brother hopes to gain from your assessment that he doesn't already know. There's little to make anyone think that Papa will be able to survive much longer. I dread the day. I dread the day my father dies and my brother takes his place." She seemed to have forgotten they were in the room for a moment. "Never mind my ramblings. Tell me what you think."

"Princess Sophia, my brother is yet examining the king. Would you care to remain and watch?"

"Of course. Forgive me. I'm worse than Dr. Halford, so be warned." She smiled nonetheless, and her expression softened her stern features.

Mercy caught her brother's attention and nodded. "That's it, Your Majesty," Devlin said, as the king took one weak step and then another.

"Why do you speak to him?" the princess asked.

"Because we really don't know if he can hear anything or not. Even if it's just sound he picks up when we are with him and he has no ability to distinguish words, it may make him feel more a part of things if we address him. Does that make sense?"

She laughed. "Hardly."

Devlin frowned.

"I see I've injured the young doctor's feelings. Forgive me. I am not one for sentiment. Am I, Papa?" She turned her attention back to Devlin after receiving no answer. "See? It makes little difference."

"Princess Sophia, he is your father, and if you spend time with him, you may as well speak to him. You don't know for certain what he hears."

"Well, I'm sure he'll tell me when we are both with our Maker. Until then, we will just have to muddle through as best we can. But don't despair. I will take your recommendation into consideration."

"What is your signal to alert your father when you approach? Will you show us and let him know you are here?"

She nodded, then reached out and put her hand on her father's chest, just over his heart.

"Is there anything he enjoys doing?" Mercy asked. "Anything from which he derives any pleasure at all?" She continued to hold the king's hand.

"Not anymore. Not even food, I'm afraid. You can see how thin he is. Why do you ask?"

"I have an idea. One that the king may enjoy a great deal."

"What would that be? I'm all ears."

Devlin raised a brow. "As am I."

"I need a basin, a pitcher of warm water, soap, a soft cloth, and two or three plump cushions."

"What on earth for?" asked the princess.

"I'll show you."

Princess Sophia nodded to her maid, who curtsied and hurried from the room.

"I want your father to experience something pleasant. He's lost his wife, his vision, his hearing, his ability to rule. He has very little left."

"I know all these things, Lady Mercy. There is nothing to be done unless you believe, as my brother does, that this spear Lord Eden lost has the capability to heal our father. I think my brother only wishes to assuage his guilt at the way he is becoming king—not that he is becoming the king."

Mercy ignored the remarks, though she thought they were probably true. "I want to wash your father's feet just as mine were washed upon our arrival. I think it will help him feel better and know in an unusual way that others care for his well-being. And when I am done it will be up to you, Princess Sophia, if you want to do the same."

"I–I don't know. It's unusual and servants' work. I never thought about anything so intimate. It is intimate, isn't it?"

"Something a daughter would do for a father she loves. When there is no longer a way to communicate with words and looks, then we must look for alternatives." Mercy poured the water into the basin and felt the temperature. "Nice and warm. Devlin, would you seat the king on this chair? I will sit on the floor. Thus the need for the cushions."

She lowered herself to the floor and made herself comfortable at the feet of the king. The servants stood nearby with all the necessities. She easily slipped off the king's slippers after she'd reintroduced herself. The odor of his unwashed feet almost made her wretch, but that was something else she'd prepared herself for just as she'd had to get accustomed to other odors in the dissecting and exam rooms in Scotland. Then she picked up his right foot.

"Nooo." He resisted and pulled his foot back, not knowing what to expect.

"Mercy," Devlin said, still holding the king's arm as he sat next to him, "rub the cloth against his foot before you pick it up."

"That might do it." She took the cloth and gently touched the king's foot with it. He jumped at first. Then she stroked his foot from toe to heel and the king relaxed. She took it a step further and picked up his foot. Receiving no resistance this time, she settled it into the basin.

The king sighed and nodded.

"This is one way to show love when all else is lost. It must be through the power of touch." Mercy thought this an ideal time to also use her understanding of the foot's pressure points to bring healing to other parts of the body.

"I do believe I will arrange the same treatment for myself," Princess Sophia said. "Look at the expression on his face."

"He's in his own state of heaven." Devlin smiled. "This is a wonderful doctoring for the king. I commend your thoughtfulness and good thinking, Mercy."

Mercy looked up at her brother and grinned. "Why, thank you, brother." She applied medium pressure to the bottom of the king's right foot. "I consider that—"

Water drenched Mercy's gown, and the basin flew over her head in a sudden eruption. The king laughed and nearly slipped from his chair. Then everyone chuckled along with him.

Mercy looked up from the floor, shaking the water from her hair. "He's ticklish."

Chapter 14

There is no charm equal to
tenderness of heart.
—Jane Austen

Eden sat in the breakfast room sipping a cup of strong coffee and reading the morning *Times*. Jasper Kane was presenting a lecture this evening. If anyone might have heard of the whereabouts of the spear, it would be Kane.

"Good morning," Mercy said from the doorway. "Don't tell me my brother has left you and me here together without a chaperone."

Cook bustled into the room with a plate of eggs, bacon, toast, and potatoes. "I daresay your brother has wits better than that, Lady Mercy. I'm to be your chaperone until your sister arrives. Your brother was called away to Bethlem." She set the plate on the table. "Well, sit down or the food will be cold before you get to it."

Mercy laughed. "And when did cool food prevent me from eating?" She hugged Cook. "I've missed you."

Cook flushed and waved her away. "Aye, not enough to drag yourself back from the north for a visit. I thought you'd gone off and eloped with a Scotsman like your aunt did."

"I've no interest in marrying anyone, Cook." She sat down at the table and breathed in the aroma.

"That's what they all say. Then you look away for a moment and a wedding's being planned."

Lord Eden enjoyed the banter. "If you think that's too much food for you, Lady Mercy, I'll help you finish it off." He tried not to stare at her. She wore a dark green velvet pelisse over a lighter green walking dress. Her short, dark hair swept forward in wisps about her face. And then he remembered cutting off her beautiful long curls on the beach. The effect made her eyes sparkle, and when she looked at him, he would swear he saw humor there.

"Still feeling guilty?" She playfully slapped his hand away as he reached for her bacon. "Not if you're planning to keep your fingers. How's that eye this morning?"

"About the same. Still fuzzy vision when I take the patch off. I'm beginning to think that it may stay this way. And, yes, I'm still feeling guilty, but I'm getting over it."

"Be patient. Your eye needs more time to heal before anyone can determine the quality of your vision. And as far as the guilt is concerned, I give you permission to carry it about for a while longer."

He watched her shovel the scrambled eggs into her mouth without spilling a bit. "What is 'more time'?"

"When it's all better, of course." She poured some tea and wafted her hand over the top to cool it off.

"Of course. Why didn't I think of that? And what would you consider 'a while longer' regarding the guilt?"

"I'll let you know. What's in the paper today? Anything of interest?"

"Not really." He forced himself to return to the paper in order to quit staring at her.

"May I have that section if you're done with it? I'd like to see if there is any talk of the physicians coming to St. Guys or any of the other hospitals to teach this spring. One of my brother's old professors, Dr. Langford, comes to town from Yorkshire now and then. I thought I might sit in on one of his lectures."

The sound of the knocker echoed through the downstairs. "That must be Victoria," Mercy said.

But it was the sound of male voices that carried into the breakfast room.

Devlin's butler, Henry, entered the room. "Your driver has arrived, Lord Eden. He said he will wait for you outside so as not to interrupt your morning meal."

Eden shook out the paper, folded it smartly, and handed it to Mercy. "Duty calls." He stood and bowed. "I hope to see you later, Lady Mercy."

"Where are you going?" she asked with a surprised look on her face. "You're not well yet."

"On the contrary, I'm much stronger. I was hoping to see your sister in order to thank her for putting me up in her home while I healed. I owe her and you and your brother a great deal, and I hope to someday repay your kindness."

She sat up straighter as if to argue with him. He smiled, picked up his napkin, and ever so gently wiped a piece of egg from the corner of her mouth. "Thank you, Lady Mercy." Then he tilted her head up and softly kissed her lips.

Mac awaited him with the team of dappled grays and the crested carriage. "Mac, take me to Jackson's. I've got so much restless energy pent up after these past weeks that I could box all afternoon."

"Aye, restless energy is looking out through the curtains at ye."

Eden turned and looked before he caught himself acting like a lovesick puppy. She waved at him and he waved back. Then he growled at Mac as he swung up into the carriage.

Mac shoved his hat up off his brow and said, "It's going to be a long time till we sail again. I can see that now." He flicked the reins over the horse's rumps and pulled out onto Grosvenor Square.

Eden walked up the flight of stairs and opened a door that led into Gentleman John Jackson's Salon, the foremost emperor of pugilism. A pudgy-faced man with a black eye and a short but strongly built body met him with a quick smile when he entered the premises. Jackson's catered to some of the richest men in England, including the noblemen of the aristocracy.

"Welcome, Lord Eden. I heard you was back in town. Looks like you got hurt."

"Thanks, Pug. I'm glad to be back. And don't go acting like you don't know what's happened. You know everything that goes on in this town. I need to work off a bit of steam and tone this body up a bit before I turn completely soft."

"You'll never go soft, yer lordship. It's not in you to do so. You might want to observe the men sparring in the corner." He tilted his head toward them.

"And why would I want to do that?" Eden stared off at the two men boxing, but from this distance he couldn't see who they were.

"Word on the street is that the muscle-bound gentleman is working for Kane. It's a well-kept secret, if you know what I mean."

"You never disappoint, Pug. I think I'll go watch." He pulled a coin from his pocket and threw it straight up. Pug caught it with a well-practiced slice through the air.

Eden joined a few of the others who were watching the men spar. They were well matched and had been going at each other for a while. "Who's the favorite?" he whispered to a man on his right who was mirroring the ducking and dodging of the pair.

"Just practice, your lordship. No betting allowed in these rooms, you know."

Eden pulled a bill from his coat pocket and handed it to the man, who looked as if he hadn't gone home after the pubs closed last night. "Of course."

The man looked around. "Marks there, with the beefy arms."

"Put my money on the other gent."

"Not meaning to tell you how to do business, yer lordship, but that might not be wise."

"Why?"

"'Cause he's losing, of course."

"Sometimes," Eden said, studying the fighters' footwork, "things are not as they seem." He wondered if this was the coward who had nearly blinded him.

The man sparring with Marks threw a left jab to the other's jaw at his first opportunity. Marks hit the floor, out cold.

Eden smiled his satisfaction.

A wave of disappointment rolled through the sparse crowd of onlookers. "About time you showed yourself, Eden," the man said, jogging toward Eden.

"No, Jackson. I've got my best clothes on. Jackson, wait." He was grasped in a bear hug that threatened to reinjure his healing ribs. He grunted, and the other man released him immediately.

"I'd heard you'd been injured. You should have stopped me," Jackson said, stepping back and eyeing his friend from head to toe.

"I tried."

"I didn't realize it was serious. I thought it another of your midnight brawls over a woman."

"Hardly. I came over to work off a building restlessness and see how out of condition I am since the attack."

"Attack? What happened? When?"

"It's a long story. I just want to punch the bag a bit and stretch these muscles."

"I'll work with you, and we shall save the talk for another time."

Mercy read with interest the information about the Legend Seekers Club and the evening's lecture to the members of the ton that would be held in Piccadilly at Egyptian Hall. A special announcement was mentioned but would not be discussed until the assembly had gathered. The knocker alerted her, and she thought this certainly had to be Victoria.

Mercy hurried to the front door, where Henry was letting her sister in. Thankfully Lazarus was not in tow. "So you left the beast at home, did you?"

"He's so sad. But I told him I would bring him back a treat." Victoria hugged her. "What about your hair? Don't you want to go out? I know I want to hear all the details of your trip to Windsor. And where did you get the green pelisse? And the walking gown?"

"Madeline's, of course. But Dev said she wouldn't mind, and he's right. I'm just glad she leaves some of her clothes here. Otherwise I'm not sure what I'd have done for today. I just finished breakfast. Devlin's at Bethlem, and Lord Eden has disappeared with his driver, Mac. He says he's better, but he still has much healing to do. And, being a man, of course he won't listen to reason. Come sit down and have a cup of tea with me before we leave."

"I'd love a cup of tea. And a biscuit, or something a bit heartier." She leaned in and whispered. "I'm feeling a bit queasy."

"How exciting."

"Only if you are not the one feeling queasy."

"I'll have Cook bring something." She rang for Cook and watched Victoria sit down across the table, imagining what her only sister would look like pregnant. "I can't wait to see how Jonathon takes the news. He'll probably lock you up in the country and forbid you to lift a finger until you are safely delivered. And then, of course, there's the effect it will have on our brother. Can you imagine Devlin as an uncle? There'll be no stopping the amount of spoiling he'll do."

"And that is exactly why I don't want to tell either of them for as long as possible. I'll lose my freedom and my snooping time in London."

Cook entered the room. "Countess." Cook curtsied. "I didn't know it was you that arrived. There's been too many comings and goings this morning. Would you like a fresh pot of tea and a warm scone? Fresh from the oven, they are."

"That sounds lovely, Cook. Thank you."

"And I'll bring two for you, Lady Mercy. I know how you love them."

"And if I'm not careful I'll be too embarrassed to be fitted for the clothes I need."

Cook left them, and Victoria studied Mercy. "I would much prefer that we solve this situation with your Lord Eden before I am forced to be pampered."

"*My* Lord Eden? He is not mine." She felt the blush rise above her gown and creep into her cheeks. "His mind is full of only his most pressing plans: locating the spear, handing it over to Prinny, and diving into his next adventure, I imagine. He doesn't seem the type to remain in one place for very long."

"Ah. You are attracted to him. I thought so. It would be difficult to spend so much time with an available and handsome man and not be attracted to him."

"Snoop, stop it. Lord Eden and I have no serious affection for one another. We were just thrown into circumstances that kept us together for an unusual amount of time. Now he is going his way and I am going mine."

Cook bustled in again with a fresh pot of tea and cinnamon

scones on a silver tray. "This should satisfy both of you." She set the scones and tea on the table. "Will there be anything else?"

"I think you've spoiled us, Cook," Mercy said. "Thank you. We'll be leaving after we've done sufficient damage to these lovely smelling scones."

"Eat hearty. Enjoy your day." Cook bobbed another curtsy and was gone.

Mercy waited until she was certain Cook was out of earshot. "And have you forgotten about my dilemma? What am I to do, Snoop? And what about this?" She pulled the onyx and gold amulet from around her neck. "What am I to do with this? I haven't told Dev or Lord Eden. You're the only one who knows." She put her hand to her head. "I think I'm getting a headache. This is all overwhelming when I think what must be resolved."

"You're leaning too heavily on your own abilities. Trust God. He is strong when we are weak, remember?" Victoria took a long sip of tea.

"You're right. I'm always trying to take control of problems I turn over to God. It's just so hard not to keep trying to do the work."

"You do the best you can, sister, without the worry, and then the rest is up to God, no matter the outcome. That's where faith comes in." Victoria bit into a scone. "This is heaven."

"I know you're right. I know you are. But sometimes it's just so hard to wait while God does what He does. I've never been patient, Victoria. You know that." She picked up a scone and waved it under her nose, enjoying the aroma. Then she bit into it. "Mmm. Pure heaven."

"I'm always right," Victoria said teasingly. "Except when I'm wrong."

"Well, speaking of right and wrong..." Mercy grabbed the

folded newspaper and found the section about the evening's lecture. "The Legend Seekers are meeting at seven at the museum. I haven't mentioned it to Devlin or to Lord Eden, though I suspect that Lord Eden will be there. If I were looking for a lost relic, I'd wonder if this speaker, Jasper Kane, might be able to help." She handed the paper to her sister. "You've heard him speak before?"

"He's a fascinating man and handsome too. Not in the way that Jonathon is handsome, of course, but intriguing nonetheless." She read the article and sipped her tea.

"What do we do about Devlin? Do we tell him we're going? He knows that many of the ton will be there. I hoped to discuss it with him this morning, but he was gone when I came down."

"We'll simply leave him a message when we shop. If he hasn't come back by the time we're ready to leave tonight, then we've done all we can. Since I am a respectable married lady, I will be your chaperone. Devlin can meet us there."

"It's a plan then."

"Now," Victoria said, "tell me everything about your excursion to Windsor yesterday."

Devlin stared into the black eyes of the huge African man through the bars of the cell in a secluded part of Bethlem Hospital below ground. "I don't know if you can understand a thing I say, but you are in great danger. There's a reason they call this place Bedlam. If you want to get out of here, you must tell me what you were doing, what you were planning, and most important of all, what you are thinking."

The African stood with arms outstretched to the heavens chanting in an unknown language from an unknown place in

Africa where he practiced things Devlin imagined not to be of God. "How am I going to help you? Should I help you? Why have our paths crossed? There must be a reason. There's always a reason." The African put his arms down and walked to the bars where Devlin stood on the opposite side. He put a fist over his chest. "Sakpata."

"Is that your name? Or where you are from? Or something completely different?" Devlin asked. He placed a fist over his chest and said, "Ravensmoore."

"Sakpata!"

Devlin ran a hand through his hair. "This is getting us nowhere. Lord, a little help please."

"Lord Sakpata!" The African nodded and strutted around the cell. "Lord Sakpata!" He pulled an ebony amulet with gold markings from his shirt seemingly as an attempt to prove what he said was so. "Sakpata!"

Devlin bowed. "Lord Ravensmoore."

Sakpata did not bow in return but stood with his arms crossed, unmoving. Devlin thought he was being put in his place by this man who wanted to make it known that he was more in charge than anyone thought him to be.

"All right, we're getting somewhere now. I just don't know where. You are either suffering from delusions of grandeur, completely out of touch with reality, or you have been practicing something like witchcraft or some tribal vodun that will not bode well for you here in England."

The African moved toward the bars of the cell again. He wrapped his hands around the bars and said, "Vodun lord."

Chapter 15

With foxes, we must play the fox.
—Thomas Fuller

"I'm growing excited about the prospect of this evening's lecture and announcement," Victoria said as she gathered her gold silk gown to mount the steps with Mercy and enter the lecture hall at Bullock's Museum in Piccadilly. The Egyptian façade gave the building an adventurous aura. The archaeologist and expeditionist Jasper Kane was drawing quite a crowd.

There were lords and ladies of the ton, as well as the very wealthy who were not considered aristocracy but were well known in England for their position in society. This included men in the shipping business, bankers, and wealthy land owners.

Mercy heard a young woman behind her whisper to her friend.

"I've heard that he's recently been to Africa."

"I thought it was Egypt."

Victoria looked at Mercy, and they both stifled laughter that came near to giggles. They were approaching the receiving line where Mr. Kane was greeting his guests. Mercy said, "He is a handsome man, isn't he?"

"The ladies dote upon him," Victoria said. "I think his opinion of himself grows too large."

"It's the *on dit* that he's in love with one of the young dowagers," a woman said to her husband on their left. "He's gaining quite a reputation, and it's not all good."

"It appears there is gossip everywhere about this man," Mercy whispered to her sister behind the fan she held. "I'm intrigued. Now, how does the wig look? Is it holding up well?"

"You look magnificent. Your new wig is near perfection. The way the back sweeps off your neck is so natural looking, no one would ever know."

"And I love what your maid did with the peach-colored flowers and white pearls she looped through my hair. It accentuates the peach in the gown, and the feel of this silk is incredible. Thank heaven the modiste was able to fit me in so quickly. The minor adjustments to the gown that had been rejected by a previous customer proved a treasure to me. I love it."

"You will have every man's interest focused on you this evening. I'm afraid not many will pay attention to Mr. Kane."

The line moved quickly, and Mercy found herself standing in front of a gentleman at least as tall as her brother with dark blond hair and blue eyes that questioned. She squirmed under his gaze.

"Hello. I don't believe we've met before. I'd recall someone as memorable as you." His voice lowered to husky, and his eyes assessed her like he might a brood mare. "Forgive me. I am Jasper Kane, and you are?"

Mercy heard Victoria saying, "This is my sister, Lady Mercy Grayson of Ravensmoore."

"Lady Mercy, a pleasure." He bowed. "And Countess Witt." He took her gloved hand and bestowed a kiss upon it. "Where is your very fortunate husband this evening?"

"He's still in the country on business, Mr. Kane. I expect him any day now. He's bringing some new horses into Tattersall's."

"I'll be certain to keep my eyes on the paper for that sale.

He has an incredible breeding stock and an exceptional eye for beauty. Lady Mercy, I hope you will spare me some of your time after the lecture. There are some unique pieces I would like to show you myself."

"As long as you do not mind me following along as chaperone, Mr. Kane," Victoria said, smiling. "I don't think your tastes run to antiquities alone."

"You underestimate me, Lady Witt. I'd be happy to show both of you about. Now I must greet the rest of my guests before the lecture begins."

They moved past Jasper Kane and into the large entry hall milling with the ton. Mercy pulled Victoria aside. "Really, Snoop. 'I don't think your tastes run to antiquities alone'? How could you say such a thing?"

"Did you see the way he was ogling you? I thought he might gobble you up there on the spot. The two of you were drawing attention. I know just what he's thinking, and you'd better stay close to me tonight. I believe he's a wolf. He's out to devour you, make no mistake about it. He didn't even bother with the sheep's clothing."

Mercy smiled. "Thank you," she said as she hugged her sister, "for watching out for me. It's lovely having a big sister."

"Don't you think it's about time I started playing the part? You were like the older sister for so many years taking care of me. Now it's fun to be the big sister and tell you what to do."

Mercy smacked her gently on the arm with her fan. "Come on. Let's go look around and see the displays. I'm more than curious."

They passed some of the more crowded displays and stopped farther into the hall. Victoria said, "Look at this." She pulled Mercy over to a display that showed large and small blowguns with the poisoned darts used in them. "Grisly, isn't it? How awful to be hit with a dart. It reminds me of a miniature bow and arrow. You'd have to have great skill to blow one of these out of the tube and actually hit something."

Mercy read the information about the display. "It says here that they were carried in quivers, just like arrows. These are from the Amazon jungle and can fly faster than an arrow."

"They're pretty." Victoria marveled over the display. "I wonder why they decorate them. There's one with colorful feathers, another with monkeys. That seems culturally suitable, doesn't it?"

"They may be pretty, but I wouldn't want to get in the path of one." Mercy's eye was drawn to an ancient statue of Asclepius, whom the Greeks considered a god of healing. "Look at this, Victoria. It's so hard for me to understand all the different gods the Greeks believed in. I don't know how the lowly mortals kept them all straight. It's fascinating to decipher other cultures."

"Perhaps fascinating, but beware of Greeks bearing gifts, so they do not draw you away from your beliefs, sister." Victoria was looking at the next display of surgical instruments—supposedly discovered in Rome—of forceps, bone chisels, and needles. "I think I'm going to find it difficult to get you out of here this evening, and it will have nothing to do with men. Look at these, Mercy. Our brother would be infatuated."

Mercy joined her sister and studied the glass-enclosed artifacts. "As am I. Don't you ever wonder how they managed life in that time? I dread to contemplate too much what surgery looked like in that day, though I understand from my studies that it was attempted."

"There's not much to be done regarding surgery even today," a familiar male voice said from behind them.

She turned to see Devlin, but her eye caught a figure watching her from the balcony, where even more exhibits were on display. She gasped.

"What is it?" Devlin asked, turning to follow her line of vision.

"I'm not sure. I thought I saw someone up there. Someone watching me."

"I don't see anyone," Devlin said, but he continued to scan the balcony. "Probably just a trick of the light through the windows."

Mercy tried to pull her thoughts together, but Devlin was too quick for her. "What's wrong? You look pale."

"I'm fine. Just taken aback for a moment. I've just realized the enormity of this room and the balcony. It's incredible the number of artifacts and antiquities on display." Her heart hammered as the figure she'd thought she'd seen took form in her mind. John Marks. It had looked like John Marks from Scotland, the one man who knew her secret, and maybe more.

Victoria stepped next to her sister as another gentleman spoke to their brother. "What's happened? You saw someone, didn't you?"

Mercy once again hid behind her fan while she talked to her sister. "I think it was him. The man I was running from in Scotland. The man who followed me to the ship I was thrown from."

"You're in danger. We must tell Devlin."

"No, I'm not sure. As he said, it may have been a trick of the light."

"I hope so, for your sake. And I don't like keeping this secret. I want you to tell him before the evening's out."

She nodded. "I will." Still, she was apprehensive, for once she told her story about John Marks, then it wouldn't be long before she'd have to reveal all about what she'd really been doing in Scotland. Her brother would not be happy about the deceit.

Devlin finished talking to the man who had approached him with some question of lunacy law. Her brother was well known now for his work within the lunacy trade and the changes he'd made when turning Ashcroft Asylum into Safe Haven.

"Well, now, it looks as though the ton has made a nice showing this evening," Devlin said, looking around the room. "Not as many as I expected, but enough curiosity seekers."

"Our host is working his way toward the podium," Victoria said, looping her arm through his.

"Allow me to escort you to your seats, my sisters."

Devlin found three seats nearby that had not yet been claimed. They didn't supply the best view of the podium, but they did offer a splendid opportunity to observe the surrounding areas yet not be easily spotted.

They settled into their seats—Devlin on the outside and then Mercy and Victoria.

Kane walked to the podium. "Welcome. Welcome to an amazing evening of discovery. You've come to the right place to unearth treasures never seen before in England from as far away as Egypt, Africa, and even Asia."

Mercy listened with interest as Kane walked his audience through adventures in jungles and on the high seas as he and his men traveled and explored many lands. He captivated the men with stories of near death and astounded the women with stories of love and adventure.

"Now I want to show you a piece from Africa." He held up a large mask. "This is said to have belonged to the leader of a very frightening tribe led by a vodun king, or sakpata. The sakpata is said to rule over the earth and can bring diseases such as smallpox and leprosy to those he wishes to curse."

Kane held the mask high, and Devlin squeezed Mercy's arm so hard that she cried out. The mask was black and sculpted with yellow feathers near the headpiece.

"What's wrong? You nearly bruised my arm," Mercy whispered loudly and looked at Devlin, who was captivated by the mask.

"I'm sorry. So sorry, Mercy. But something is terribly wrong here."

"What is it, Devlin?" Victoria asked, leaning across Mercy and grabbing her fan to conceal her question as much as possible.

"That face. That face is one of my patients in Bethlem."

"What are you talking about?"

"I must talk with Kane tonight. There's some connection between him and my patient, and I'm going to find out just what it is. Stay here. I'll be back soon."

Kane went on at length about tribal vodun rituals and curses and such, details Mercy found disappointing. He was sensationalizing superstition to seduce his audience, and, from the looks on most of the faces, she could see he was doing a fine job of it.

"And now I want to offer you a proposition—an opportunity for you to go on an expedition. An expedition both dangerous and alluring to what we know as New South Wales in Australia. But beware that the expedition will be expensive, and only the hardiest of men should even consider such a journey."

Mercy saw a shadow move near an alcove to her far left. She felt certain someone watched her. She tried to pay attention to what was being said.

"What is it that you hope to discover on this adventure, Kane?" asked a man in the audience.

Mercy saw something flutter in the shadows once again. She kept her eyes focused on the area past the displays and deeper into the recesses behind them. Mercy whispered, "Victoria, where did Devlin go?"

"I'm not sure. Shhh, listen."

"A good question, indeed," Kane said. "The answer is diamonds."

A wave of excitement filtered through the audience. A man near the back stood up and asked, "How do we even know any diamonds exist in Australia?"

"Because I have proof, of course," Kane said. He opened a piece of emerald green cloth, cupped it in his hands, and walked to the rear where the gentleman stood. The man gasped. "These must be worth a fortune!" The crowd stirred again.

Another man asked, "Why should we believe those diamonds came from Australia? And how do we know there are any left?"

"I will answer all your questions." Kane walked back to the podium and settled the diamonds into a leather pouch.

Then the atmosphere changed and the audience hushed. There was a slight undercurrent of restlessness that started at the podium and worked its way to the back of the room.

"Look. It's Lord Eden." Victoria went to grab Mercy's arm, but she wasn't there. Victoria's eyes swept over the room. *Perhaps she's with Devlin. She must be.*

"Pardon me, Mr. Kane. But I have a question."

Kane's eyes narrowed. "What would you like to know?"

"There's a piece of information missing here. A very valuable piece, I'm wagering. If you have these diamonds and you know where there are more, why would you share that information with us? Why not keep it all for yourself?"

"First of all, sir, I'll answer the questions that were asked in the back. I have documents that guarantee these are genuine diamonds discovered in Australia and that there are indeed thought to be more, many more, in fact."

Lord Eden walked down the center aisle dressed in doeskin britches, a coat the color of spice, and a cream-colored shirt with matching cravat tied in intricate knots. The patch on his eye gave him the look of not only a pirate but also a formidable one at that.

"Thought to be more? Or are more? How certain are you?"

The room hushed.

"I'm very certain."

"Then," Eden turned back to those gathered and quirked a brow, "why *do* you need anyone else?" He swung back around to face Kane.

"Because expeditions are expensive, and I don't want the burden of the entire trip on my shoulders. I need help. That's what it comes down to, but there's a fortune in diamonds to be brought back if anyone is brave enough and adventurous enough to join me. Have I answered your questions, Lord Eden?"

"Indeed you have, Mr. Kane. Indeed you have." He turned to address the audience. "Forgive me for aggressively questioning the details of this possible expedition. But I would encourage each of you—"

Countess Witt captured his attention, and she was looking most worried.

Kane said, "You seem to have lost your thought."

"Well, I–I encourage each of you to consider wisely. I, for one, will not be chasing rainbows." Lord Eden moved away from the podium and circled around to where the countess sat, alone.

"What's wrong?" He slid into the seat where Devlin had been. Kane continued his plea for adventurers.

"They're gone. Both of them," she said in a rush. "Both my brother and sister. Dev said he would be back, but Mercy just disappeared. One moment she was here, and then I turned to her and she was gone."

Eden surveyed the room. "I don't like the sound of that, Countess. I'm going to look for them."

"Not without me, you're not." She thought he was about to refuse her.

"Very well. But remain close. I don't want you disappearing too."

They left their seats and quietly walked behind the displays on the main floor. From the shadows Victoria could see the eager faces of young men clearly under Kane's spell of treasure hunting. She scanned the crowd for her brother and Mercy, but they were not there.

"Look." Eden pointed to stairs that led up to the balcony or down to the basement of the building. "Let's go down."

They descended the stairs. Wall sconces flickered in the dimness to reveal boxes and crates. Victoria's senses heightened, and she hoped that the pounding of her heart would not give them away if someone else were in the basement with them.

She pulled up for a moment. Eden had hold of her wrist, and her hesitancy stopped him. When he looked at her, she shook her head and mouthed, "I don't think they're here."

He held up two fingers. "Two minutes," he mouthed back. Then they quietly moved forward. The program upstairs must have ended then. Voices with an edge of excitement could be heard as the crowd continued to move about the room.

Eden stopped so fast that Victoria bumped into him.

"What is it?" she whispered.

"A trunk. It has markings on it I recognize from the ship. Stay right behind me. I don't think anyone is down here with us, but let's proceed with the utmost caution."

She nodded and followed him. The trunk did indeed have markings on it—unusual markings that seemingly caused her blood to surge faster through her veins. It had the same markings as the amulet around her sister's neck, the necklace that had been thrown over her head just before she'd been tossed overboard.

He opened the unlocked lid. It was filled with African clothing and an assortment of beads and masks. She watched Eden rifle through the contents in search, it seemed, of his prize.

"I feel something." He leaned deeper into the trunk.

"Lord Eden, do be careful. What is it you seek?"

A large calloused hand clamped over her mouth. She tried to scream.

The lid of the trunk slammed hard against Lord Eden's back.

Then all went dark.

Chapter 16

There are some that only employ words for
the purpose of disguising their thoughts.
—Voltaire

"I've been looking for you everywhere. Where did you go?" Mercy found Devlin returning to the building just as she went to search for him outside.

"It's a long story and growing more complicated. Where's Snoop?"

"Inside with Lord Eden. When I left, he was confronting Mr. Kane about the diamond expedition he hoped to gain financing for, and I think he may have talked some of the young fools into the venture."

Devlin shook his head. "No doubt." He offered her his arm. "Come on. Let's find Snoop and go home. I'm hungry."

When they entered the building, many of the crowd had dispersed, though some still lingered over the displays and four gentlemen encircled Kane, listening to him with wide, curious eyes and open wallets.

Mercy scanned the room and the balcony. She hadn't been able to locate the shadowy figure she thought she'd seen earlier, and perhaps that was best. What would she have done if she'd caught him? And the possibility that it had been John Marks was remote. "I don't see them anywhere."

"Nor I, and I don't like it. I thought I'd told Victoria I'd be back."

"Maybe they're looking for us. I don't think I said anything to Victoria. I wasn't planning on going far. "

"It's Lord Eden," Mercy gasped. "He's hurt."

Eden clung to a balustrade as he made his way up the stairs from the basement.

"What's happened, Eden?" Devlin demanded. "Where's my sister?"

"I–I don't know. Someone attacked us. I was hoping she'd gone for help."

"Blast the wicked devil. Kane!" Devlin yelled. "Get down here immediately. My sister, the Countess Witt, is missing. If anything's happened to her, I'll hold you responsible. This was your event! Where was your security?"

"I'm sure there's a logical explanation," Kane said, wearing a look of complete annoyance as he approached the three. "I'm trying to conduct affairs of business here. Now what's happened?"

"I'll tell you what's happened," Eden said, grabbing Kane by the lapels of his green velvet jacket. "I was knocked out when someone slammed a trunk lid on me in this basement, and when I came to, the countess was gone."

Kane smirked. "What were you doing in the basement?"

Mercy spoke up. "They were looking for me. I'm sorry, but I thought I saw someone I knew, and I failed to tell my sister I was leaving."

"Well, let's go to the basement and see if we can find her," Kane growled. He turned to the gentlemen who were waiting. "I will return shortly. Please be patient."

The men nodded, conveying their own looks of annoyance to Kane, and continued talking to each other.

"I swear," Kane said, descending the long curving staircase

into the basement, "if you cost me their agreements to finance this next expedition, I will demand satisfaction."

"Let's concentrate on finding my sister," Devlin said, "because I swear I will have you put in Newgate if anything has happened to her."

Mercy yelled, "Victoria! Victoria, are you down here?"

"Show us where you were when the attack occurred," Devlin ordered.

They all shouted her name as Lord Eden led them to the trunk. "The markings are the same as I saw on board the *Agwe*. Vodun symbols." He lifted the lid. "Valuable vodun masks and clothing."

"Victoria! Where are you?" Devlin yelled.

"If she's hurt..." Mercy's eyes filled with tears as she thought of her sister and the baby. The baby! *Please, God.* And then she thought she heard something. "Listen!"

"It's coming from that wall." Devlin pointed to the right, where a mountain of crates and trunks were stacked.

"Victoria," yelled Mercy, "we're here!"

Again came the thumping.

"If it's Victoria, she's hitting up against one of the trunks over here, I think," Mercy said, leading the way to a distant corner.

The thumping grew louder. "Back here." Mercy pointed to a large trunk that was quivering from inside movement.

Devlin and Eden pushed other trunks out of the way and quickly unfastened the trappings of the trunk that was now vibrating beneath their hands. "Hang on, Victoria," Devlin shouted, and with a heave he lifted the lid to find clothes and blankets filling the trunk.

"Get her out!" Mercy said, throwing the contents onto the floor. "She's going to suffocate."

Victoria lay in the bottom of the trunk with hands and feet

bound and a gag stuffed into her mouth. Her blue eyes, wide with relief, were now filling with tears.

Devlin easily lifted her from the trunk that could have soon become her tomb.

"Victoria." He cradled her in his arms while Eden removed her gag and bonds.

She took a deep breath. "Thank God. Oh, thank God you heard me. I was so afraid." She wrapped her arms about her brother's neck and shook as great sobs escaped her throat.

Mercy looked at Devlin's pale face. He needed no words to express the fear and relief vying for control of his features. She put her arms around both of them and silently praised God.

"I'm all right now—I think," Victoria said, breathing hard. "I was just so scared. I didn't think any of you were going to hear me, and if you'd left, we would have perished." Her hand went to her abdomen.

Devlin gaped. "Snoop, are you with child?"

She nodded. "You don't think I'd be crying if it were just me, do you? It's all these emotions. They just come pouring out at the most awkward moments. Now look. All of you know about the baby, and I haven't even told Jonathon yet. Don't you dare tell him you know. Not any of you." She looked past Lord Eden and saw Mr. Kane. "That goes for you as well, Mr. Kane."

He nodded and smiled. "Your secret is safe with me. I'm just sorry you had to experience such an awful thing and at such a time. What can I do?"

"I want to go home," Victoria said. "Mercy, will you stay with me at the house? I don't want to be alone."

"Of course."

"First," Kane said, "can you give any kind of description of who attacked you?"

Victoria shook her head. "Everything happened so fast.

I remember a hand covering my mouth and seeing the trunk lid come down on Lord Eden. I tried to scream and must have fainted. The next thing I knew I was in darkness and could barely move."

"There must have been more than one wretched devil," Eden said, and cursed.

"I'm taking you home immediately," Devlin said. "I'll be staying with you as well. I want to keep an eye on you. This is too much for a woman carrying a babe."

"Please put me down, Dev. I can walk now."

"Not bloody likely. We'll put you to bed immediately, and I'm sending for your husband."

"He'll be in town soon. The horses, remember?"

"Good. I'll send for him anyway, just in case he's taking too long," he said as he carried her up the stairs.

Kane followed them back to the first floor. "Let me know if there is anything I can do. I'm very sorry for all this upheaval." He turned and left them to rejoin his supporters.

Lord Eden put his hand on Mercy's arm as they entered the deserted foyer. "Are you all right? Do you want to talk?"

"I don't know. I'm so unnerved. It's too much..." She held out her hand to steady herself against him. Mercy hadn't felt so helpless in a very long time, not even when she was in the ocean, terrified and fighting for her life. Almost losing Victoria and the unborn baby had started an avalanche of emotion inside her that now nearly caused her knees to buckle. Eden enfolded her in his arms, and she felt safe.

She loved the leather and clove scent of him, the strength of his arms, and the way he rested his chin on her head. She knew she should pull away, but she didn't want to. She didn't want this embrace to end.

He ended it. "They're waiting for you. I'll walk you to your brother's coach." He kissed her forehead. "I'll see you tomorrow," he whispered in her ear. Then he led her to the coach and handed her inside.

Eden dreamed of his next adventure, his next treasure hunt, his next journey into the unknown. But into each dream now entered a vision of a woman with raven hair and tempting green eyes and the smell of sunshine and sea on her skin. Her touch made his senses reel and his heart beat faster, and he wanted nothing to do with the fear it invited into his soul.

He woke in a tangle of bedsheets and a mounting sense of agony that all connected to the one thing he couldn't afford in his life, and that was complications that would interfere with what he'd decided he wanted a long time ago, a life free of entanglements and heartache. He could find a woman to ease his body anytime; he didn't need a wife. Blast it all! He didn't want a wife!

He threw the sheets aside and poured himself a liberal helping of brandy from the dressing table in his room, grateful to be back in his own townhome in London. The drink burned his throat the whole way into his stomach, where it rumbled like the tempest-tossed thoughts in his mind.

An internal whisper made him squeeze his eyes shut. *What are you running from? Why are you running away?* Maybe he could block it out with enough brandy. *It's time to stop.*

He pressed both hands to his temples, trying to erase the memories.

His father sat in the library and stared at the empty, cold hearth. "Sometimes I think I hear her talking to me, Vincent. Do you ever hear her?"

Vincent shook his head as he sat in the chair opposite his father. It was the eighteenth of June.

"No, you wouldn't, would you. When she died giving birth to you, my whole world crumbled. You're ten now. She would have loved you, but I–I just can't. You look just like her. You have her unique eye colors. The one blue eye and the other green."

"I'm sorry, Father. I know you don't love me, but I wish you would try."

"I'm sending you to live with your sister, Caroline. She'll love you. When I'm gone, Eden will be yours. And then you will learn what it means to have a wife and children. I pray you never experience the horrific grief I've known."

Vincent St. Lyons forced the visions of the past from his mind and drank more brandy, and then even more brandy, until he could no longer remember or care.

"Lord Eden? You've an urgent message from His Majesty the prince regent."

Vincent heard his valet through a haze too heavy to disperse. He groaned and rolled over onto his back, taking the pillow with him, and ineffectively tried to muffle the onslaught of unintelligible words he was certain he did not want to hear.

"Lord Eden! You must awaken. Lord Ravensmoore awaits you in the library, and he doesn't appear to be in a good mood."

He threw the pillow aside, being careful to keep his eyes closed. "Tell Ravensmoore—"

A deluge of cold water splashed over his face. "What the devil?" He bolted upright. "Pooles, have you lost your senses? What do you—" He blinked and blinked again, wiping the water from his eyes and shaking the excess from his hair, and then groaning at the agony that sliced through his head.

"It's not Pooles you need chastise," Devlin said. "I don't care how foxed you became last evening. You are going with me to see Prinny, and you will act sober."

"I don't take orders from you or anyone else. Now get out of my house, or I'll throw you out as soon as I find my pants." He stood up and Pooles handed him the basin.

Eden sat down hard on the bed and vomited into the basin. "I feel like a herd of horses trampled me in my sleep." He vomited again.

Ravensmoore said, "Pooles, would you be kind enough to mix the contents of this draft together and bring it to your pitiful excuse of a master?"

Eden turned his head from the basin and squinted at his valet holding a piece of paper. "Don't do it, Pooles. I'm not drinking anything except some strong coffee."

"Do it, Pooles. I insist," Ravensmoore said in a no-nonsense tone. "And if Eden here is dense enough to dismiss you from your post, then I'll hire you."

"Yes, sir," Pooles said, smiling. "Right away, sir." He left the room and could be heard whistling a jaunty tune as he descended the stairs to the first level of the house to prepare the concoction.

Ravensmoore picked up the crystal decanter of brandy. "This stuff will pickle your brain and land you in Bedlam, Newgate, or the grave. Which do you prefer?"

"I have other plans."

"Yes, I imagine you do." Ravensmoore set the decanter down

with a firmness that echoed through the room. "However, if you think they involve my sister, you are mistaken."

Eden's pulse quickened, and he wished his thoughts were less foggy so he could discuss this matter with intelligence. However, intelligence was not something he possessed at the moment. "I have no intentions toward your sister, Ravensmoore. You've nothing to be concerned about."

Ravensmoore walked to the bedroom window and whipped open the heavy blue drapery to let in the bright morning sun.

"Blast it! Close the drapes. I am not yet ready to face the day, and well you know it. Where's that patch?" Eden buried his head in his hands to relieve the stabbing pain in his injured eye. "Some doctor you are. I'm nearly blinded already in one eye, and you seek to complete the deed."

"I'll close the drapes when you agree to a truth session. Here and now. Or I'll simply see you at Carleton House. It's your choice."

"Hardly a choice." He grimaced and nodded. "Agreed. Now close the drapes."

The drapes were yanked back into place. "You butchered my sister's hair, disguised her as your valet, slept with her in the same cabin, nearly got yourself killed, and then my sister cared for your injuries. Yesterday, when Victoria and I awaited Mercy in the coach, I saw the two of you embrace."

"I was simply comforting her. She'd been through an ordeal, and it just happened. How are your sisters?"

"They are both fine, but don't try to distract me from what I'm telling you." He pulled up a chair and straddled it with the back facing Eden. "I would die for my sisters. I am not going to allow Mercy to throw her life away on someone who has no respect for her or God. From the way you're drinking, I suspect you may not even have respect for yourself."

"How dare you suggest that I have no respect for Lady Mercy. I protected her from all the men onboard the ship the only way I knew how when I discovered her on the beach. I only added to the disguise she wore already when I cut her hair."

Ravensmoore's eyes narrowed. "What disguise?"

"She was dressed in men's clothing when she washed up on the sand. Didn't she tell you?"

The lord doctor's face paled. "No, she didn't tell me. In what manner of dress did you bring her into town?"

"She remained in disguise as a valet until she entered your sister's home." The onset of understanding swept through his bewildered senses. "They didn't tell you."

"Mercy will be fine. Victoria needs rest."

Vincent cocked his head to the side. "Now who's changing the subject?" He tried to stare at his unwanted visitor, but he couldn't keep his left eye open and it began to tear.

"Let me examine that eye." Ravensmoore reached out and waited for Eden to permit his attention. "It's not healing the way I'd hoped."

"Can anything be done?"

"Perhaps an ointment. I'll see what can be found. Prayer is always at our disposal."

"I can't remember the last time I prayed," Eden said, and a feeling of awkwardness settled over him.

"I will pray for your healing and wisdom to know how to treat the eye. God willing, you will have good vision and relief soon, and then you can dispose of the patch."

He nodded. "God willing. That is an interesting term, don't you think? What happens when God is not willing?"

"You don't believe in God, do you?"

"I haven't much considered God for a very long time. He gave up on me long ago, and I am certainly not pursuing His attentions. They lead to nothing but trouble."

"You have a skewed knowledge of God."

Pooles entered the room with a large glass of yellow liquid. "As you requested, your lordship."

"I'm not drinking it." Eden snapped his lips shut as a young child would who feared the taste of a new vegetable.

"I said that once." Ravensmoore nodded to the valet. "Hand it over to him, Pooles, and ready his bath. He needs one. I'll take care of this."

Pooles followed the orders and left the room, another round of whistling in his wake.

"Enough foolishness. You got drunk enough to need a remedy, and I've provided one for you. Don't taste it and don't smell it. Just drink it down and don't stop until it's gone. Trust me. I know from experience."

"You?"

"Drink it," Ravensmoore said, ignoring the question.

Eden closed his eyes and drank as quickly as he could. "I think I'm going to be sick."

"No, you're not. Now go take a bath and get ready. I'll meet you downstairs in fifteen minutes. Do not tarry overlong. We're going to be late."

"You're late," the prince bellowed. "Come in and tell me what you thought of my father's condition and that the lost relic has been found."

The regent was lounging in a purple-cushioned, high-backed chair upon a slightly raised dais.

Eden grumbled under his breath, "As if my head didn't hurt enough."

Ravensmoore bowed. "Careful," he whispered. "He's not happy with you as it is, and your demeanor will not improve the outcome of this appointment."

Eden followed suit and said, "I'll try."

"Come forward." The regent motioned with his hand. "My sister, Princess Sophia, thinks well of your sister, Lady Mercy. She said that your sister washed my father's feet and that he kicked the basin of water all over her because he was ticklish." The regent roared with laughter. "How I wish I'd been present to see it. Understand, Ravensmoore, that I'm not laughing at the predicament your sister was in, but the fact that my father's feet are ticklish. I never knew that."

"My sister has always been one to seek ways to make others comfortable. She has a gift."

"She does indeed. And now your report, sir. I'm interested. Tell me everything."

Eden bristled at the fact they were not offered seats. Prinny's social punishment. His head ached and his patience grew thin.

"I spoke briefly with the king's physician," Ravensmoore said. "Although we may agree on the fact that your father will probably not live another complete year, we disagree completely on how he is currently being treated."

Ravensmoore stepped closer, and Eden took note of his confidence as he went on to explain in more detail.

"My sister was shocked to see the king in restraints, as was I. He needs to be taken out of doors and permitted to breathe fresh air on a daily basis. His hair is long and unkempt, and so is his beard. He needs more attention than he is currently getting. He may be old and infirm, but I'd wager that if any of us could not see or hear, it would add to our madness as well."

The regent stood and walked about in front of them with his hands behind his back. "Is it your opinion that he is completely blind and deaf? I want to know your assessment of his incapacity."

"He is able to sense vibration of those walking around him and doors opening and closing, but, as I'm sure you must be aware from your own experiences with the king, he is not improving. He continues to deteriorate mentally and physically. Due to the extent of his deafness and blindness, his true mental capacity is difficult to ascertain."

Prinny stopped his pacing and nodded. "I understand."

"Lord Eden, come closer."

Vincent had no idea what to expect. "Your Majesty."

"Have you had any luck in locating the missing relic?"

"I have not found it, sir, but I have some leads, and other men searching along with me."

"That is not good enough. I need that spear, and I need it soon. You saw the king and talked with Symes. You know the situation. I must insist that you turn all your efforts to finding the relic as quickly as possible. My father's life depends on it if any of the myth surrounding the spear is true. I'm running out of time, and so is England's king."

"Sir," Eden said, "you understand the gravity of the king's health. A legendary spear is unlikely to change anything."

Prinny's more than ample chin trembled. "You know not the power of this spear or what it may be capable of. Just find it!"

"I will do everything in my power to place the relic into your hands." Eden thought it best not to aggravate the regent further, but he found it difficult not to ask him what would happen if he could not locate the spear.

"I have been more than patient. I believe the power of this relic to be the key to many things, including England's safety and my power. Princess Sophia tells me that the Roman soldier who pierced the side of Christ to prove His death was healed from blindness when the blood and water from Christ's side splashed over his face and entered his eyes. I will find out the truth about the power of this spear."

Ravensmoore said, "Excuse me, sir, but I trust you will not allow your hope of healing for your father to deceive you from your faith. Only the Christ has the power to heal your father, not the relic."

"I will be the judge of that, Ravensmoore. I will be the judge. And Eden, you have a week. If you do not bring the spear to me within seven days, then you will suffer the consequences."

Eden's hands clenched at his side. "What kind of threat is this?"

"I see no reason to supply you with your own ship if I do not get the relic that was part of our agreement. In addition, you will be confined to the boundaries of your estate until another representative of mine can locate the spear."

"I committed no crime. I—"

A quick elbow in the ribs cut off his words.

I'm doomed. He said, "I understand, Your Majesty."

Chapter 17

Oh what a tangled web we weave,
when first we practice to deceive.
—Sir Walter Scott

What do you think he's going to say?" Mercy asked, sitting across from her sister in an upholstered wing-back chair of burgundy damask. She knew her visit to London would be changing in some way soon. She wouldn't be staying here at her sister's home for long since Victoria's husband, Jonathon, was due to arrive shortly.

"My husband or our brother?" Victoria stretched out on the comfortably cushioned gold silk settee with matching pillows under her head in the parlor of her home with Lazarus on the floor next to her.

"Our brother, of course. He's more likely to arrive before your husband. I hope the appointment with the regent goes well."

"He's not pleased, so I imagine it will not be agreeable," Victoria said.

Mercy couldn't help smiling. "The meeting with the regent, or when Dev speaks with us?"

"With us, silly. Whenever he's worried, he's harsh. And yesterday he was very worried, so today I expect he will be very harsh."

Lazarus lifted his head and sighed. "His way of showing sympathy." Victoria smiled and ruffled the big dog's ears.

"I can't really blame Dev. You could have died. I had nightmares the whole time I slept, which was very little, by the bye."

"Dev sat by my bed all night. I don't know what he thought was going to happen. I slept like the dead—however it is the dead sleep—and Lazarus was there to protect me."

"I think he just had to reassure himself that you weren't dead. If he hadn't known about the baby, I don't think he would have reacted so calmly. He wanted to keep you calm."

"I know he was surprised about the baby, but even though it was not my fault, he'll use this situation to limit our activities and keep us out of mischief. You'll see." Victoria wagged a finger through the air. "He's hovered over me most of my life, just like you did through all those years when I was ill. And then to find me practically suffocated in that trunk at the Legend Seekers Club." She shrugged. "I think he would have ranted and raved like one of the poor souls confined to Bedlam, but as you say, due to my condition he curtailed his temper."

"He seemed to be simmering just below the surface."

Victoria's mouth curved into a knowing smile. "That simmering was not because of me. That was because he caught you and Lord Eden in an embrace."

"No. Tell me he didn't."

"Yes, he did. I saw him staring out the coach window while we waited for you. And though I was distraught, I was coherent enough to note his deep frown. Our brother saw something he didn't approve of, and that is what the simmering was all about."

"So you didn't see anything and you don't know what he saw. You're just guessing." Mercy's head hurt, and she put her fingers to her temples. "Life is getting far too complicated."

"And it's about to get more so. Here comes Devlin."

"Well, I guess it's best to get this over with and move on with what needs to be done."

Victoria continued to stare out the window. "And Lord Eden is with him."

"What?" Mercy jumped from her chair. "I can't be here. Not now. Not with him."

Lazarus barked and ran to greet their guests.

"I thought nothing happened," Victoria teased as she sat up and smoothed out her pale blue morning gown and patted her blonde curls. "Collect yourself immediately and sit down."

Mercy pinched her cheeks, brushed her rose silk walking dress with her hands, and sat down only a moment before Myron entered the room. She gripped the arms of the chair and tried to steady her nerves. *This is ridiculous behavior.*

"Your brother and Lord Eden have arrived, Countess."

"Have them come in, Myron, and ask Cook to prepare some sandwiches and tea."

"Immediately, your ladyship." He gave a quick bow and departed.

Devlin and Eden entered the room "Are you feeling well enough for a visit?"

Victoria laughed. "Of course. I thought perhaps you might not be up for a visit. Come in and tell us how your appointment with Prinny went."

"I'm sorry to intrude, Countess, Lady Mercy." Lord Eden bowed. "Your brother insisted."

Mercy studied their guest and leaned forward a bit. "You don't look well, Lord Eden. Has something happened?"

Eden grimaced. "It's been a challenging morning."

Devlin sat next to Victoria on the settee and motioned for Eden to take the seat near Mercy. "It's a bit complicated."

Victoria put her hand on her brother's arm. "Don't you dare try to wheedle out of telling us what happened. Out with it."

"Prinny is a stubborn mule and still insists that the relic may have powers to heal the king." Devlin described the conversation between Eden, the prince regent, and himself.

Mercy looked at Eden. "What are you going to do?"

"The only thing I can do. Recover the relic."

Myron entered with sandwiches and tea and set the tray of contents on the table next to the countess. "Will there be anything else?"

"I think we may need smelling salts," Victoria said.

Myron frowned. "Smelling salts?"

Devlin coughed and said, "The countess was making an attempt at humor, Myron."

Myron looked to Victoria for assurance.

"Forgive me, Myron. I was only jesting."

"Of course," he said, not looking quite convinced. "Is that all, your ladyship?"

"Yes, Myron. You may leave us."

Myron exited the room, and Mercy caught him shaking his head when he turned the corner out of the parlor. She couldn't help but smile.

Lazarus got up and padded over to Lord Eden. He put his chin on Eden's knee.

"Well, hello, Lazarus." He patted the big dog's head.

"You *aren't* feeling well, are you?" Mercy asked. "He does that when Victoria's sick. He's used to you since you were here with your injuries."

"He's a very astute animal." Eden stood. "I think I need to leave. You're right, I'm not feeling well, and I think I will go home and rest."

"My coach is waiting for you. I'll bring you ointment for the eye later," Devlin said, getting up. "I'll walk you to the door."

Mercy's heart sped up. "Ointment? Are you certain you don't want to rest here?"

"No. No, thank you, Lady Mercy. I need to go home." He turned to Victoria. "I hope you are well and not just putting on a brave face, Countess. You are a courageous woman, very much like your sister." He bowed and left the room with Devlin.

Mercy let out a breath of concern. "What do you think is wrong?"

"I'm not sure." Victoria poured a cup of tea, added sugar, and then delivered it to her sister. "This will help your nerves," she said, handing Mercy the cup. "Tea makes all things better." She returned to the tray and poured another cup for herself and Devlin.

Devlin returned and sat down in the chair where Eden had been. "I'm sure you were stretched out on that settee before we arrived, Snoop." He took the tea. "Now lie back down. I thank you for the tea, though after this morning I'm tempted to add something a bit stronger. But I've learned my lessons."

"That bad, was it?" Victoria stretched back out on the couch. "Is there something else you want to tell us?"

"We need to talk, about last night." He turned to Mercy. "Why don't we begin with what you were doing in Scotland that led you to wash up on the sand in England wearing men's clothing. And perhaps more important, why haven't you told me what I'm guessing you have already told our sister?"

Mercy's eyes filled with unexpected tears. "I was afraid to tell you. I'm still afraid to tell you." She looked out the window, avoiding his eyes, those eyes that always knew when she was lying. He knew his sisters well. She knew he loved them, loved her. But how could she explain this to him?

"It's time you told me everything, Mercy. Maybe I can help."

She wiped the tears away and looked into his face. "I want to be a doctor."

"I know."

Her mouth sagged open in surprise for a moment and then she closed it quickly. "How could you know?" She looked at Victoria then. "Did you tell him?"

"Now, you know I would never betray a confidence. He's our brother, Mercy."

"And if you recall on the road to Windsor," Devlin continued, "you told me you felt called to heal the sick. I didn't quite understand at that point that you wanted to be a doctor, but you obviously love this ancient medicine about pressure points on the body. Then when I felt better after you'd ministered to me and to Lord Eden, I began to put more of the puzzle together. Your acts of kindness to the king, to Eden while he was injured, and then all those years with Victoria and her illness."

"He knows us better than anyone other than God," Victoria said. "Tell him everything."

She nodded and took a long sip of tea.

"When I came to London last year, I had already started my studies at the Royal College of Physicians in Edinburgh. Uncle Gordon taught me everything he knew about herbs and the work done in the apothecaries. A friend of his was visiting from China, and he taught me the art of using needles or pressure to relieve distress within the body. He showed me how applying this pressure to certain parts of the body accelerates healing. You experienced that on our trip to Windsor."

Devlin nodded and continued eating the sandwiches that Myron had brought from the kitchen. "I must learn that technique. Go on."

"Aunt Kenna and I frequently visited the theater together, and she introduced me to an actress friend of hers. I later met with this friend to learn more about the application of makeup for the purpose of disguise. I did all this with one thing in mind."

"Attending medical school?"

Heat crawled up her neck and into her face. "Yes. I advanced quickly, and no one suspected that I was a woman. I kept my voice low, tried never to call attention to myself, and with the help of Aunt Kenna's actress friend I was able to keep up the pretense of being male without much difficulty."

"So what happened that led you to arrive on the beach where Eden discovered you?" Devlin asked.

Mercy looked at Victoria, who was calmly eating a cucumber sandwich and seeming to enjoy the telling of this tale. She simply nodded her encouragement and smiled.

"One day someone followed me back to the house. It had been a long day, and as soon as I entered the foyer, I took off the hat and wig that kept my hair well hidden. When I was fluffing my hair out, I caught a movement outside a window. Someone was watching me. I saw his face only for a moment, but I knew who it was."

Victoria sat up. "You didn't tell me this. What else have you been hiding?" She took another long sip of tea. "Who was it?"

"I now know him as John Marks. He was also studying medicine. I felt that someone had been following me for weeks but had no proof. I was so afraid of being discovered that I contributed to my fears."

"What does this John Marks look like?" Devlin asked. "Do you think he followed you from Scotland?"

"There's a bit more." Mercy stood, poured cream into another cup of tea, and carefully added two teaspoons of sugar. "I began receiving blackmail letters. The letters said that if I didn't pay a certain amount of money, then my secret would be revealed to the academic authorities of the medical school."

Devlin stood up and began to pace at this revelation. "Tell me you did not pay him anything, Mercy."

"I didn't pay him money. I gave him my jewelry. Mother's emeralds."

Victoria gasped. "No."

"Mercy," Devlin said as he came to stand directly in front of her and took her hands in his. "Why didn't you ask me to come to you? I would have dropped everything."

She squeezed his hands and let go. He moved away and stared out the window. "And that is why I couldn't ask you. You had too much to do. You and Maddie hadn't been married all that long, Mother was back at Ravensmoore, and Maddie's mother had need of attention. The estate and Safe Haven needed looking after. I just couldn't bring myself to further burden you."

He turned from the window. "I never consider my family a burden."

"And what of me?" Victoria asked. "You know you could have come to me and Jonathon."

"I wanted to solve my own problems, to use my own resources. But the problem became more complex and dangerous. One day I visited an antique shop, and I was attracted to a strange-looking amulet. It was made of ebony and had odd gold markings carved into it and hung from a long cord. I thought I'd seen it somewhere before, but just couldn't remember."

Devlin sat down next to her again. "I think I've seen it. I think I know it. Describe this amulet again."

Victoria said. "We can show it to you. It's hidden in my room upstairs. I'll go get it."

The three looked at each other, and they all headed for the stairs.

"Where do you think you've seen it before, Devlin?" Mercy asked as they climbed to the second floor.

"Around the neck of a patient at Bethlem."

They hurried to Victoria's room, and she went straight to the dresser drawer where they had hidden it. She dug deep for the amulet.

"I can't find it," Victoria said.

Mercy looked for herself. "It can't be gone. I saw you hide it. I'm sure it was this drawer as well."

Devlin said, "If it's not here and neither of you have it, then someone has broken into the house and taken it. This is getting far too dangerous."

Victoria pitched everything out of the drawer.

A small, ragged doll tumbled onto the floor among Victoria's intimate clothing. Made of burlap, the figure was dressed in fabric from the clothes Mercy had been wearing when she arrived at her sister's home.

"What is this?" Mercy picked up the doll. "It has a needle thrust through both hands. Is this supposed to be me? What does it mean?"

Devlin grabbed it out of her hand. "It's a vodun doll. It's a message left in place of the amulet, a warning to stay away or trouble will follow." He stuffed it into a pocket inside his jacket. "Superstition and religious misinterpretation."

"Devlin, you said you'd seen the amulet on a patient at Bethlem. What does he look like?"

"He's a huge African man who refers to himself as Sakpata. It's not his name, it's a term for a type of healer, but he says he can also cause illness."

A shiver of dread raced up Mercy's spine. "Sakpata! That's what the man on the ship said before I was thrown overboard. He carried a real serpent about his neck. He said I must never part with the amulet until *Sakpata* asks me for it. Then when he does ask me, I must have it on my person or harm may come to my family."

"Some Africans express their beliefs in this way," Devlin said, "but doing so can bring harm when it is exploited by others. We have no reason to be afraid, however. Our God is more powerful than any vodun priest or practice."

"What do we do now?" Victoria tossed her undergarments and chemises back into the drawer.

"You will stay here and await your husband. Please do not leave the house, Snoop. I know how a mystery can affect you, but this is a dangerous situation, and I don't have all the facts. You had a close encounter yesterday. I do not want you to risk yourself or my nephew again. Do you understand?"

"I didn't know I was risking myself when I went looking for you and Mercy. And what makes you think it's a boy?"

"A divine premonition?" He hugged her.

"Or perhaps just an uncle's hope?" She hugged him back and held on for a moment. "Thank you for being here."

"That's what all good brothers do. They try to be there when you need them, and they hope for boys to play with. Frankly this brother—" He pointed to himself. "—has been surrounded by women for too long." He laughed, and Mercy punched him lightly in one arm while Victoria punched him in the other.

"Is that any way for ladies of the realm to treat their brother who is an earl?"

"We don't care," Mercy said, "if you are an earl or a duke. You are our brother, and we will treat you accordingly."

"I believe I will be on my way. I've much to do, including another trip to Bethlem to see the African. I will show him this doll and see what kind of response I get. Of course, he doesn't speak English, but his physical reaction may tell me much more than any words could." He turned to Mercy. "You must remain here with Snoop and make certain she doesn't get into trouble. I have a thought about something you said. Trust me. I'll explain later, but for now, please do not go out. I'm going to find Simon and have him and a couple men from Bow Street keep an eye on the house."

"Now you're making me nervous," Mercy said. "You will be careful, won't you?"

"Of course." He departed the room then, and Mercy turned to Victoria and in unison said, "Men!"

Chapter 18

The wisdom of the prudent is to understand
his way: but the folly of fools is deceit.
—Proverbs 14:8

Kane slammed both hands down on the table in the drawing room. "Idiot! You are a blundering idiot! You told me you planned to keep out of sight. What were you thinking?"

John Marks's nostrils flared. His broad nose took up much of his face, making his eyes seem unjustly narrow and dangerous. "It's not as though I can read others' minds, Kane." His thin lips turned down and his dark brown eyes raged under heavy brows. "I saw them enter the basement and knew they'd be snooping around. If I'd let them search much longer, they would have located the spear."

"I don't care about Eden," Kane said, wiping his hand across his mouth, "but you could have killed a countess, one that I now know to be carrying a child. We would have had all of London down on us." He slumped into his chair.

"Where's the relic? We need to sell it off to the highest bidder immediately. It's become too much of a risk. I'd hoped it wouldn't come to this, but better to get rid of it now and divert suspicion."

"I have an anonymous bidder." Marks prowled the room. "He doesn't wish to be identified, so I've dealt with his man of affairs."

"What's he willing to pay?"

"Fifty thousand pounds."

Kane grinned, and his eyes widened with his greed. "Sell it. But first I want to meet this man of affairs and his money. Bring him here tonight at midnight, and we'll seal the deal. Bring the relic, but do not take any risks. We cannot afford to lose it now."

Marks nodded and left.

Devlin entered the underground corridor that led to the African's cell. The torches on the walls provided a medieval quality to the hall that caused him to shiver. He almost expected to see old torture devices hanging from the walls and hear the sounds of the poor souls subjected to such cruelties. He turned the corner, and there sat the African on his cot. His black eyes widened, but he did not stand when he saw Devlin.

Pacing in front of the cell, Devlin wondered if he shouldn't just leave, and maybe, maybe everything would settle down. He prayed quietly for guidance. He knew that until the spear was found and placed in the hands of the prince regent, nothing would settle down. *What's the point of all this?* he wondered. Nothing was making sense.

He stopped pacing, looked directly at the man, and pulled out the vodun doll.

The African smiled, big yellow and broken teeth in a black face.

"I know you cannot understand me, but—"

"I know."

Devlin's eyes widened in shock. "You speak English?"

"Enough."

"All this time. And you haven't spoken a word of English."

"Better to listen," he said in a deep, mocking voice.

"You mean, better to spy," Devlin said, disappointed that he'd been duped. But there was nothing for that now, nor any way he could have known. He held up the vodun doll again. "Do you know anything about this? Do you know what it is?"

"A warning. Trouble coming."

Trouble here, thought Devlin. "It was in a drawer where my sister had left an amulet of ebony with deep gold carvings in it. Almost identical to the one you wear."

The African pulled out the amulet. "Sakpata. Houngan."

"Are you going to tell me what houngan means? Is it your name?"

"Priest. Lord." He pointed.

"And sakpata?"

"Healer. Like you. But able to bring sickness too. Smallpox spirit."

"No one can cause another human being to get smallpox through a curse as you suggest. They must be exposed to the illness by others who have it."

"Sakpata strong."

"And who is this Agbe? He threw my sister into the ocean. She could have died."

"Agbe. Spirit of the sea. She not die if Agbe throw her in the sea. Protection strong."

Devlin shook his head and rubbed the back of his neck. "I understand you do not believe in Jesus, but—"

"Jesus. Yes. Jesus come to Dahomey."

"Africa?"

"Home. Africa. Dahomey."

"What do you mean by 'Jesus came to Dahomey'?"

"White people bring Jesus. Long time ago. Sakpata chase them away."

"Do you understand why you are sitting here in this cell? In this hospital?"

"I kill and sacrifice chicken for spirit of sakpata. No believers bring me here. I need to go Dahomey."

"The British are not used to Africans sacrificing chickens in front of their churches. They believe you have lost your mind, and I think they may be right except that I understand you are under the influence of evil."

"No evil. Sakpata!" He hit his chest with a fist.

Devlin closed his eyes. *Dear Jesus, help me know what to do for this man. It is not within my ability to save him, but You can. Your will be done.* When he opened his eyes, his thought was of one thing. "I'll find a way to get you home."

Cloying tendrils of mist searched the city like skeletal fingers reaching deep into crevices, hoping to capture the elusive prey needed to satisfy gnawing hunger. Two figures watched from the shadows.

"Here he comes," Pooles said. "That's the man I discussed the transaction with. He will take us to Kane's house."

Vincent St. Lyons, Lord Eden, studied the man as he approached. He couldn't help but wonder if this was the man who had inflicted the injuries on him when they had tried to make their way to Windsor that first night. The same man at Jackson's Salon. "When they discover that I'm the one who is buying the relic, there might be trouble."

"You have the element of surprise on your side, sir. Kane wants his money and wants to be rid of the spear now that he can make a profit."

"I understand the meaning behind your well-thought-out

words, Pooles. This is not the time for revenge." Vincent pulled the hood of his cloak around his face. It wouldn't do to have someone recognize him. There was too much at stake.

"He's waiting next to the entrance of the Black Hawk Tavern. That's our signal to join him." Pooles stepped into the cobblestone street, and Vincent followed. He assured himself by patting the pistol hidden in his greatcoat pocket. He still wore the patch over his eye, but the ointment Ravensmoore had delivered into Pooles's capable hands earlier that day lessened the pain. For that he was grateful.

"Are you ready, Mr. Marks?" Pooles asked as they drew close. "This is the gentleman I told you about."

Marks did not extend his hand. "Kane awaits us. Let's get off these streets before the footpads target us. I wouldn't want you to lose your money before the deal is made." He smiled. "Follow me."

When they arrived at the handsome townhome on Bond Street, Marks used the knocker three times, and a grim-faced butler opened the door within moments. He brought them into the elaborate foyer decorated in a royal blue wallpaper and two large mirrors. A heavy unlit chandelier hung from the high ceiling. Wall sconces illuminated the stairs leading up to the second floor.

Kane awaited their arrival in a plush drawing room with heavy burgundy drapes. A magnificent ebony table filled the center of the space. "Welcome, gentlemen. Please allow my butler to take your cloaks. Our London mist is a chill one this evening."

Pooles and Vincent lowered their hoods at the same time. "Hello, Mr. Kane," Vincent said. "I hope my appearance here as the buyer doesn't surprise you too much."

Kane's face showed a moment of surprise that he quickly masked. Vincent had to give the man credit. He probably bluffed well at the gaming tables.

"I have to admit I am a bit taken aback. After your public discourse at the Legend Seekers Club last evening, I wouldn't have thought you a man interested in relics."

"Let's just say that it's for a friend." Vincent wondered what Prinny would do when he delivered the spear. It would be a relief to have it off his hands. He hadn't relished the idea of being banished to his estate until the spear was located. He much preferred doing things his way. If he had to pay for the relic and in that way redeem himself and his freedom, so be it. He could afford it.

"Have a seat, gentlemen. And is this your man of affairs that Marks mentioned?"

"Yes. Mr. Pooles."

The four of them sat at the table. Kane flicked open an ebony and silver snuff box, caught the tobacco between his thumb and forefinger, lifted it to his nostrils, and inhaled deeply. "Would anyone else care to indulge?"

Eden shook his head. "Let's get on with it."

"Anxious, are we?" He clicked the snuff box closed and slipped it into his pocket. "Marks, the relic."

The gold ring on Kane's right hand brought back a flood of painful memories. It was him. Eden had seen the ring but hadn't remembered it till now. Kane was the one who beat him the night they'd tried to make Windsor.

Marks pulled the box that contained the relic from inside his coat and laid it on the table. The gold inlay sparkled under the brightness of the room's chandelier.

"May I?" Vincent asked, looking directly into Kane's deceiving blue eyes. It galled him that he couldn't deal with this thief the way he wanted at this very moment. He struggled to conceal his emotion and wondered if he'd done near as well at masking his feelings as Kane had just done. Vincent tamped down the anger roiling inside him. It took all his strength.

"That's why you're here," Kane said. "Inspect your merchandise. I'm sure you'll find it all as it should be."

Vincent grasped the box with one hand and slid the lid off with the other. The spearhead lay in the padding of the box. He picked it up and inspected it. The silver and gold bands still held the artifact together. The nail from the crucifixion had not been tampered with, and for that Vincent was grateful. Ever since he'd heard the story of the lance of Longinus from Lady Mercy, he'd developed more respect for what it represented, even though his faith was shallow.

"It appears to be intact and of good quality. How do I know this is not an excellent forgery?" He handed the spearhead over to Pooles, who pretended to know something of antiquities. Pooles simply nodded and handed it back to Vincent.

"If you are not confident that this piece is what you seek, then I will simply sell it later to the next bidder."

Vincent placed the relic back in the box and closed the lid. "I seriously doubt you will find another to offer you such a profit." Vincent wanted to make Kane sweat, but Kane was winning the mental battle.

"Do we have a deal or not?" Kane asked.

Marks loomed behind Kane as if to intimate that no game playing would be tolerated or someone might get hurt.

"Yes. We have a deal."

Pooles reached into an inner pocket of his jacket, pulled out a thick stack of bills, and handed them to Vincent, who pushed the money toward Kane. "I assume you'd like to count it?"

"Of course. I'm not one to trust gentleman of the ton."

Kane counted the money. "It appears that you now own a valuable relic. I'm certain you will have no difficulty recouping your costs." He stood. "Good evening, gentlemen. My butler will show you out."

When they were outside Kane's townhome, Vincent said, "I'm glad Mac is waiting for us with the coach. Something is not right. That was too easy. Keep your hand close to your pistol, Pooles."

They made their way through mist-filled streets barely able to see two feet ahead of them. When they neared Piccadilly, they couldn't even see the coach. "Where are you, Mac? We may need to employ a couple of the link boys to light the way."

"I'm over here, Lord Eden," Mac said from the mist directly in front of them.

Vincent elbowed Pooles, who must have been thinking the same thing. Both pulled their pistols.

A familiar guttural voice cut through the fog. "Throw the guns down. Come, come. 'Tis yer old friend, Fox." The African from the ship held up his hand to motion them forward.

"Fox." Vincent's gut twisted. This was not good. He wore ill-fitting clothes from one of the secondhand shops in the poorer sections of the city.

"Lord Eden." Fox's grin seemed to cover his entire face.

"What the devil are you doing here?" Vincent asked. "And we will not throw down our guns."

Vincent considered praying when he saw a dozen or more of the Africans from the ship appear out of the mist. Mac walked with them, a machete at his throat.

"They took me by surprise, sir. I never heard them coming, and then all of a sudden they were on me. Sorry, sir." Mac stood with his head back, unable to look at them due to the machete ready to slice open his neck.

"Our luck seems to have run dry, Mac," Vincent said, lowering his pistol to the ground as Pooles did the same. "What do you want, Fox?"

"The relic."

"Why?"

"*Geheim*."

"What kind of secret? What geheim?"

Fox shook his head. "*Medisyne. Slaaf.*

"What's he mean?" asked Pooles.

"I'm not sure, but it has something to do with medicine. And I have a feeling we are again parting with the spearhead. Give it to him, Pooles. We can't let Mac get his throat slit over this. And even if we could fight, there are too many."

Pooles removed the box from his greatcoat and handed it to Vincent. "All that money for nothing, and you're back where you started. Devil of a shame, sir."

"A shame indeed." Vincent handed the relic to Fox.

"*Danke*." Fox nodded. Then he ordered one of his men forward to take their pistols. "*Vergeef*."

Vincent blew out a deep breath. "Are you finished now?"

"Finished."

The Africans backed into the mist, and moments later Mac came through the curtain of fog. "It's been a hell of a night."

"I can't disagree with you there, Mac."

Pooles said, "We need to make a plan."

Vincent patted the shoulder of one of the dark bays standing with the coach. "Let's go home."

CHAPTER 19

Two are better than one; because they have a good reward for their labour. For if they fall, the one will lift up his fellow: but woe to him that is alone when he falleth; for he hath not another to help him up.

—ECCLESIASTES 4:9–10

CHILLS SPREAD OVER Mercy's skin in the warm morning sunshine of the garden. She read the letter that had been delivered by a street urchin just minutes earlier. Myron explained that he'd opened the door and the young boy had shoved the letter into his hands and run out of the yard as fast as his legs would carry him.

"What's wrong, Mercy?" Victoria asked. "You look quite pale."

Mercy handed the letter to her. "It's a threat."

Victoria sat down on the garden bench beside her. "Let me see." She snatched the letter away and carefully read the note.

"This is evil. Anyone who threatens a woman is a coward. Do you think it's from the same man who was blackmailing you in Scotland?"

"I don't know who else it could be." She allowed herself to feel the fear that swept over her, but she would not allow it to control her. "It must be Marks. Snoop, you cannot be drawn into this. You and the baby need protection from whatever this might bring. I cannot remain here."

"Don't be silly. We must tell Devlin and Jonathon immediately. They'll know what to do. One thing is for certain. You need protection too." Victoria put her arm around her sister. "I'm so glad Jonathon came home last night. I've missed him so much, and this makes it all the more important that he be here with us. He will not allow anything to happen to you, and neither—"

"Neither will I." Lord Eden stepped near. "I'm sorry to have overheard, but Myron let me in and directed me out here. He was wrestling with Lazarus over who was going to walk whom."

"Lord Eden." Mercy rose. "You don't understand."

"I understand that someone is trying to frighten you. It was you who helped me on the ship when I was sick and you who cared for me when I could hardly move from the beating I'd taken. Let me help you now."

"That's very kind of you, sir. But it's not right to impose on you."

"May I read the letter?"

Mercy hesitated, looking from him to the letter and then back to him.

"Please?"

> I have not forgotten how you escaped me onboard the ship. However, I have been following your movements since you arrived. I know you disguised yourself in Scotland. I thought there was something odd all along. You are a master of disguise, but I know you care for me. You cannot disguise that, and I will no longer hide my love for you. But now that I know your secret, I think we can come to an understanding. You will marry me, and your family will be expected to dower you well and accept me with open arms. If you do not agree to this offer, then I will go to the prince regent and the

> lords and ladies of the ton and discredit you. One way or another I will have you. Make no mistake about that, my love.

Eden looked at her. "He's lost his mind, or he's an evil, manipulating pig of a man."

"Who's a pig of a man?" Jonathon, Lord Witt, asked.

"Yes," Devlin said, following on Witt's heels, "I'd love to know what's going on out here. You all look as though you're plotting some kind of conspiracy."

Victoria hurried to her husband. "I'm so glad you're here. This is Lord Eden."

Witt shook Eden's hand and then put a strong arm around his wife's waist. "I can tell by the worry in your eyes that something is seriously amiss, and I will not allow anything to upset you."

"What's happened?" Devlin looked to Mercy, and his gaze narrowed. "Mercy?"

"Give him the letter, Lord Eden."

"She's being threatened," Eden said and handed him the crumpled missive.

Devlin read it. His jaw was rigid and a pulse beat in his neck, a sure indication of his ire. "This is mad." He handed the note to Witt.

"What should we do?" Witt asked.

"Mercy," Devlin said, "you're going back to medical school."

"What? That's impossible. I can't go to medical school. I'm not going back to Scotland if that's what you're thinking."

"That's not what I'm thinking at all," Devlin said. "Doctor Langford is in town to begin his series of lectures. I'm helping him with the lectures that concern treating the mind and how to care for those with physical illness and madness. You are going to become one of his students. And together he and I will help you complete your medical training and hide you from this man who is hunting you."

"I can't. It will never work." Mercy started pacing.

"Now you are picking up my habits." He smiled. "Pacing is what I do best when I'm thinking. Remember?"

Eden cleared his throat. "I have an idea. But I don't think you'll like it, Ravensmoore. And Lady Mercy may not like it either. I think I should attend medical college with her and be everywhere she goes. If you tell this Dr. Langford of our plan, I think it will work. Then I can help protect your sister while we search for this deluded stalker."

"That might actually work, Eden," Devlin said. "But what of others in town who know you're an adventurer?"

Mercy smiled. "Too bad you don't have long hair. I could cut it for you and help with your future disguise."

"Touché," Eden said. "But in all seriousness, you used a disguise for a long time while you were north and know what to do. I will use my own disguise. Together we can pull this off until this man is caught. When I'm not with you, you can stay here. Lord Witt looks quite capable of taking care of any intruders."

"Or," Devlin said, "it may be better for her to stay at my house. Madeline will be coming to town tomorrow with our mothers to visit. I can alert Simon."

"I hope all of you don't think I'm going to remain locked up in this house just because I'm having a baby. I will be involved in capturing this culprit one way or another."

"Not without me by your side," Witt said. "This is my first child, and I will do all I can to protect both of you. No snooping, my Lady Snoop." He smiled down at her.

"We shall see about that. Women have many methods of spying."

"And if you would not object, Ravensmoore," Eden said, "I'm

sure my valet and Mac could also act as guards for your home."

"Good, this is all good. But we will have to firm up our plans. There is much to be done. We don't know who this person is, and we don't know everything that is going on in his mind."

"I might know who it is, but I'm not certain." Mercy explained what she'd told Victoria about her experience with John Marks in Scotland. "I think I saw him at the museum. He could be working for Kane."

Devlin looked a Mercy with disappointment. "Why didn't you tell me? It's a very dangerous situation, and the deeper we delve into this, the more dangerous it will become."

Mercy's frustration raged. "I have no proof that it is Marks. I just think it could be him."

"At least we can be cautious and investigate further. Once Marks or whoever the culprit is understands we are not just going to hand Mercy over to him, and his delusions shatter, he could become desperate. Then who knows what he might do?"

"Let's go into the house," Witt said. "We'll eat and discuss more of the details. I'm glad I got to town before anything else happened without me."

Mercy pulled Victoria aside as they filed into the house, talking to one another. "You haven't told him, have you?"

Victoria evaded her sister's scrutiny. "It was too much. I didn't want to ruin my announcement about the baby with the information that the baby and I were almost lost. I'll tell him later."

"Well, then, you'd better make sure Devlin and Eden don't tell him first." Mercy looped her arm through her sister's. "I'll warn Lord Eden and you warn Devlin not to say anything."

Victoria smiled. "You like him, don't you? And don't try to play coy. I know you too well."

Lazarus trotted outside to meet them. "Back from your walk, dear dog?" He nuzzled against Victoria's skirts and nearly knocked her over with his bulk. "Lazarus! I do believe you are jealous." She looked to Mercy. "I really think he knows I'm having a baby. He's not been acting himself."

"Wait till the baby arrives. He'll be a nuisance with his jealousy," Mercy said.

"How do you feel about him?"

"Lazarus? Why, I think he's lovely." Mercy laughed. "I'll talk to you later. This is an awkward time to be speaking of such things when he's just inside the house. Be patient."

Victoria put on her pout. "That just gives you more time to rehearse something to say."

"In we go," Mercy said as she slipped her arm out of her sister's and walked ahead, leaving Victoria behind with Lazarus. She turned back and said, "He's going to lock you in your room."

Chapter 20

Trust in the Lord with all thine heart; and
lean not unto thine own understanding.
—Proverbs 3:5

Kane unfurled the map over the desk in his personal library. "I'll show you what I'm talking about."

Marks puffed on a cigar and bent over the map from his position in a chair opposite Kane. "We'll have to be very careful. It's not wise to take too many risks."

Kane laughed and smoothed his hands over the map. "Ah, but that's half the fun. The other half is all the money we can make."

"Let me see if I understand this." Marks' heavy brows knit together as he surveyed the map. "You have five investors. They've all agreed to fund tens of thousands of pounds to go on an adventure that will get them killed."

"They don't know they aren't going to make it to New South Wales. They have diamond lust, and they're only interested in adventure and wealth."

"They sound exactly like you, Kane." Marks shifted in his chair and ran a finger over an area of the map. "The sea is unpredictable, as you know. Just how do you expect to manage the sinking of a ship and be assured all onboard will die?"

"That's where it gets complicated." Kane pointed to an area

of the map about a day's sailing out of London. "I think it will be best if we disappear the day the ship goes down and allow everyone involved to think we died as well." Kane went to a side table and picked up a decanter of brandy. "Care for a glass?"

"Yes. But what of everything we've built here?"

Kane poured two glasses of liquor and handed one to Marks. "I'll arrange something, locate someone trustworthy." He sat down. "Sell this house and the Legend Seekers Club and have the money delivered to a predetermined place."

"We'll never be able to come back here. The families of the men killed in this venture would certainly be suspicious. It's a very dangerous plan, Kane."

"And this may be the time for us to part, permanently. I will go to Australia, and you can return to Africa if you want. You have talent, though, my friend. Having lived among the Africans and appearing more black than white simply because of your exposure to the sun has its advantages. I'm not sorry I rescued you from that illegal slave ship. You've been a great asset. You're sure you're not of mixed blood?"

Marks snorted in contempt. "Nor would it have worked if I'd drowned," he said. "I will return to Africa. My parents are getting old and need my help."

"You have much to offer them now." Kane swirled the brandy in his glass. "Of course, being God-fearing missionaries they may not want to know how you came into all your wealth. The entire tribe may be converted by now."

"That is not likely. The vodun is strong in Dahomey. They will be busy saving souls."

"All but yours."

Marks laughed. "There are others, but their parents are not Christian. If my parents knew I practiced vodun, it might kill them. That's why it is best they think me dead. It was one way to keep them from finding out. I would not have been on that slave ship if I hadn't been trying to rescue one of my tribal friends."

"It is too bad he was lost."

Marks swallowed a large gulp of brandy. "This stuff is almost as warming as a good woman." He set down the glass. "What must be done next?"

"Even though Eden possesses the spearhead until he gives it over to the prince regent, I think he is too dangerous. He could ruin all our plans. You heard his speech at Egyptian Hall."

"I heard. And he is close to the Lady Mercy. I don't like it. There are too many people involved around them. I say we leave him alone and set sail as soon as you can arrange a ship."

"There are some who think the regent as mad as his father. Given his obsession with the relic, I wonder if it might not be true. The House of Hanover may be cursed with madness. Perhaps it is time to help Prinny along the road to Bedlam."

"What are you thinking?"

"I'm not certain. The idea has just begun to form in my mind, but I may need you to do a little vodun magic, Marks."

"Possibly. But I'm still wondering how we're going to survive the destruction of the ship that carries your investors. We have to have another ship nearby. If any detail of our plan goes wrong, we might not make it either. This is beginning to look impossible."

Kane got up and poured another brandy and refilled Marks' glass. "Hmm." He moved to the window and looked out onto the street below. "What if the ship never makes it out of the harbor?"

"This is sounding more to my liking."

Kane turned around. "What if we go our own ways the night before? Then, when the investors gather the following morning, we simply don't show up because we will be well on our way and headed in different directions."

"It's not that easy," Marks said. "There may not be ships leaving to the ports we want to go when the investor ship leaves."

"This is giving me a headache. There's got to be a way. Something obvious we're missing." Kane lit and puffed on a cigar until he drew smoke. "What if we purloin Eden's ship? The one Prinny agreed to give him when he brought back the relic. The investors will think I'm going to Australia. Instead, I will go with you to Africa. There is much to be discovered there."

"It sounds more reasonable than getting ourselves killed at sea." Marks got up and paced back and forth from the window to the desk. "We must be sure of the plan."

"And," Kane said, "we must not leave any loose ends."

Mercy peeked around the corner of the drapes to watch Dr. Langford enter Devlin's home on Grosvenor Square. The butler answered the knock almost immediately, and Mercy could hear the men conversing in the foyer. She swallowed back her fear. She'd been tossed overboard and nearly drowned, but she thought her heart beat faster now than it did when she faced the possibility of never again finding solid ground.

"Dr. Langford." Devlin greeted the distinguished older gentleman. "I'm so glad you've come. I know you're getting ready to deliver a series of important lectures."

"You make a very good spy," Eden whispered near her ear. "Your sister would be proud."

Mercy jumped and turned around. "It's most unkind to creep up on a person like that. You know how nervous I am."

"They're coming. I thought I'd rescue you from acute embarrassment." He offered her his arm.

She took it gratefully. "Thank you. I think I might faint, and I'm not one for dramatics."

"You'll be fine. Remember, you and your family have helped me. Now I'm going to help you."

She nodded and held tightly to his arm. Devlin was ushering his guest into the drawing room.

"Breathe, Lady Mercy." Eden let go of her arm. "Steady now."

She inhaled deeply as advised and hoped her smile wasn't as tremulous as it felt. She prayed for courage.

Devlin was saying, "Dr. Langford, I'd like you to meet my youngest sister, Lady Mercy, and our family friend, Lord Eden."

"A pleasure, Dr. Langford." Mercy curtsied and then stood to find herself being studied by the doctor's curious gray eyes. His hair too was completely gray, and he wore wired spectacles that gave him an added air of authority, if that were possible. He wasn't very tall—in fact, he was only about an inch taller than she—his mustache and beard were neatly trimmed, and his well-cut coat and trousers were dark.

"Lord Eden." They shook hands.

"Let's sit down," Devlin said. "Cook has created a delicious meal."

A footman seated Mercy first and then Dr. Langford directly across from her. Lord Eden sat to her right, and Devlin sat across from him. The table was beautifully set with fine silver, candelabra, and colorful tulips in two exquisite vases.

"You are missed in York, Ravensmoore. I hope you don't plan on spending all of your time here in town. After a while you can forget what fresh air smells like, and I'm sure your mother and wife miss you, as well."

"I don't enjoy being away from home, but there is much to learn here in town. And in fact, Madeline and our mothers are arriving today. Soon the house will be overrun with women, and the shopping expeditions will begin."

"There's something nice about that, Ravensmoore. It's been a long time since my home has been overrun by anything or anyone. In fact, it may have been Simon who last brought any excitement to my home. Where is he these days?"

"Simon is assisting Bow Street. He quite enjoys investigations."

"I'll have to make sure I see him while I'm in town."

Cook delivered a wonderful meal of beef and carrots and roasted potatoes. Mercy thought it was impossible to actually taste food when she was so nervous. She was glad for the easy banter and stories of Devlin's student days.

"Now that we've enjoyed an incredible meal, why don't you tell me why I was sent for, Ravensmoore. I know you wouldn't have sought me out so soon if something—what should I say—unusual wasn't going on?"

Devlin looked at Mercy and then at Langford. "My sister is being threatened."

"I'm sorry, my dear," Langford said, turning to Mercy. "How do you think I can help? Tell me what's happened, everything."

Mercy was surprised by how easy it was to tell her story to this man. She'd been so intimidated by all the tales she'd heard of him from Devlin's medical training. She didn't really see any of that man in this kind-eyed doctor who sat across from her. She told him everything, including her desire to practice medicine, what had happened in Scotland, and what the latest threat had included.

"That's an incredible story. If you weren't Ravensmoore's sister, I don't know if I'd believe it. Again, what can I do to help?"

Eden took her hand under the table and squeezed gently. She loved the closeness of him; his presence calmed her. She pressed his hand in reply and at that moment realized she was falling in love with him. And that complicated her situation even more.

"I know this is highly unconventional," Devlin said, "what the ton would call beyond the pale, but—"

"I want to study medicine with you, Dr. Langford," Mercy blurted. "I want to finish my degree and if necessary practice medicine as a man." She knew her face flamed, and she must look the color of the Indians she'd heard about in America. "Can you help me?"

Dr. Langford's bushy eyebrows gathered together like thunderclouds above his glasses. He rubbed his bearded chin between his thumb and forefinger and stared at her as if he were trying to see what her mind was made of, whether she was mad or just ridiculous in requesting such a thing. He said nothing.

They all seemed to be holding their breath when Langford finally replied, "Take a walk with me, Lady Mercy. Ravensmoore, Lord Eden, kindly permit me this indulgence."

They all stood, and the butler helped her on with her green pelisse and handed Dr. Langford his walking cane.

Outside the air was fresh after an evening of rain. Dr. Langford offered his arm, and Mercy took it as they proceeded down Grosvenor Square.

"You are a beautiful woman, Lady Mercy. You were born into privilege, and, as you well know, the ton and society in general expect you to fulfill your obligations as a wife and mother. Tell me, why would you want to expose yourself to death and disease and all the horrors that come with being a physician?"

"Do you believe in callings, Dr. Langford?" Mercy didn't look at him but stared straight ahead as they walked.

"I do. But some people think they hear the call of God on their hearts when in fact it is simply their personal desire. How do you know that this is more than desire?"

"Because there is a part of me that is afraid. Part of me that wonders, like the prophet Jonah, if God might be mistaken. I'm not ready, or capable, or male. Still, I know in my soul that I must proceed."

"Even though the prince regent would forbid you to practice and you would be ridiculed to no end if anyone discovered the truth? The ton would ostracize you. You would be considered socially undesirable. And how long could you carry on this charade as a man?"

"Forever, if necessary. I don't care what others think. I must find a way, and I can only hope that my secret does not come out. Are you afraid to teach me? Do you think women below your station?"

"Not below my station, Lady Mercy, but beyond my ability to defend you should you be found out. I have other students to teach, and they would be appalled to find out that a woman was training in their midst."

"I will not be without an escort. If you will permit it, Lord Eden will also be one of your students. If anything violent occurs, he will assist me."

"Let's hope that is not the case. I see no reason Lord Eden cannot attend. He may be uncomfortable with the situation, but I doubt we'll have any concerns unless he faints dead away."

Mercy laughed and then thought about Vincent's seasickness. Hopefully dead and diseased bodies would not affect him.

"As far as your question about women in medicine—" He shook his head. "I don't know if it will happen in my lifetime, but women will enter medicine sometime in the future."

"And in my lifetime?" She felt dread crawl in her stomach.

"I don't believe so, but only God knows the answer to that."

"So you won't teach me then?"

He stopped walking and faced her, letting go of her arm. "I

will teach you. I don't think it's the wisest decision I've ever made, but, then, look at your brother. Who would have thought a lord of the realm would choose to continue in medicine after he came into his title?" He laughed. "Poor judgment obviously runs in the family." He slanted a teasing look at her, offered her his arm again, and continued their walk.

"When will your lectures commence? I'd like to be there for the beginning."

He ignored the question. "I'm guessing your brother has told you more than one story about his training with me in York?"

"Of course. You were quite the ogre." She stumbled over her words. "I mean, I mean, he said... Oh, dear, I've put my foot in it now. I do apologize. I just know that it was difficult."

"Lady Mercy, you will be treated like the men in my class because all will think you are a man. I may be forced to be harder on you than the others in order to keep up the pretense, and it will not be pleasant for you or for me. Do you understand this?"

Mercy knew of what he spoke from her experience in Scotland. "I understand."

"You cannot break down like a hurt child and cry. You will have to deal with all the unpleasantness of my teaching style and the naked human body if we do an autopsy or a procedure on needy patients. Are you strong enough to manage this? Be completely honest with yourself and with me."

Mercy swallowed hard. "In truth, I don't know. But if you will accept me, I will give every ounce of courage and strength I possess to completing the task. And the rest will come from God Himself."

"Far be it from me to argue with what God can do. I've seen Him accomplish many things in medicine, and often I've watched men take credit for what could have happened only through the grace of God."

"I'll have to work out some kind of *quid pro quo* with your brother. Understand it is pure selfishness and nothing to do with my willingness to have you as a student. But men do have their pride. I'll just tell him I have some students following me back to York when I'm finished here, and I would love for him to tutor them in the intricacies of the mad-doctoring trade."

"I don't think he'll consider it an intrusion. He loves his work. That's what makes him such an anomaly in society."

"Indeed. Now, let's return to the house. You will have to be at the lecture, in your disguise, by eight o'clock tomorrow morning."

"Thank you, Dr. Langford."

"And your name will be?"

"Mr. Snow. Mr. William Snow."

Chapter 21

Things do not change. We change.
—Henry David Thoreau

Mercy was in her room at Devlin's home when she heard the family arrive. She set down the wig, makeup, and clothing that she and Victoria had purchased earlier in the day. The attire she'd pulled together was perfect. Once again she would enter medical school in the guise of a man. A sense of freedom soared in her spirit. She hurried from her room and down the winding staircase to the foyer entrance, which was already empty. She followed the voices into the parlor.

"Mother!" She ran to their mother, who was currently embracing her son. She still wore a light veil over her face to hide the scars from the smallpox she'd survived two years earlier.

Everyone in the room turned toward her and stilled. "Mercy, whatever happened to your hair?" her mother asked.

Mercy ran her hands over her shortened locks. In trying on her new disguise, she'd neglected to put on the wig she wore every day. "Oh, no, I forgot. I'll tell you later. Just let me get a hug from all of you."

Her mother, Madeline, and Madeline's mother, the Countess Richfield, all surrounded Mercy and took turns hugging her close and planting kisses on her cheeks. She'd missed them so much, but she knew she'd made the right choice when she followed God's call and went to Scotland. But it was lovely being reunited with her family again.

"How was your trip?" Mercy grabbed her mother's hand and pulled her to a settee, while Devlin hugged his wife and kissed her, and then kissed her again. Devlin's mother-in-law joined the couple, and the three of them took up chairs by the empty hearth and started to catch up with each other.

"Our trip was uneventful, thank the Lord. It is you I want to know about. Do you realize how long it's been since we've seen each other?"

"I know, Mother. It's been almost a year. I'm so sorry, but it was important that I stay in Edinburgh. I have much to tell you, and you probably won't be happy when you've heard my story—especially when I tell you I'll be busy most of tomorrow morning."

"I don't understand, Mercy. What could be so important that you must leave us so soon?"

Devlin stood. "I think we should answer that question, Mother, with everyone hearing the same story. You've only just arrived. Take some time to rest from your journey, and we will explain everything at dinner."

"Perhaps you're right, Devlin," the dowager countess of Ravensmoore conceded. "But I expect a full account of what has been happening. I have three children, and I want to see you all at dinner. So, while I'm resting, I expect you to notify Victoria and Jonathon. We will have a true family gathering this evening."

Two hours later, at six o'clock, they assembled in the drawing room at 3 Grosvenor Square. "It's wonderful to have everyone together again," Devlin said. "It's been too long." He could barely take his eyes off Madeline, who looked radiant in a gold silk gown. A strand of pearls wove through her dark hair that was swept up in a simple chignon and matched the pearls draped around her neck.

"I don't like us all being separated for long periods of time," Madeline said. "And I especially don't like being separated from you, my husband." She graced him with a smile that made her eyes dance.

That's what I want. Mercy watched them. *I want that easy way they have with each other, as though they are best friends picking up where they left off the last time they were together.*

"Mercy?" Madeline asked. "Mercy?"

"I'm sorry, Maddie. What did you say?"

"I was asking you what you wanted to tell us this evening. The suspense is just too much. Out with it, my dear."

"I think there is one more thing of great importance to discuss before I tell you what I wanted to talk to you about." She looked meaningfully at Victoria and Jonathon. Victoria glowed. Mercy was amazed her mother hadn't already guessed. "Victoria?"

Jonathon put his arm around his wife.

Victoria looked at her mother. "I'm having a baby."

The table sat silent for two seconds and then exploded into congratulations and hugs and the joy only an announcement of this nature creates. Mercy was grateful that this special news would help ease the shock of what she would reveal.

An hour later, after the excitement and dinner had nearly ended, Devlin turned to her and said, "Mercy, you may want to explain to Maddie and her mother, and especially to our mother, what kind of an adventure you are involved in and what they might expect in the coming weeks."

"An adventure?" Madeline turned toward her. "How intriguing. What are you doing?"

All eyes turned in Mercy's direction, and she had to grip the table with both hands to keep from bolting out of the room.

Her stomach churned. *O Lord, help me find the words, the right words.*

"Mercy?" Her mother tilted her head in anticipation.

Mercy took a deep breath and allowed all that had happened, and all that was about to happen, to tumble out of her, an avalanche of explanation and emotion. She didn't notice she was crying until Devlin gave her his handkerchief.

She took it and dabbed at her eyes. No one said anything. Of course, Victoria and Jonathon already knew most of the story, though not what was to transpire tomorrow, and Devlin knew everything.

"You're in danger," her mother said. "I don't like this, Mercy. You are putting yourself at risk for a dream that cannot possibly come to fruition. Such things are not accepted; you are a woman."

"Mama," Mercy said, gaining strength, "I'm dressed as a man when I study, and a man will get the medical degree, not me. I will never be able to call myself Dr. Grayson. If I get my medical license I will be Dr. William Snow. Devlin did it, and although his gender wasn't against him, he still had to stare down society for daring to break the boundaries of social status. Many of his naysayers backed off, but some will never retreat. I have to try."

Her mother lifted her veil to reveal her scars. "You will have to examine women who will think you a man—" Her green eyes focused on Mercy with profound intensity. "—and men who think you a man. You will be an imposter."

"Only because I will be forced to be an imposter because of an unjust, small-minded society that wants to keep women in our supposed place. It's not right. It's not fair."

"But it is what it is," her mother said. "And you will be in constant danger of being found out. You may even find yourself in physical danger, depending on the situations you get yourself into, my daughter."

Mercy no longer wanted to cry. She wanted to scream, but anger choked her, not anger at her mother but at the way things were.

"Perhaps I can help," a familiar voice said from the doorway.

Everyone turned to look at their visitor, but Mercy saw her mother hurriedly lower her veil before turning to see their guest.

Devlin and Jonathon stood.

"Come in, Lord Eden," Devlin said. "Allow me to introduce you to everyone. My wife, her mother, the dowager Countess Richfield, and our mother, the dowager Countess Ravensmoore. This is Lord Eden, who rescued Mercy and brought her to Victoria."

Eden bowed. "It's a pleasure to meet you. You are a large family, are you not?"

"And growing larger," Mercy's mother said. "The Countess Witt has announced there will soon be another and, who knows, possibly an heir." She smiled.

Mercy sent a wide-eyed panicked look straight at Eden along with an almost imperceptible shake of the head. "But I suspect it will be a girl," she said hurriedly, praying that Eden understood.

"Well, we won't know for certain till almost Christmas," Victoria said, sending her sister a glance of gratitude.

Mercy had considered the idea that Victoria may not have yet told Jonathon about the incident at the Legend Seekers Club. She now knew she was right. "Please join us, Lord Eden."

He settled into a seat near Madeline as she directed him. "Please tell us how you think you can help keep Mercy safe, sir." She poured him a cup of tea as he explained.

"I will be attending the medical lectures with Lady Mercy, and anything else that may be necessary for her studies at the college."

"I've already arranged this with Dr. Langford," Mercy said, "and he is in agreement."

"Devlin," his mother said, turning to him, "you know my past and that I do not say this lightly, but perhaps you should lock them both up in Bedlam and then throw away the key. I don't know why you would have anything to do with this plot. It's utterly insane."

Victoria tried to cover a laugh with her hand, but the laugh slid out between her fingers. And then her husband joined in. Devlin cracked a smile, and within seconds they were all laughing, with the exception of Lord Eden, who didn't seem to know whether to join them or get up and run for his life.

"I'm sorry, Lord Eden. It's a family trait," Mercy said. And then she knew they would all help her in any way they could. Even her mother, who was only concerned for her welfare and happiness. Now, if she could only convince herself that all would go according to plan.

The next morning Mercy looked in the mirror, and Mr. William Snow looked back. She thought she'd done a fine job of disguising her femininity as she scrutinized her makeup that showed crow's feet at the corners of her eyes. She wore a mustache and close-shaved beard the same color of her own hair that was concealed by a wig that looked quite good with the black hat she used to top it all off.

Her cravat of white silk was tied better than most men's valets were capable of doing, and her black waistcoat and trousers along with a gold pocket watch, donated by her brother, completed the ensemble. The quizzing glass in her outer coat pocket would add to her male authority if needed.

When Mercy descended the stairs, her mother gasped. "Is it you, Mercy?"

"Aunt Kenna's theater friend is a magician when it comes to makeup and costumes. I've had lots of practice." She lowered her voice. "I mean, my dear lady, are you not impressed with my transformation?"

"Indeed."

Henry the butler had to look twice. Then he cleared his throat, bowed, and said, "Your gloves and walking stick, Mr. Snow."

The air, heavy with moisture, held the promise of rain, and the gathering dark clouds confirmed the probability. She slipped out the rear door so as not to draw attention in the front of the townhome and entered a hackney that had been arranged for by her brother.

"Simon! I didn't expect you. How wonderful."

"Your brother insisted." He grinned. "I mean your brother insisted, Mr. Snow. I hope you don't mind. You're a mighty fine-looking gent."

Smiling, Mercy adopted a lower octave and said, "Is that any way to speak to a stranger?"

"You even sound like a man. How'd you learn to do that?"

"Practice." She settled in and closed her eyes for a moment, taking a deep breath. "Now let's go. I'm nervous."

Simon maneuvered the single-horse hackney expertly through the streets toward the East End. "I don't like that this fancy school is so near to Newgate Prison. It's a bad spot for learning." Simon kept his eyes on the crowds and neatly avoided a dray hauling barrels of beer.

"The Royal College of Physicians is more than just a school, Simon. It's where the great future minds in medicine will learn the intricacies of the human mind and body. But I agree with you on its location here in the West End, although it's not far from where the old college burned down on Amen corner, and St. Paul's is also nearby. I am pleased, though, that Lord Eden will be attending along with me. There has been too much happening of a dangerous nature, and I am not one to tempt fate."

"Is he now?" Simon glanced at her. "Seems you've been spending quite a bit of time with the good Lord Eden." Simon held the reins in one hand for a moment while he ran a stubby finger around the collar of his coat. "It's a might sticky out this morning. I'll be waiting for you across the street when you've finished. Your brother said not to let you come home without an escort—even if you are a man for the time being. I'll be your chaperone."

Laughing, Mercy said, "It is an unusual family I'm part of. There it is, Simon." She pointed to the building on the left.

The school sat in a very crowded area that detracted from its solid and noble architecture. Mercy had never been inside, and she carefully studied the structure. Six columns accentuated the front of the two-story brick and stone building on Warwick Lane, a distinguished atmosphere for those studying medicine.

"Thank you, Simon. I'll look for you after the lectures are completed, near noon. It's nearly eight now."

"Be careful, Mr. Snow."

Mercy swallowed and tried to calm the fear roiling in the pit of her stomach. She carefully considered what she'd learned in Scotland about molding herself into another character. It hadn't been easy, but she'd become quite accomplished. Now, as she walked up the six steps to the entry door on the octagon-shaped porch, she became Mr. Snow.

She fell into the crowd of other students making their way through Spanish oak paneled hallways to the lecture hall where they would register prior to entering the room. The floors gleamed nearly as much as the windows, and the sound of their boots and shoes echoed through the building. Once she made her way into the lecture hall, she looked for a seat where she could easily escape if need be. Then she looked for Lord Eden, who would also be in disguise as a Mr. Worden, so as not to bring attention to his sudden need to study medicine.

Dr. Langford walked to the front, where he took his place on a slightly raised platform.

"Let's get started. As you know, I'm Dr. Langford. I will be your instructor for the next six weeks, and I've come in from York to teach on three major areas. The first one is blood disorders, the practice of blood-letting, and what we are seeing in the way of these illnesses today. The second is madness, its root causes, current treatment, and what the future holds. The third is what I call 'physician as surgeon.'"

A thin, pale man in the front row stood. "Dr. Langford, my name is Mr. James. I believe it is beneath the physician's duties to act as a surgeon. Indeed, it goes beyond the pale to even suggest touching a patient, let alone acting as a surgeon; it is abhorrent. I believe—"

"I believe you've said enough, Mr. James. Sit down and keep your mouth closed until you have a better question."

Laughter rolled through the room.

"Mr. James, if you would have allowed me to finish my thought, you would have learned a bit about my beliefs on the subject of physician as surgeon. It is precisely the attitude of which you speak that needs changing, and I will tell you why in the course of this series of lectures."

James looked as if he were about to protest, but with a stern look from Langford he simply said, "Yes, sir."

"I expect each of you to be on time, answer questions when asked, and to think differently than you've been taught to think thus far in medicine. Are there any questions?"

"Excuse me, Dr. Langford. My name is Mr. Worden. I'd like to know if we can expect to take part in any surgeries or dissections? I for one would like the opportunity to participate in both."

"Ah, Mr. Worden." Langford paced the platform. "It may indeed be possible to participate in a dissection. I'm not certain about a surgery, but God willing there may be a chance."

"Thank you, sir." Mr. Worden sat down.

"Are there any more questions before I begin?"

Mercy knew that he'd asked this question because he didn't know where she was in the large lecture hall. She followed his lead.

Mercy stood. "Dr. Langford. My name is Mr. Snow. I was hoping that you might take us into Bethlem when you lecture on the subject of madness. Will that be possible?"

"Mr. Snow, I'm glad you asked that question. You all will indeed have the opportunity to enter what the city calls Bedlam, the oldest asylum in the world. However, I will be assisted with the lectures and the trips to Bethlem by a past student who is now a physician. Many of you may know of Lord Ravensmoore, who, I understand, has picked up the nickname of lord doctor. He will be assisting, and we will be splitting up the students into groups for that adventure."

"Thank you, Dr. Langford." Mercy sat down, and when she glanced across to where Lord Eden had been sitting, she saw that he was gone.

Chapter 22

And out of darkness came the hands that
reach thro' nature, moulding men.
—Alfred Lord Tennyson

Eden scanned the entryway and hallways on the first floor. "Did you see a man leave here just a moment ago?" he asked the gentleman sitting at the desk where all the students had registered before signing in.

"Yes, sir. He went up to the second floor." He pointed above them.

Running through the hall and up the stairs, Eden searched the area for any sight of the man in the greatcoat he'd seen sitting in the rear of the lecture hall. A library filled most of the second floor. He methodically scoured the area.

"Did anyone see a man of average height wearing a greatcoat run through here?"

Several men scowled at him. One said, "This is a library, not a circus." Another nodded toward the opposite side of the room.

He raced in the direction the man had indicated. His heart sank when he saw another set of stairs leading down to the first floor. "No, no, no," he murmured to himself. He hurried down the stairs and saw a door open to the outside. He rushed through it and into the rain that was just beginning to fall. He looked both ways but didn't see the man he was tracking. Then he chose and ran down the alley instead of toward the front of the building.

When he reached the street that the alley emptied into, all he saw and heard were hawkers selling their wares and row upon row of stalls with merchandise that included old clothing, fruit, flowers, and goods. The thunder rumbled overhead, and the sky unleashed a torrent of rain, sending everyone scrambling.

"Blast it!"

By the time he got back to the lecture hall, his coat and clothing were soaked through. He couldn't leave because he had to keep an eye on Mercy, but he wasn't beyond entertaining a heartfelt longing for a warm bath and hot coffee.

"Are you going back in there like that?" asked the student at the desk. "You're dripping."

"I'll sit in the rear." He slipped into a seat behind the section where Mercy sat listening to Langford.

"Ah, I see you have decided to rejoin us, Mr. Worden. I suggest next time you take a walk outside that you dress more in keeping with the weather."

Every face in the room turned to stare at him, including Mercy, who looked relieved. He felt himself sliding farther down into his seat, wishing he could simply slither away. Instead he only nodded.

"Tell me, Mr. Worden, what did William Hewson discover about the lymphatic system?"

Vincent stood and said, "I'm afraid I don't know, Dr. Langford."

"Sit down, Mr. Worden," Langford said. "Can anyone else answer that question?"

Another student stood and said, "My name is Mr. Lawrence. I think Hewson discovered that blood coagulation was dependent on the lymphatic system."

"I suggest you stop thinking for the day, then, Mr. Lawrence. That is not correct. I want you to write a paper this evening about the lymphatic system and its functions."

The red-faced Mr. Lawrence nodded. "Yes, sir."

"Mr. Snow, would you happen to know the answer to my question?"

Mercy stood. "Hewson let it be known that the lymphatic system was not part of the circulation system, which doctors had previously believed."

"Exactly," Langford said. "Very good, Mr. Snow. You may sit down."

For some inexplicable reason Vincent felt something like pride swell in him for Mercy. He liked that she wanted to be a physician, he liked that she pursued with passion what she referred to as her calling, and he liked the way she had taken care of him on the ship and at her sister's home. But he didn't like that he was falling in love.

Vincent knew he could never live with himself if his wife died in childbirth as his mother had and as many women still did. There was no way to know whether it might happen to the woman you loved. He could reason as an adult, but his heart always felt the vulnerability of the child he'd been at ten. His father had died from guilt. There couldn't be a God, not a loving God, anyway—a God who would allow such wretched things to happen to women during childbirth.

"Why did you leave?" Mercy stood in front of him as Mr. Snow.

He tried to clear his thoughts. "What? It's finished?" He squinted up at her.

"Mr. Worden," she whispered, "you're not wearing your eye patch?"

"The miracles of modern medicine." He grinned. "Your brother cured me."

"The ointment?"

He nodded.

"Would you like a ride home?" she asked. "If you don't get out of those wet clothes, you could end up as a cadaver on one of Langford's dissecting tables."

The other students were quickly exiting, probably looking forward to getting something to eat, he thought as his stomach growled. "I think I will accept that ride, Mr. Snow. Thank you, but I'll see you safely home first." He offered her his arm and then caught himself, looking around to see if anyone had seen the faux pas.

"You're going to have to be more cautious than that," she whispered. "Follow me."

When they arrived at the rear of Number 3 Grosvenor Square, there was no longer a need to remain in character. Vincent helped Mercy from the hackney as Simon sat back and laughed.

"If you two aren't the odd couple."

"Simon, I'm too soggy to impose upon Lady Mercy. Would you take me to my home? If you agree, I'll share a meal with you."

"Don't have to ask me twice."

Mercy's mother met them at the back entrance. "I'm glad I caught you, Lord Eden."

"How did you know it was me under this rather damp façade of Mr. Worden?"

"It's your eyes, of course. You're not wearing your patch, and Mercy told me you had a green eye and a blue eye."

"I see where Lady Mercy gets her cleverness," he said.

"Mercy, we want to go on a shopping expedition in a couple of hours. Your sister wants to go to the Burlington Arcade, and Maddie wants to come as well. Devlin wants us to take Lord Eden with us because Jonathon wants him to look at some horses he brought in for Tattersalls. Are you able to come with us, Lord Eden?"

"I would love to accompany you. I'll return in two hours, and I'll bring my coach so you don't have to bother." He bowed and then turned to Simon. "Let's go, my friend."

Women flocked to the Burlington Arcade, which sat on the western side of the huge Palladian style manor known as Burlington House. Mercy and her sister, their mother, Devlin's wife, and her mother were thoroughly engrossed with jewelry at the moment. Vincent scanned the street, wondering how they could stay so interested in such baubles for so long a period of time.

"Lord Eden, don't you think this necklace accentuates the color of Mercy's eyes?" Victoria asked.

He turned to see an exquisite double-strand emerald green necklace laced together with gold chains about Mercy's neck. But it wasn't the necklace that captivated him as much as the sparkle in her green eyes. She was enjoying herself, and he hadn't seen her look so at ease since he'd met her.

"You're beautiful. I mean, it's beautiful."

Victoria laughed. "I think we know what you mean."

Rough voices raised in argument across the street caught his attention. A group of six or eight men sparred in verbal combat over the problems that would continue to go unresolved within the city if the Tories remained in power.

"You're a blithering idiot is what you are," one man said to another.

The other man responded with a fist to his antagonist's nose. With that, all chaos broke loose and moved in the shoppers' direction.

"Get into the store," Vincent yelled. "Now!" He blocked a wild misaimed punch that was headed straight toward his face. He turned to see the women hurry into the shop. When he turned back, he received a blow to the right side of his jaw that sent him sprawling into the street.

The rage that had built in him since he'd been attacked on the way to Windsor exploded, and he put his boxing talent to use, easily incapacitating all who tried to better him. When a large man came barreling at him, he simply rolled into a ball that threw his challenger off balance and sent him over the top of another ruffian.

Two of the horse patrol entered the fray within several minutes, along with three of the foot patrol, and took charge of the situation. He brushed himself off and entered the shop where he'd left Mercy and her family.

"Are you hurt?" Mercy immediately rushed to his side. "You could have seriously injured yourself again. Let me see that eye," she demanded.

Vincent laughed. "I'm fine. In fact, I haven't felt this good since we arrived in London."

Mercy's mother laughed from behind her veil. "Men always judge their prowess by the outcome of a good fight."

"Let me see anyway."

He allowed Mercy to assess his eye. Her soft touch on the side of his face was more potent than the surge of excitement from the fight. He caught her hand for just a moment.

She stared up at him. "Amazingly, you are right. No damage done."

"I don't know how you avoided that huge man," Victoria said. "It was like watching David and Goliath with fists, but it all happened so fast."

"I'll tell you a secret," he whispered. "Just as Mercy learned the art of pressure points from a gentleman from the Far East,

I learned the ancient art of fighting from a Far Eastern expert when I visited his country."

"It was fascinating to watch, but I hope you aren't soon engaged in this ancient art again," Madeline said.

Mercy studied him, and he caught her eye.

"What are you thinking?" he said, rubbing his jaw.

"I'm thinking there is much I don't know about you, and all along I thought you were an open book, easy to read with no hidden mysteries."

"I don't know if that's a compliment or an insult," he said.

Madeline's mother looked wistful. "Unfortunately, Lady Mercy, I know just how many mysteries a man is capable of hiding, and they are many. The male gender is not to be quickly trusted. I'd wager that Lord Eden has a few mysterious secrets he has not yet revealed."

"Don't we all, Countess? Life would be boring without mystery," he said, wondering what had happened in her past that she would share her thoughts so openly. "If you've all had enough excitement for one afternoon I suggest we locate Mac and the coach and return home."

"I hate to disappoint you, Lord Eden, but we've only started. We still have to finish here, and then we wanted to look for some special items for Victoria's baby," Mercy said. "And then I thought we all might stop at Gunter's for ices. When was the last time you were at Gunter's, Lord Eden?"

He smiled and tried to remember. "I admit it was a very long time ago. Alas, I am at your command, ladies. Carry on." Then he whispered into Mercy's ear, "Tomorrow morning will come quickly, so when you want to cover your head with your pillow and go back to sleep, don't blame me. I, on the other hand, will be wishing I'd never volunteered to go shopping. Madness must be catching."

The next morning they followed their same routine. She swore she suffered no ill effects of the day's shopping expedition. He, on the other hand, nodded off during Langford's lecture.

"Mr. Worden!"

Vincent bolted upright. *Not again*, he thought miserably. Then he stood for the severe chastisement that was inevitable. He felt like the small child his father used to shout at when he got drunk.

"If this lecture is so completely boring to you, then I insist that you add to it by sharing your knowledge of the current effectiveness of bloodletting." Langford glared at him in all seriousness.

Didn't the man know this was only a pretense and not to be taken so seriously? "If it's my blood to be let, sir, I'd have serious doubts about its effectiveness."

The others in the room laughed despite the warning expression on Langford's face. "If you fall asleep in class again, you are dismissed. Is that clear?"

Perfectly. "Yes, sir." He sat down and found Mercy's sympathetic smile behind the mask of Mr. Snow. She turned her attention back to the lecture, and he turned his thoughts toward the limited time he had to locate and deliver the Spear of Destiny to Prinny. He had to find the spear, but he could only do that in the afternoons and evenings when Mercy didn't need him.

He hadn't yet told anyone he had recovered and lost the relic within the same hour. Maybe he could use that information to his benefit, maybe not. One way or another he would get the spear back, because he knew Fox had it and he also knew where Fox might be. But he was going to need help, more help than Mac and Pooles could provide. He needed a small army, and maybe, just maybe, he was beginning to believe he needed God. Mercy and her family were having an effect on his disbelief, but he no longer knew who God was and still blamed God for the death of his mother. How could—

"And now," Langford was saying, "I want to introduce you to the doctor who will take you through Bethlem Hospital and teach you what madness can do to a person. Man or woman, adult or child, insanity can kill just as surely as any other disease. Lord Ravensmoore is a physician and a surgeon. He can teach you things about the behavior of humans and why they do the things they do, better than many who have studied the aberrations of the mind for a much longer time."

Ravensmoore walked up on the platform. "Thank you, Dr. Langford."

Langford stepped back and took a seat near the rear of the platform.

Vincent glanced at Mercy, whose attention was completely on her brother, and then focused on Ravensmoore.

"I know you are anxious to become doctors," Ravensmoore said, "but there is valuable information about the human body locked in the human brain. Too often physicians forget that the brain is part of the body and offers possibly more insight into illnesses and ailments than other organs."

A young blond man stood. "My name is Mr. Peck. How is that possible? The brain is not more important than the heart or the liver."

"Mr. Peck, without the brain you would not be studying to become a physician. I suggest you all think carefully about what you plan to ask before the words escape your mouth. Sit down, Mr. Peck."

"If any of you have delved into your Bibles, you know that within the Gospels are words about the church and her people. Romans 12:5 says, 'So we, being many, are one body in Christ, and every one members one of another.' Imagine that the brain is Christ. He, Christ, directs the rest of us in this life, just as the brain directs what happens in the human body. And that, gentlemen, is what you must recall when you enter Bethlem tomorrow. There are many reasons the hospital is referred to as Bedlam. But remember that the people who are patients of Bethlem are human beings like you and me."

"Excuse me, my name is Mr. Snow." Mercy stood and addressed her brother. "Can you explain who it is we may encounter tomorrow, Lord Ravensmoore?"

"Mr. Snow, you will encounter what we might all become, at any time, for a reason unique to each individual mind. You will encounter hopelessness, despair, and the deepest horrors a mind can imagine."

Chapter 23

For God shall bring every work into
judgment, with every secret thing, whether
it be good, or whether it be evil.
—Ecclesiastes 12:14

Seven Dials encompassed the poorest and most dangerous the city of London had to offer. If Fox and the others were hiding out here, no one would likely know because most men would not venture down one of its six streets during the day, let alone in the evening hours.

Vincent and Simon hugged the walls leading down Great White Lion Street. "This place smells like rotted death." Simon poked Vincent in the side with a finger. "I think I'm about to cast up my accounts."

"You'll not draw attention to yourself if you do," Vincent said. "I think someone beat you to this spot for just such a need." He covered his mouth and nose with a handkerchief trying not to gag.

Simon muffled a squeal.

"What's the matter with you? Do you want every footpad or worse on us?"

"A rat nearly made its way up my trouser leg. Nasty monster. Big as a dog."

"Shh." Vincent watched shadows dancing along the wall about twenty feet in front of them. He turned, grabbed Simon by the collar, and pulled him back into a tiny alcove. "Someone's coming." He felt for the knife in his boot and pulled it from its hiding place, then flattened himself against the wall, Simon next to him.

A prostitute was leading a willing customer down the alley. Vincent just hoped they weren't planning on using this alcove for their entertainment. They passed by, laughing and groping each other and smelling of gin. When they were far enough away, Simon stuck his head into the alley. "It's clear."

They left their hiding place and ventured out into the alley again. After several minutes Vincent stopped. "Listen."

"I don't hear anything," Simon said and cocked his ear forward with his hand. "Wait, it's coming from inside."

Vincent pointed to the building at his left and then brought a finger to his lips. He nodded toward the building and led the way. The continuous droning of a chant pulled Vincent closer. He'd heard this before. He'd heard it on the ship. "I should have trusted my gut," he whispered to Simon. "There will be too many for us."

"Look." Simon pointed to a small wooden door half hidden by boxes piled in the alley. Simon examined the door. "There's no lock on it." He pulled and the door creaked, but the chanting continued.

Vincent's heart skipped a beat. *Turn back.*

"I think I can wiggle through here, Eden." Simon lay on his stomach and tried to get through the narrow opening.

"Can you see anything?" Vincent asked, getting down on his knees next to Simon.

"Africans. They're sittin' round a fire," he whispered.

"How many?" Vincent looked about the alley. No sign of trouble.

"'Bout a dozen."

Simon wiggled back out. Dust and cobwebs clung to him. "No sign of the spear, but it would be hard to see from here." He sat back against the wall to catch his breath. His eyes widened and locked on Lord Eden and the Africans surrounding them with machetes drawn. "Guess there's more than I thought."

Inside the building Vincent and Simon watched the Africans with interest. Unfortunately, they watched with their hands tied behind their backs, their feet bound, and both propped against a far wall. They weren't going anywhere soon.

"What do you think they plan to do with us?" Simon asked.

"We're a danger to them now," Vincent said, wishing he'd listened to his gut and left. But this had been his idea. He couldn't blame anyone but himself. "I don't know if they'll kill us or just throw us on whatever ship they plan to leave on when they're ready. I should have organized the small army I thought I needed instead of dragging you into this with me."

"Lucky for you that I work for Bow Street. You don't really think I'd go into Seven Dials at night without telling someone, do you?"

Vincent's body sagged with short-lived relief. Fox strode toward them.

"Come," Fox said. Another African with huge eyes and a broad nose joined them. He yanked Vincent to his feet, while Fox pulled Simon to a standing position.

They were gagged and hoods were thrown over their heads. Then they were flung on top of something that smelled of urine and feces. Soon enough Vincent realized he was being rolled into a piece of carpeting. If he didn't die from the smell, he'd likely suffocate before long.

The sensation of being lifted and dumped into a cart or wagon occupied the next several minutes. Then they began to move. He couldn't hear much because the carpeting muffled sound, and though he tried to yell through his gag, it was useless. He wasn't getting away, and they'd taken his knife from him in the alley.

He thought this might be a good time to reacquaint himself with God, but he couldn't quite fathom how to do that, so he simply thought, *If You really exist, You'll get Simon and me out of this wretched mess, and then perhaps we can get to know each other. Perhaps.* It was all rather irreverent, and he figured no God worth His title would waste a moment on him and his predicament. *If You're there, save Simon.*

He lost perception of time. When he spilled onto a hard, cold floor, he knew Simon's friends from Bow Street were not coming. At least he could breathe again, but with the hood still in place he couldn't see. Something rolled into him with a resounding *thwack*. Vincent groaned. He guessed that Simon had just slid out of a carpet he'd been transported in and now lay on the floor as well. Moments later his suspicions were confirmed when the hoods were removed and, surprisingly, the gags as well.

Shadows chased each other in dim light on stone walls. "Where are we?" he asked.

They were pulled to their feet. Off balance and still adjusting to the light and the surroundings, Vincent fell back against a wall, smashing his left shoulder into the barrier.

Simon said, "Protect us, Jesus."

Looking out behind the bars of a cell stood a huge African. "You are Eden?"

"Where in the depths of hell are we?" Vincent said and looked around to see Fox and three of his friends who had accompanied them.

"This is Bedlam. My hell," said the man.

Fox leaned close to Vincent's face, his breath a heavy stream of gin and rot. "Meet my father, the sakpata."

"Your father? How'd he get here, and what are we doing here?"

"And," Simon asked, "how did we get inside? Past the guards?"

"Power of vodun." Fox pushed Vincent against the bars.

The sakpata snaked fingers with long, dirty nails around the back of Vincent's neck. "Agbe sent the woman. Bring her to me."

"Who is Agbe? And what woman are you talking about?" Although Vincent knew before he heard her name mentioned. A strange puzzle with missing pieces was taking shape.

"Agbe placed the amulet on her. Bring her to me."

"None of this makes sense. Get these ropes off of us if you want our help, but we are not bringing any woman to you."

"Lady Mercy. Ravensmoore's sister. Bring her."

"That's impossible." Eden twisted his wrists against the ropes.

"If Agbe entrusted her with the amulet, then the power must come through her while wearing the amulet. If she appears in front of me without the amulet, then she will die by the power of vodun."

"She will not die." Vincent felt the sakpata's nails push into the skin on the back of his neck. "If you seek to commit murder, then you will pay the price," Eden said. "And I will not allow you to harm her in any way. Is that understood?"

"We can't do anything if ye keep us tied up now, can we?" Simon said. "You understand that, don't ye?"

The African removed his hand from Vincent's neck and stared at Simon. "The power of vodun is greatly misunderstood, small one," the sakpata said. "The power is ancient like the relic you seek."

"Wrong," Simon blurted. "Yer all mixed up. The power doesn't come through the relic, the spearhead. The power comes through Jesus Christ, not an old thing but a living God. Ye wouldn't understand, but I'd be happy to explain it to ye."

"I am a living god. I have power."

"Then why are ye still behind them bars if yer so all powerful?" Simon asked.

"There are ways to be followed," the sakpata continued. "There are ancient ways to be followed, and only then will the power come. Bring the woman," he turned to Vincent with fire in his eyes, "and I will give you the relic you seek."

Vincent nodded. "I'll do it, but I must receive the relic, the spear, at the time she comes to you. You must give me the amulet now."

Sakpata looked at two of the men who stood behind them and said something in a language Vincent did not understand.

Fox came forward. "You will not get the relic until you bring the woman here. You must place the amulet over her head before she approaches the sakpata or you will not get the spear."

"But I don't have the amulet."

Fox grinned. "Then you must find it."

"If any harm comes to Lady Mercy, you will never live to see your country again."

"We're not leaving this place in those stinking carpets either," Simon said.

"Bring the woman." The sakpata raised his hand.

"Eden!" Simon yelled.

Pain splintered Vincent's skull as a dark void swallowed him.

Mercy spent much of her evening thinking about Vincent when she was supposed to be studying. Her brother was out, and he'd allowed her to use his library. He'd said, "If you are surrounded by books, it may help you keep your mind on your studies. Tomorrow will be an emotional day, and you will need your strength, so get to bed early. Bedlam has a way of sucking the life out of you." She imagined that he meant the sadness of the place.

Then her thoughts had drifted back to Vincent and the difference in the color of his eyes, the right one blue and the left one green. He was no longer in need of the eye patch, and she found that when his gaze stilled on her, she was lost in that mysterious and fascinating gaze. She couldn't help but wonder if he would father children with the same eye coloring. And then a tingle of anticipation swept through her when she thought about seeing him in the morning dressed as Mr. Worden. She didn't care what disguise each of them wore. Somewhere along the way they had acknowledged there was more to their friendship. Perhaps it was the way he'd looked at her just before the fight broke out at the Burlington Arcade. She sighed.

"I'd love to know what that sigh meant," her mother said. She tilted the book so she could read it. "I seriously doubt that *An Introduction to the Comparative Anatomy and Physiology* would elicit such a sigh. I thought you may have been reading Byron. Would you like to talk?"

Mercy laughed and looked up into her mother's veiled face. "Yes and no."

"I've never known you to be indecisive, child of mine. Come, sit over here by the fire. It's uncommonly cold tonight for early June."

Mercy followed her mother to the cozy fire in the hearth, and they both dropped into comfortable tapestry-covered chairs. "This fire will put me to sleep in minutes if I'm not careful, and I have much yet to study tonight."

"Tell me what is troubling you, dear."

Her mother reached out and covered Mercy's hand.

Mercy studied her mother. "I will talk if you will remove your veil. I love to see your eyes when I talk to you. The scars don't bother any of us, Mother. Please."

"If you're sure. I hate the sight of them." She lifted the small blue veil off her face and pushed it back over her hair. "There. Better or worse?"

"Mama, you must stop being so hard on yourself. You are still a beautiful woman despite the scars. They have diminished over the past two years. I believe it may be time for you to venture into society again."

"Rubbish. I have no need of society, and they certainly have no need of me. I love and prefer the country. London is not a place I care to remain long. After you are through with your medical program, perhaps you would consider coming back to Yorkshire with us. I'm sure you could do a lot of good at Safe Haven, and you would have your own brother to work with, and even Dr. Langford on occasion."

"I don't know if I will get my medical degree. And even if I do, I must hide my true identity from the public. It would be a double life, as we discussed. I would be much like Jonathon was during the war, a spy of sorts. Not really me and not really Mr. Snow. It's all beginning to look quite impossible. But I must try. I simply must."

"Remember the verses in Colossians, Mercy. 'And whatsoever ye do, do it heartily, as to the Lord, and not unto men; knowing that of the Lord ye shall receive the reward of the inheritance: for ye serve the Lord Christ.'"

Mercy smiled. "That's an excellent verse for me, and Mr. Snow, to remember."

"Now, when I came in I heard you sigh. And it wasn't a sigh of weariness. It was a sigh regarding your Lord Eden, wasn't it?"

Mercy felt exposed. Was it that obvious? She couldn't even bring herself to look at her mother now, so she stared into the flames dancing in the hearth. "I hoped it didn't show. I don't think there is any place for him in my life or for me in his. We are simply friends."

"Does he know?"

"Know what?" Mercy asked, turning to her mother.

"That you're in love with him. What do you think I've been talking about?" She stood and walked behind Mercy. "I'm going to put my hands over your eyes. Now sit still."

Not being one to disobey, Mercy sat compliantly while her mother covered her daughter's eyes.

"Now, what do you see?"

Mercy laughed. "Nothing. You're covering my eyes."

"That's the point. What do you see when I cover your eyes and all is darkness?"

"Is this some sort of chicanery?"

"Suspicious child." Her mother laughed. "What do you see? Give attention to your thoughts."

After about a minute she gasped. "I see him. I see Lord Eden."

"Now you know the sigh was for him and not your studies."

Mercy pulled her mother's hands away and turned around in the chair. "How did you do that?"

"I didn't do anything. He is what you were thinking about, so that is who your mind chose to see. If I learned anything after all those years at Ashcroft it was that when I closed my eyes, I could see my children. Every night I closed my eyes I fell asleep dreaming of you, Victoria, Devlin, and Edward. We see those we love, my darling girl."

She stood and embraced her mother. "I've stayed away too long. It was selfish of me after missing you for so many years. Forgive me."

"There is nothing to forgive. You are following your heart. I just wish you would have told us. All of us. Sooner. Perhaps we could have saved you the difficulties you now find yourself in. Trust God, trust your family."

Mercy felt the weight of a burden lift. "I'd better get to bed, or I'll be late to lecture in the morning. We're going to Bethlem, and Devlin is teaching. I'm hoping Mr. Snow will be his brightest pupil."

"I just hope he remembers to call you Mr. Snow. Now off to bed with you. Happy dreams, Mercy."

But Mercy's dreams were not happy. She watched herself emerge from the mist on the London streets. She didn't know where she was or where she was going, but she was looking for someone. Then she heard steps behind her and she was running. She was back in Scotland. Fear gripped her so tightly she couldn't move. She understood that something evil was hunting her, cutting through the fog.

Chapter 24

Therefore trust to thy heart, and to
what the world calls illusions.
—Henry Wadsworth Longfellow

The stars faded one by one as the night sky bloomed into dawn. "So much for help from your Bow Street friends." Vincent's head ached as though someone had beaten him with a hammer. He knew he couldn't stop now. Mercy needed him whether she knew it or not. His steps quickened.

"She will never forgive you," Simon said.

"You're probably right," Vincent agreed. "But I'd rather be unforgiven than see anything ugly happen to her." Though the morning mist clouded the way, Vincent's sight focused only on getting to Bethlem before Mercy and her brother visited there today with the other students.

"What will everyone think when you show up and you're not dressed as Mr. Worden? And how will you find this sakpata African again? And how will you get Mercy to where he's imprisoned?"

"Simon, you are nothing but a voice in the mist. You have been swallowed up, and if you're not careful, I may very well step on you by accident. Other than that, you ask too many questions."

"I'm right beside you."

"Ouch." Vincent slapped at the hand that reached up out of

the mist and pinched his arm. "You try my patience, Simon."

"But what are you going to do? If I'm going to help you at all, I need to know the plan."

"I'm going to put an end to Lady Mercy's fears of John Marks. He can come after me when he finds the amulet missing. If it's so important to him that he chased Mercy from Scotland to London for it, then I suspect its value lies in what Marks and Kane think they can make from the piece and not from any magical power the sakpata believes it harbors."

They turned a corner onto Amen Street about a block from the entrance of Bethlem Hospital. The high walls of the lunatic asylum burst into view, and Vincent felt for the amulet in his pocket. He was turning into a fine thief. The sun shot through the dissipating mist, and Simon reappeared at Vincent's side.

"How did you know where Marks was living?" Vincent asked, picking up the pace.

Simon had to walk faster to keep up, his breath coming fast. "They use me as an assistant at Bow Street. I do have some experience at locating fugitives. Besides, I saw him duck into an alley known for harboring those with something to hide for the right price. I just didn't know it was him at the time. His landlord can always be bought, and you gave him no reason not to allow you into Marks' rooms. He won't breathe a word—unless Marks is willing to part with a great sum of money."

"When he discovers he's missing the amulet, he'll probably think Fox took it. We might not be the first he suspects," Vincent said, talking to himself more than to Simon. "And that will give us the advantage."

"Watch out there," yelled a driver. "I near ran ye over." Two large bay workhorses pulling a wagon laden with straw plodded next to them.

Simon and Vincent moved closer to the stone wall of a church to allow the driver more room. "Ye could give a body a warnin'," Simon yelled at the driver. "If'n ye ain't more careful, I'll drag ye over to Bow Street and you can complain to the magistrate."

The driver shook a fist at Simon. "I'm late for getting' this 'ere load to Bedlam, and yer tryin' to make me morn'n worse. The devil take ye, I say."

"My friend's had a difficult night," Vincent said. "Did you say you were taking this load to Bedlam?"

"Aye, what's it to ye?" The horses plodded along, and Vincent easily kept pace with them.

"Now what are ye doin'?" Simon growled.

"Just listen and learn, Mr. Bow Street man. I'm about to be brilliant."

"This should be interestin'." Simon stopped walking. "I gots to catch me breath."

"Sir," Vincent called to the driver, "a half crown for a moment of your time."

"Whoa, whoa there, Maggie. Whoa, Topsy. I'll be seein' that 'alf crown now that ye got me team stopped in the middle of this 'ere street."

Vincent pulled himself up next to the driver. He looked into the dull eyes of a ruddy-complexioned man with dark stringy hair, the odor of cows upon him, and a glare to match that of any sea pirate. "My friend and I need to get into Bedlam without anyone seein' us. If you allow us to hide in your wagon until we're safely through the gates, I'll give you another half crown to match this one." He pulled the coin from his pocket and handed it to the driver, who immediately bit down on the piece with broken, crooked teeth.

"Ah, 'tis real enough, it is. Must be me lucky day. Aye, I'll take ye in. Most queer folk is usually tryin' ta get out o' Bedlam, and 'ere ye are pay'n' me to get ye in. A fine lot the world's come ta.

But won't be so easy for ye to make yer way out once they find how loony ye both is. Make yer way into the straw—and without bein' seen. Wouldna want ta sully me reputation."

Vincent nodded and lowered himself to the ground. "We've got ourselves a ride, Simon."

"You must have been hit on the head harder than I thought," Simon said. "Are you mad? We're almost there."

"This is our camouflage. Now no one else will know we've entered." He looked around, and when no one was nearby, he picked Simon up and tossed him into the straw, climbing in after him.

Mercy tried to listen to her brother talk about the needs of patients in Bethlem and in other lunatic asylums throughout Great Britain. But neither her mind nor her eyes could focus on Devlin. Instead she looked about the room, wondering why Simon hadn't come for her this morning and concerned that Lord Eden was not present in the lecture hall. Something was not right. He would not have knowingly left her in a vulnerable situation. But there was little she could do about it now. Devlin had assured her he would stay with her until the others could be located.

"Listen closely." Dr. Langford addressed the group. "We will assemble at the main entrance of Bethlem in an hour. Don't be late. We will not wait for you."

Vincent and Simon slipped from the wagon. The driver waited with an outstretched palm, which Vincent filled with another half crown. As they maneuvered past a guard, the driver could be heard singing a song extolling the virtues of a warm hall, a full mug, and a bulging coin purse, among other things.

"We have no idea where this sakpata's cell is, and Bethlem is a big place," Vincent whispered to Simon from behind several barrels where they watched the comings and goings of those working within the asylum and those bringing in goods.

"We must wait for Ravensmoore to arrive with Lady Mercy and the others," Simon said. "Follow me."

"Follow you, where?" Vincent asked, looking about and seeing no place they could go without being seen.

Simon dusted the straw off his clothing and pulled pieces of it from his hair. "I'm here on official Bow Street business, and you are with me. We're searching for a criminal posing as a madman to escape justice. If anyone asks, simply say he attacked you and stole a valuable item from your person."

"Then why didn't we just go through the main entrance if you were planning on using your Bow Street ruse?"

"Because, Lord Eden, at the front gate they will be more diligent than those in this area of the asylum."

"How do you come up with these schemes? You're good, almost eerily good."

"I lived in a lunatic asylum for years. I know how the places work."

"You jest, of course." Vincent dusted himself off as well and tried to look somewhat presentable after the evening's chaos. "You forget that we stink worse than pigs."

"Let me handle it." Simon strutted into the busy aisle where deliveries were being attended and walked with determination toward the entryway. Vincent shrugged and followed, thinking that at worst they would be thrown out.

They'd walked past two guards before one stepped in front of them—a burly man with wide-set eyes and thin lips.

"And who 'ave we 'ere?" the guard asked. "If yer visit'n' ye need to come in the front entrance."

"I'm Simon Cox of Bow Street. I'm here on official business with Lord Eden."

"If yer a lord," he said, looking Vincent up and down, "then why is ye dressed like that and smellin' worse than the lot of Seven Dials?"

"Because I was accosted and followed the vermin who attacked me into Seven Dials. I have reason to suspect that the man's accomplice is hiding out here in the asylum pretending to be mad, when he is quite sane. Mr. Cox believes he knows the thief."

"And as your nose is telling you, we don't carry the odor of petunias, now, do we?"

The guard backed away. "Git on with ye, then. And if ye finds the crook, ye'll 'ave to follow proper channels to 'ave 'im moved to Newgate or take 'im to Bow Street."

Simon scowled. "Whad ye take me for? An amateur?"

"Humph. Git on yer way."

Simon and Vincent moved past the man and into the interior of Bethlem. A satisfied smile had just passed Vincent's lips when Simon turned back to the guard.

"Ye wouldn't happen to know where I could find a patient I need to talk to—big African man?"

"Course, I know. Ye think me daft?"

Simon frowned. "Well, then, where is he?"

"Ye need authority to git down there. From the lord doctor."

"And where is down there?" Vincent asked.

"The old dungeons. He's the only one down there."

Mercy had never been inside the walls of Bethlem. She'd almost met her brother and sister there a year ago to minister in a section Devlin had set aside for women he thought might be able to leave their prison with a little more help. He was the only one willing to do that, and it did help. It also cost Victoria, but Mercy didn't want to think about that now.

Devlin guided her and nine other students through the various wards of the asylum. He still treated women in the west wing of the hospital whenever he came to town to work. He tried his best to get them back with loved ones—if they had any—or to find them other places in the community where they might do some good and not be tortured by those who were too ignorant to understand them.

One of the students, a Mr. Martin, asked, "Where do the criminally insane patients live? Are we going to see them today?"

"The dangerous patients are in another area on the other side of the hospital. We will not be going there today. There is a patient nearby, though. I had not planned on taking you to see him. He's an African who was sent here by the Bow Street magistrate after the man sacrificed a chicken in front of a church."

The skin on the back of Mercy's neck prickled. "What are you going to do with him?" she asked.

Her disguise as Mr. Snow was wearing on her nerves. The constant pretense around the other students was difficult to maintain, but so far she'd been able to manage. But now Devlin wanted to introduce her to someone who must be involved with the strange events Mercy and Eden had experienced since they'd arrived in London.

"I'm not sure," Devlin said. "It's unlikely many of you will get this kind of opportunity again. I've never known the hospital to have a practicing vodun African within its walls."

The word *vodun* spread through the ten students like a crack in the spring ice. The others were excited, but Mercy felt only dread. She believed there was a connection between the sakpata and the Africans who were on the ship she'd been on just before Eden rescued her. She looked at her brother and knew he thought there may be a connection as well.

"Follow me," Devlin said.

The group wove through various hallways until they came to a heavy oak door with a barred window built into the top. Her brother drew a set of two keys from his waistcoat and used one to unlock the door. He pulled it open, and the rusty hinges creaked, adding to the eerie sense of impending doom that Mercy couldn't shake.

A student named Smith asked, "There are no patients running around loose down here, are there, Lord Ravensmoore?"

"No," Devlin said. "The only patient here is the African, and he's confined to a cell. I ask you not to say anything that might upset him. He's going to feel even more vulnerable because there are so many of us staring at him."

They followed Devlin down a circular stone staircase. Spiders clung to cobwebs, and sconces on the walls lit the way.

"The guards come and go from this area," Devlin explained. "They don't like coming down here, but the patient must be fed, and the sconces are the only source of light and must be kept lit."

The farther into the dungeon they went, the harder and faster Mercy's heart beat. She wanted nothing more than to turn and run, but how would she explain that? And Devlin had locked the door anyway. When they turned a corner, Lord Eden and Simon Cox awaited them.

"Simon, what are you doing here?" Devlin bristled. "Lord

Eden. How did the two of you get in here without my knowledge? You both have much to explain."

The African stood in his cell, staring out at them. He turned to Eden. "Where is the woman?"

Eden walked toward Mercy. "Forgive me," he whispered.

"Stop, Eden! You have no right," Devlin growled.

"Don't," Mercy whispered. Her vision blurred with tears.

Eden removed the hat and man's wig she wore. Then he ran his hands through her hair. "Here is the woman you seek, sakpata."

The other students gasped. Mr. Martin said, "Snow is a woman! How can this be? It's outrageous."

"Where is the amulet?" the African asked.

Devlin stepped between Eden and Mercy. "Stop this at once. I don't know what you are doing, but it ends now."

"It can't end yet. Here is the amulet." Eden removed it from his pocket and draped it around Mercy's neck.

The African sakpata held his arms through the cell bars. "Face me, woman."

Devlin stood in front of her. "She will do no such thing."

Mercy didn't care anymore. She didn't understand exactly what Eden was up to, or what this African wanted from her, or how Simon was involved. All she knew was that she'd been betrayed by the man she thought she loved. She stepped in front of her brother.

The African stared at her as if she were a coveted sweet to be consumed. She walked toward him. "Come here."

The sakpata placed his hands on her shoulders and seemed to go into some sort of trance. He chanted unintelligible words, and Mercy simply stared at him, not understanding his intent and not caring. When the chanting stopped, he pulled the amulet over her head and placed it around his own neck with the amulet's twin. He took both parts and fitted them together. "It is done."

He turned, went to the cot in his cell, and pulled the box containing the relic from under the thin mattress. "Lord Eden, the spearhead is yours."

Vincent took the box containing the treasure. He turned to Mercy. "I hope you understand that I didn't do this for the relic. I honestly thought your life in jeopardy."

She ignored him and turned her attention back to the sakpata. "Who was it that placed the amulet on me before he threw me overboard?"

"My brother, the agbe. He sent you to me."

"And why would he do that?" Mercy asked.

"To free me. He sent my freedom to me through you; you were the entrusted one. You had to bring it to me. If not, you would have died. Agbe would have killed you."

"I don't believe you," she said. "You practice vodun and believe in your own power. I know that Jesus is the truth, the way, and the life. Your vodun is nothing. There is no power in objects. No power in the amulet or—" She turned and looked directly into Eden's colorful eyes. "—in the spear the regent seeks to heal the king. The power comes through the Holy Spirit, through Jesus Christ, my living God, and, in truth, your God as well."

Mercy turned to her brother. "I want to leave. I want to go home."

Chapter 25

Forsake her not, and she shall preserve thee:
love her, and she shall keep thee. Wisdom
is the principal thing; therefore get wisdom:
and with all thy getting get understanding.
—Proverbs 4:6–7

The relic Eden had traveled to Austria to retrieve and then returned to England with was now sitting on the desk in his library. The journey he'd been on had all started with this spear and the myth surrounding it. He would now deliver it to the regent. He should feel satisfied, but he wasn't.

A tap on the door turned his attention elsewhere.

"My lord, you have visitors."

"Who is it, Pooles? I'm not in the mood to see anyone."

"The Countess Ravensmoore and the Countess Witt, sir."

"Both of them?" He stood, thinking his appearance needed attention before he greeted them. And then he wondered if he should meet with them at all.

"My lord?" Pooles said.

"Show them in, Pooles. And bring some tea. Lots of tea."

"I thought you might turn us away," Countess Ravensmoore, Lady Madeline, said, studying him. The gentle fragrance of jasmine wafted into the room with her.

"And that," the Countess Witt, Lady Victoria, said, following her sister-in-law, "would not be polite."

Eden went to them and bowed. "Countess Ravensmoore, Countess Witt, I apologize for my appearance and for what I can imagine is the reason for your visit. Please, sit down."

Devlin's wife, Lady Madeline, was a vision in a mint green gown with a forest green pelisse pulled over it. She wore her dark brown hair swept under a becoming cream-colored hat with green feathers. Hazel eyes flashed with intense intelligence and possibly sympathy.

"I understand that you've gotten yourself into a fine mess. My question is, what do you plan to do about it? My husband is raging, which is something he never does."

"And my sister is calmer than I've ever seen her," Victoria said, "which can only mean that she is determined to do something that will most likely cause us all concern, such as disappearing into Scotland again."

Lady Victoria looked radiant in her gown of blue silk, her dark blonde hair pulled up in the back and laced with pearls throughout. Blue eyes were filled with concern. "You have betrayed her, and now she is forced to consider her options."

"I'm sorry, I—"

"Is that the spear?" Madeline pointed to the intricately designed box on his desk.

He nodded.

"May we see it?"

"Of course." He picked up the box and slid the spearhead out into his hand. He handed Victoria the empty box to examine and her sister the relic. "What do you think?"

"The thought that this spearhead actually pierced the side of Christ is very powerful," Madeline said. "I can see why anyone would be drawn to it. Still, it is only an object to be preserved for history's sake. The power of Christ comes not through objects but through Him who sacrificed all for our sin, through His grace and mercy to each of us who believe in His power and not the belief of an object that may or may not have come in contact with His person."

The two women then traded the pieces and examined them further. "It's incredible," said Victoria. "I can see how easy it would be for some to worship this as an idol that has power rather than worshipping Christ Himself. It's tempting, alluring, because it possibly came into contact with the body of Jesus Christ, but it is not Jesus."

They handed back the box and the relic. "You will take this to the regent soon?" Madeline asked.

"Tomorrow." He gently returned the spearhead to the box and then slid the box into a desk drawer.

"The entire ton is in pure heaven this morning with the gossip of yet another Ravensmoore attempting to enter the practice of medicine," Victoria said. "But you can imagine how horrid the talk because Lady Mercy was brilliant enough to disguise herself as a man, hoping to better society, only to be slapped in the face by the one man other than her brother she thought she could trust."

"I–I don't know what to say."

Madeline sighed. "That is why we're here, Lord Eden. To tell you that you'd better say something quickly, or I'm afraid she will return to our home in Yorkshire with no intention of ever seeing you again. In addition to telling her you are wildly in love with her, you'd better appease my husband, or he will never give you permission to marry her."

"Marry? She would never marry me now." He couldn't even believe those words spilled so easily from his lips. "I won't marry her. I can't marry her."

"What do you mean you won't marry her?" Lady Victoria said. "You do love her, don't you?"

"Yes, I love her, but I can't marry her."

Madeline sat forward, a grimace on her pretty face. "You make about as much sense as a drunken fool. Explain yourself, sir."

"It's a long story, and you'll never understand. Forgive me."

"We are not in the mood to forgive you anything yet, Lord Eden." Victoria took a deep breath. "Out with it."

He arched a brow.

"Every young man has a story about why he doesn't want to get married. We want to hear yours," Madeline said.

Victoria asked, "Do those different-colored eyes run in your family?"

Pooles knocked and entered with a silver tray heavy with tea and sandwiches. "Pardon the interruption. It will only take a moment to serve you."

"Pooles," Countess Ravensmoore said, "I will serve. Thank you."

"If you insist, your ladyship." He bowed and left them alone.

"Please, Lord Eden," Lady Madeline said, "tell us your story while I serve the tea."

"As I said, it's a long story. But I will share it with you. And yes, Lady Victoria, these eyes of mine do run in the family." He got up and walked to the mantel where the hearth lay empty. He laid an arm across the white-enameled top. A picture of the gale-tossed HMS *Victory*, Lord Nelson's flagship, hung on the wall above him.

He told them of his childhood, his relationship with his father, and how his mother had died in childbirth. He talked of being sent away at the age of ten to live with his sister and how his father had died a guilt-ridden, lonely man.

"I pray this talk of my mother dying in childbirth has not greatly upset you, Lady Victoria. I hesitated sharing all of this because of your delicate condition." He left the mantel and returned to his seat behind his desk.

Lord Eden," Victoria said, "I understand the dangers of childbirth. Every woman does. We take the risk because we love our husbands and want to have children. We don't expect it to be easy. I know you are not a believer in God, but if you'd simply open a Bible, you'd begin to understand. The apostle John said, 'These things I have spoken unto you, that in me ye might have peace. In the world ye shall have tribulation: but be of good cheer; I have overcome the world.'"

"I believe your father planted some very sad seeds of despair in your young head, Lord Eden," Lady Madeline said. "Instead of helping you grieve, he tried to pull you into his anguish. No wonder you're so frightened of marriage."

"I'm not frightened of marriage, only of causing my wife pain and possibly her death." He felt the rush of embarrassment flood his face. "I have shared too much, I'm afraid. I just wanted you to understand."

"I think perhaps you should have a talk with my husband," Victoria said. "He's positively terrified of my giving birth."

"We want you to know," Madeline said, "that we understand your fear. But don't let that stand in the way of a marriage. Take a leap of faith for God and for Mercy. If you love Mercy, you must tell her what you have told us. And then perhaps she will forgive you for your well-meaning but perhaps not-well-thought-out actions at Bethlem yesterday."

"There was no other way. It had to be done, or she might have been killed. I don't understand all this vodun worship, but the sakpata said she would die. I would never have betrayed her if I didn't think her life was in danger."

The two women stood.

Eden hurried to his feet. "I hope you believe me."

Madeline looked at Victoria, and they both looked at him. "We believe you. Now it is up to you to make our sister believe you."

Jasper Kane walked the deck of the clipper he'd purchased for his venture. The *Voyager*, a large and well-constructed sailing vessel, would suit his purposes to escape from England with the treasures he would use to bring him wealth wherever he decided to go. There was only one more treasure he needed to collect before he left John Marks, his investors, and his old life behind: Lady Mercy Grayson.

Devlin studied a spider crawling along the windowsill in his study. He watched it and thought of the predicament in which his sister Mercy now found herself, and his heart broke for her. For she had very much been trapped in the spider's web. "Grant me wisdom, Lord, for I find myself in a most dangerous mood and one I'm sure I would regret acting upon. Vengeance is Yours, but in this situation I would love to be of assistance." He squeezed his hand into a tight fist, wanting to hit something, wanting to smash something that very much resembled Lord Eden's face. The spider disappeared out of sight.

Lord Eden raised the knocker of Number 3 Grosvenor Square and struggled to keep his anxiety under control. But it wasn't the butler who answered the door. Ravensmoore and his brother-in-law, Lord Witt, stepped outside.

"I'm guessing that now your wives have spoken to me, I have

yet another interrogation to endure. I've come to see Lady Mercy, and I have an appointment with the regent to deliver the relic. I haven't much time."

Ravensmoore and Witt looked at each other and smiled. "This won't take long. We want to take you somewhere," Ravensmoore said. "Either you come willingly, or we may have to encourage you a bit."

Vincent backed up a step. "Is that a threat?"

"Oh, no," Witt said, "we never threaten. It's a promise we plan on seeing through."

A coach and four came from around the corner. Mac and Simon were sitting on top, and Mac, his own driver, was directing the horses. They pulled to a stop.

Eden scowled. "*Et tu*, Brutus?"

Mac shrugged.

"Some friend you turned out to be, Simon."

"Things are not always as they seem," Simon said, arching a blond brow.

Devlin opened the door to the coach. "Get in."

Looking at Devlin in front of him and turning to see Witt still behind him, Eden took a deep breath and entered the coach. Ravensmoore and Witt sat across from him, their arms crossed, their eyes all but boring holes through his head.

"May I ask where you are taking me?" Vincent said, running a finger underneath what felt like a tightening cravat.

"No," Witt said. "You'll know when we get there."

Eden stared out the window so as not to be skewered by the looks of his traveling companions. He couldn't imagine where they were going unless they meant to incarcerate him in Bethlem Hospital as a means of vindictiveness. But when the horses eventually turned on to Hanover Square and slowed, his puzzlement increased.

The coach stopped in front of St. George's Church. "Why are we stopping here?"

"Because we are taking you to church."

"But why?" Vincent asked. "It's not Sunday."

Devlin grinned. "We thought this might be a good place to talk." He opened the door and the three of them quit the coach. "Find a place in the shade for the horses to rest, Mac, after you drop Simon at Bow Street. Come back in about an hour."

"Certainly, yer lordship," Mac said.

They walked up the stone steps and past the six Corinthian columns that supported the portico of the church. Inside, the church was quite plain. Witt led the way to sit in one of the box pews. There was no one else about at this time of day.

"So, are you going to tell me why you dragged me into this church in the middle of the afternoon?" Eden asked.

"First," Devlin said, "because we wanted to hear from your lips what happened that led to your outrageous betrayal of Mercy at Bethlem Hospital. We wanted to do it here in case our tempers flared. We thought we would be more likely to remember to be respectful in the house of the Lord, and perhaps we would not be so quick to resort to violence...until we know every detail."

"And second?" Eden asked.

"Because you do not know the Lord Jesus Christ, or you've chosen to reject Him." Witt lowered his voice when his words echoed off the walls. "And we want to know why."

"Now, tell us why you did what you did," Devlin insisted.

"I told your wives what happened. Why can't you just ask them?"

He rose to leave, but Devlin put a hand on his shoulder. "Tell us."

"I wanted to save her from the threat the African made against her. Surely Simon's told you what happened. He was with me, as you know."

"It's not Simon we want to hear from; it's you. Now are you going to tell us or not?" Witt said.

"It appears the two of you have already made your own decisions regarding my behavior and are ready to pass judgment." He leaned back against the pew and looked straight ahead. "I was afraid that if I waited, something horrible would happen and I wouldn't be able to stop it. I knew you and Mercy would already be at the lecture hall and that you would be coming to Bethlem. When Simon and I found the Africans who accompanied Mercy and me on the ship, I hoped to locate the spearhead. Simon and I had been through a difficult night. Perhaps getting hit on the head and getting no sleep contributed to poor judgment, but I saw no other way."

"So you didn't intend to ruin her hopes of becoming a physician?" Devlin asked, arching a brow. "You didn't think to marry her and then keep her from following a dangerous and forbidden path and thereby ruin her chances to see her dreams come to fruition?"

"I have no idea what you're talking about. I have mentioned nothing to Lady Mercy of marriage. I'm an adventurer with nothing to offer your sister, Lord Ravensmoore."

"I believe you're running away," Witt said. "You're running away from Lady Mercy and looking for excuses. And you're so afraid of not being in control that you have ignored God and possibly ignored His will for your life."

"You know nothing about my life nor what I want of it." He

stood. "I suggest you get Mac to drive you home. I'm going to walk."

"Not yet," Devlin said. He stood next to Eden.

"Why not?"

"Because," Witt said, standing on Eden's opposite side, "you have not told us the most important detail."

"And what would that be?" Eden asked, still sitting and looking up at Witt and Ravensmoore on either side of him.

"Do you love her?"

Eden walked in circles around the streets of London paying little attention to where he was going, for in truth he had no destination. If ever a man had reason to leave the country and never return, it was him. The whole of London had turned to Bedlam. And then he thought of Mercy and started to laugh. She had indeed captured his heart, and he hadn't even told her.

All right, Lord, I bow to Your wisdom for my life, and I am Yours. But I'm going to need all the help I can get. I trust You won't abandon me as my own father did. Guide my steps and forgive my years of silence and indifference. Your will be done.

He shook off the invisible mantle of despair he'd worn for years and hurried to his townhome. "Pooles! Pooles! Where are you?"

"What's wrong, my lord? I'm right here." Pooles came running out of the kitchen. "I was just testing Cook's soup for—"

"I have no time for soup. Tell the groom to ready the coach and provide me with four of the footmen, all armed. I've an appointment with the regent to deliver the relic, and I must beg the forgiveness of the woman I love before doing so. I need you to help me get ready."

"Yes, my lord. Indeed, my lord. But I have a message for you from the regent." Pooles reached for the note with the regent's seal upon it and handed it to his employer.

Vincent ripped it open, scanned it, and then summarized it for Pooles. "The king has been brought to Carlton House. The regent is desperate to prove to his sister that the relic will not make a difference in the king's health, and his sister is hoping it will make all the difference. The regent is only curious to see if it will help him become invincible. His own power has gone to his head."

Vincent took the stairs to the second floor two at a time. Halfway up he stopped and turned. "And, Pooles, tell Cook not to hold dinner for me. I'll be seeking to change the course of my life this evening."

Chapter 26

Thinking is easy, acting is difficult, and
to put one's thoughts into action is the
most difficult thing in the world.
—Johann Wolfgang von Goethe

Mercy sat in the parlor with Madeline and Victoria and their mothers. "I wish life were as simple for me as it seems to be for dear Lazarus," she said. "All he has to do is eat and sleep and beg for treats." She patted his head and stroked his back.

"He gets much attention," Victoria agreed. "His life's not complicated at all. He doesn't even have to get dressed, fortunate beast."

Madeline laughed. "Well, he does have a simpler type of covering, but then he has to wear the same thing day after day. It may be easier, but for us it would be most boring."

The dowager Countess Richfield, Madeline's mother, nodded. "Speaking of fashion, Lady Mercy, you look lovely in that burgundy and cream walking dress."

"Thank you, Lady Richfield. It's one of my favorites that I had time to be fitted for since I arrived in London. It is wonderful to indulge in feminine dress after spending so much time in Scotland dressed as the opposite sex. Yet—"

The knocker at the front entrance announced the arrival of a visitor. Lazarus ran to welcome the unexpected guest with loud enthusiasm.

"Hello there, Lazarus." The familiar voice of Lord Eden resounded in the hallway.

"You look like a startled deer, Mercy." Madeline stood, preparing to greet their guest. "Try to look unassuming."

She'd just taken a deep breath when Henry knocked on the parlor door. "Lord Eden to see you, my lady. May I show his lordship in?"

"No," Mercy said quickly.

"Yes," chorused the rest of her family.

Henry looked totally perplexed.

Madeline nodded. "Show him in immediately, Henry."

"It's a conspiracy, and I don't appreciate this one bit," Mercy said, spearing each of them with a look of resentment. "How could you?"

"Perhaps you will find a way to forgive us...eventually," her mother said. "Now you must excuse us."

A sense of panic seized Mercy as she watched each of them file out of the room. "But you can't leave me alone with him. It's not proper."

Madeline turned and mouthed the words *just trust* and then she was gone.

A moment later Lord Eden entered the room. "I know I don't deserve it and I know you don't understand my actions, but I beg your forgiveness and I pray you will listen to me." He closed the door behind him. "Please."

"Since it appears that I have little choice in the matter, I am all ears." What was it about those disconcerting eyes of his that made her want to stare at him? It was as though he looked at her from two different angles. "You may sit down."

He walked to where she sat and lowered himself into the chair opposite her, where Madeline had been only moments before. "I've hurt you, and I didn't mean to. I only wanted to assure your safety, and by doing so I have lost your trust."

"I think I understand more than you, or my family, have interpreted in this situation. But you can't begin to realize what it has done to me. My chances of becoming a physician are completely gone now. The entire ton knows of my deception, and although society and their disdain mean little to me, I feel responsible for the difficulties and humiliation it will cause my family."

"For a few minutes I would like you to think only of yourself," Eden said. "And by that I don't mean you as a physician or not a physician, but as a woman. You've been so caught up in trying to be what you believe God wants you to be that you may have missed some of the other things He wants for your life."

"I cannot think beyond that, for that is all I've considered for the past three years and probably long before that. It's who I am, who I am meant to be."

"Is it?" Eden reached out to capture her hand.

She jerked it back. "Of course it is." She frowned. "Ever since I was a child and old enough to help, I cared for Victoria and helped her battle for health. Those experiences shaped who I am today."

"What do you want?" he asked.

"I want to be a doctor. I want to help people get well."

"And do you want anything else?"

"I haven't thought that far ahead. I'm choosing to think through one thing before I move on to the next."

He laughed. "I thought women were known to be able to do many things at once. And here you are saying the opposite. I believe you've been wearing men's clothing for too long. Today you look very much the woman."

Mercy stood and walked to a window overlooking the gardens. "What is it that you want, Lord Eden?"

He drew near, and his arms suddenly slipped around her in a manner that suggested he knew her far better than he did. "I want you. Turn around and look at me."

"No. I can't."

"Can't or won't?" He kissed the back of her neck. "Is this one of the pressure points you used on me while we were on the ship?"

Gooseflesh spread over her neck and shoulders. She forced herself to turn around. His gaze captured hers. What was it she saw there? "You betrayed me. You betrayed me for your own gain. For the relic."

"I did receive the relic in exchange for bringing you to the sakpata, but it wasn't the only reason. The Africans' beliefs in vodun are strong. They wrap up who they are in the power of what they think they can control. I learned that while I was with them on the ship before I found you. They believe and pray to so many gods for so many reasons that they lose themselves and their souls in the process. I believe they would have found a way to hurt you or even kill you as the sakpata predicted. It wouldn't have happened through what they think of as vodun power but outright murder by one of the tribe."

"You think they would have murdered me? For the sake of the amulet?"

"No, Mercy. The tribe's sole intent was to free the sakpata by whatever means it took. They used your presence on the ship and your relationship to me and your brother to attempt to prove how powerful vodun is. Really, vodun is more a power over the mind and thoughts of another than the power to control people or circumstances."

"I don't know what to believe anymore."

"Believe that I love you. Believe that we can have a life together."

She wanted to believe him, but she didn't trust her feelings. She didn't yet trust him. Then his lips were on hers and for a moment she couldn't think at all, didn't want to think, and she allowed herself to kiss him back.

She pulled away. "I–I shouldn't have done that. I don't know what to do. I don't think I can trust you." She turned away. "I need to think."

"You think too much."

"And you don't think enough."

"There. You see. A good match indeed. Together we will think just enough."

His thumb traced her lips and a desire for more than a lifework in medicine began to niggle at her heart. She pushed it away. "I think you should leave now."

"I have an appointment to deliver the spear to the regent. Will you come with me? You've been involved with this strange mission of mine, and I'd like you to see it through with me. Will you come?"

Mercy's curiosity about what would happen once the regent actually had the relic in his possession overpowered her pride. "I will go with you. Not to please you but to satisfy my need to see this through."

"I received a note today from the regent that said the king has been brought to Carlton House. I don't know what he intends to do with the spear. Perhaps wave it over King George like a magic wand."

"Whatever he chooses to do, we both know it will not heal the king."

"It's about time, Lord Eden," the regent said. "I was beginning to think the relic had fallen into criminal hands again." He rose from the chair in the Circular Room, garbed in doeskin breeches and a cream-colored waistcoat that threatened to pop its silver buttons at any moment. A fine coat the color of dark chocolate graced his heavy frame.

"And lucky for you my father still lives. You understand he is here with me at Carlton House, along with my sister, Princess Sophia. Perhaps now we will see how powerful this spear really is."

"Yes, Your Majesty." Eden bowed and kissed the regent's ring. "However, I caution you about getting your hopes up."

"I have no real thoughts or hopes of my father being miraculously healed, Eden. But I cannot ignore the possibility of its other potential. The rumors from Austria are that it protects their country and their king from harm and attack."

"You're risking much and hoping for more, Your Royal Highness," Mercy said, unable to understand how the regent could fall under the spell of a relic.

"Lady Mercy. An unexpected and pleasant surprise. However, this time I do not think my father will need his feet washed."

"I understand, Your Majesty." Mercy curtsied low.

"Give me the spearhead, Lord Eden." The regent held out his bejeweled hand.

Vincent removed the box from a red velvet bag and handed the box to the prince regent.

"We shall soon see what healing powers are available through the influence of the spear." The regent nodded to a guard. A door near them opened. King George III sat in a wheeled chair pushed by a footman. The king's daughter, Princess Sophia, walked by his side.

"Princess Sophia, you've met Lady Mercy and Lord Eden. They've brought the spear."

Vincent again bowed and acknowledged both the king and the princess, and Mercy followed suit with a deep curtsy.

The regent then opened the box and slid the spear from its nesting place. "I don't know what I was expecting, but the spearhead is quite heavy. It does indeed appear to be something a Roman soldier would carry."

Princess Sophia held out her gloved hands. "May I hold it, Your Majesty?" she asked her brother.

He handed it to her. "It's magnificent. Surely this is the real spear Longinus used to pierce the side of Christ."

Vincent watched her marvel over the artifact. "There is no way of knowing or proving this is indeed the same spear, Princess Sophia."

"The Austrians believe. There must be some truth behind the tales of this holy lance." She frowned. "It certainly cannot hurt to see if they are valid."

"How will you decide if they are valid or not?" the regent asked his sister.

"The king shall hold it and we shall pray to God. That should be enough, don't you think?"

The regent shrugged. "Place it into his hands. I am, after all, the supreme governor of the church. You shall join us in prayer, Lord Eden and Lady Mercy."

The princess followed her brother's instructions and wrapped her hands around the king's until he understood that he was to hold the spear. Then she bowed her head and prayed for her father's healing.

"I will keep the Holy Lance in my apartments and well guarded," the regent said. "We shall see if anything good comes of my father's health. And now, Lord Eden, I will keep my part of our agreement. Your ship is in the harbor and at your disposal. It should take you anywhere in the world that you choose to go."

"Thank you, sir. I will use it well."

"Have you chosen a name for ship?" Princess Sophia asked.

"I have. It will be called *Mercy's Way*." He looked at Mercy to see her response.

"But why?" Mercy asked.

"Because it honors God, you, and what I hope to provide to others through my adventures to come."

"But I thought you didn't believe in God. What's changed?"

"My stubborn, bullheaded need to do everything my own way without the help of the Creator, who made my life possible."

The regent looked at him hard. "So you have found your faith."

"I believe I have, sir. Faith is a mystery to me much like the human heart. I have much to learn, but I do believe that it may be my greatest adventure yet. I look forward to it."

"When will you leave on your next journey?" The regent came to stand next to his father and sister.

"I haven't yet decided. However, risking Your Majesty's ire, I would ask that I be allowed to return the Holy Lance to Austria when I do sail from England."

"Humph. You do risk my ire, but I am in a gracious mood today. Therefore all I will say is that I will consider the idea. I never really intended to return the relic. It fascinates me, and I wish to study it further. It is said to have great powers, and I don't see how I can discover those powers if I return it to Austria in the near future."

"I understand." Eden bowed. "We will leave you now. I am anxious to inspect my ship."

"If I may, sir," Mercy said, "might I say my own good-bye to the king? I'm guessing that he and you, Princess Sophia, will return to Windsor soon."

"I think the trip was actually good for my father. We will rest here for two or three days and then return to Windsor, unless of course we change our minds." The princess smiled. "I like London."

"Lady Mercy," said the regent, "I have heard of your recent deception in order to study medicine. You understand that I cannot allow a woman to practice medicine. It's bad enough that I let your brother get away with it, but his abilities have actually proved to be helpful to me, as you know."

"Forgive me, sir. It's been a dream for a long time, and I took risks and harbored secret hopes I shouldn't have. But I pray you will not hold it against me or my family."

"I harbor my own hopes, as you know. I will not condemn you or your family, but you must not attempt to practice medicine. You will not receive a medical degree."

Vincent's heart broke for Mercy. It was his fault this had come to pass. Guilt weighed heavy on his heart.

"May I ask a favor, sir?" Mercy asked. "I learned the skill of applying pressure to different points on the body to encourage healing and relief. May I have your permission to use this skill and midwifery skills in our British Isles?"

"I see no reason why not. We have midwives already, and as long as you don't describe yourself as a physician, you may use your skills to provide healing and relief."

"And may I touch the king behind his neck to lessen what I think would be melancholia for all he has suffered?"

The regent looked to his sister, who nodded.

"You may."

Vincent watched Mercy place her fingers on the back of the king's neck and apply pressure. The king moaned appreciation, and she kept her fingers in place for a couple of minutes. As she leaned over the king, she whispered in his ear.

When she was finished, she looked to the regent and his sister. "Thank you."

"Lord Eden," the regent said, "do not leave England without telling me. I may decide to return the relic to Austria in the near future. However, I find that possibility very doubtful."

"Of course, sir."

"You should be commended on receiving your own ship. You've suffered much to get it," Mercy said as they returned to Lord Eden's coach.

"And what of your suffering? This must be a horrible blow to your hopes and dreams for helping others."

Mercy's vision blurred with tears, but she refused to let him see them. "I can't even think about it at the moment. It's all too much disappointment, though it's exactly what I expected."

"What did you whisper to the king?"

"Remember the words of Christ: 'My peace I leave you.'"

"But they say he cannot hear."

"I spoke the words to his soul."

"He seemed to respond to your touch."

"I pray that touch brought him some peace. It's supposed to relieve the mind of sadness. Still, I don't understand the regent's thinking or that of the princess. Why can't they see that praying to God is enough? The use of the relic is near to idol worship. Princess Sophia puts more faith in the spearhead than she does in our God."

"Perhaps she is just a fearful child, albeit a grown woman, who will do anything within her power to try to save her beloved father. It may not make sense, but there it is," Lord Eden said.

"My chaperones await." Mercy waved to Devlin and Madeline,

whose curricle sat behind Eden's coach. Then she saw Simon with them. "Something is wrong."

"From the expressions on their faces, I'd say you're right."

They quickened their steps. Devlin, Madeline, and Simon hurried forward, closing the distance between them.

"What's happened?" Mercy asked.

Simon Cox, out of breath, said, "The sakpata has escaped."

CHAPTER 27

Fear is pain arising from the
anticipation of evil.
—ARISTOTLE

THE HOUSE AT Number 3 Grosvenor Square contained so many people that Mercy found it difficult to believe they could all understand what the others were saying. Her head ached, and she longed for a breath of fresh air.

"They will want to return to Africa," Eden said. "They came here to find him and take him back. That has become clear, but they have also come to take the African treasures back with them. We need to find Kane and his associate."

Mercy caught Victoria's eye and mouthed the word *outside* to her. They met each other in the back of the house, for it was too crowded with the entire family, Lazarus, and the others to even find their way to the front door.

Yellow pansies smiled up at them as they walked into the moonlit evening. The creamy white petals of hawthorn bushes flecked the path ahead like miniature lanterns. Prim gardens, fragrant with red and pink roses, filled Mercy with a much needed sense of tranquility.

"It's beautiful this evening," Mercy said, looping her arm through Victoria's. "I think they are all making too much of this.

The sakpata and his tribe don't want me. They want to get away from London and return to Africa."

Victoria sighed. "I believe you're right, but the fact that the sakpata was imprisoned in Bedlam cannot be ignored."

"Of course. It's just that I've had two incredibly emotional days. I prefer to go to bed rather than plot to capture an African who practices vodun and his tribe that urgently wants to escape the boundaries of England."

"I'm most ready to retire for the evening, as well." She let go of her sister's arm, and they sat down on a bench near the end of the garden. "My mornings are exhausting now with nausea, and all I really want to do is sleep."

"Why didn't you tell me? I can help you feel better."

"Please do. Why don't you sleep at our house this evening? No one will accost you with Lazarus in the house, and after I get through my dreadful morning with your help, we can talk about what's happened and what you want to do."

Mercy tried desperately to contain the sob that threatened to break free. And then it did, along with the tears of anger and sorrow. She laid her head on Victoria's shoulder and cried.

"Let it all out, Mercy. You're tired and have endured more than any woman should." Victoria opened her beaded reticule, pulled out a handkerchief, and handed it to her sister. Then she pulled out another for herself and indulged her own tears.

"It would appear that I've been dreadfully un-brotherly," Devlin said. "Forgive me." Lazarus padded up behind him. Devlin held out his arms, and both Mercy and Victoria fell into them with Lazarus trying to ingratiate himself among the three of them.

"Here now, blow your noses and wipe your eyes," Devlin said. "Let's go inside. I've sent everyone home but family."

"I want Mercy to stay with me tonight, Dev," Victoria said. "We need some sister time."

He hugged them close. "I'll have the coach brought around for you. I want you both to simply rest this evening."

The clip-clop of the horses' hooves on the cobblestone soothed Mercy's concerns for the moment. She looked forward to staying with Victoria, who sat across from her in the coach, dozing. She must have napped herself because she felt the coach slowing and looked forward to a warm bed.

"Whoa," the driver called. The coach stilled.

"Victoria, we are home," she said and then looked out the window as Victoria awakened. "Wait, this isn't—"

The hatch in the roof of the carriage opened. "Good evening, Lady Mercy, Countess." The masked man held something to his mouth in the darkness, and then a whooshing sound invaded the interior of the coach. Lazarus barked, let out a whimper, and then fell against Mercy's legs.

"Lazarus?" Victoria bent forward to check on him. "What have you done to my dog?"

"Who are you?" Mercy demanded. "Where are our footmen and driver?"

The door to the coach opened, and Mercy was yanked out. A gag was stuffed into her mouth, and she was forced into another coach beside them. There was another whooshing sound, and her eyes widened in the shadowy darkness as she looked into the other coach and watched Victoria slump in her seat. Anger and fear swept through her as her captors forced her to the floor of the coach.

"Where is she?" Devlin pushed past Myron, with Lord Eden following on his heels. "Witt!"

"They are upstairs, my lordships," Myron said. "Dr. Langford is with them."

Devlin and Eden bolted up the stairs, down the hallway, and into the bedroom. "Snoop! Are you all right?"

"They've been drugged, Devlin," Witt said. "Dr. Langford says they'll be fine."

Langford was kneeling over Lazarus, who lay outstretched on the floor in front of the low-burning hearth. The mastiff turned mournful eyes up toward Devlin, as though he had disappointed him in some way.

Devlin hurried to Victoria. "Snoop, what happened? Do you know who it was?"

Eden said, "Where's Lady Mercy?" He paced the room and knelt next to Lazarus for a moment to pet the dog's head.

"They took her," Victoria said weakly. "I'm fine. My shoulder is sore where the dart hit me and I'm tired, but I'm fine and the baby is fine. You must help Mercy. Go!"

Langford said, "They used this on the countess and the dog." He held up the weapon. "It's a dart from a blowgun. It was soaked in some kind of sedative. Luckily it wasn't curare, or they'd be dead."

"Dr. Langford," Eden said, "how did you find Countess Witt and the dog?"

"It wasn't me who found them. The night watch said Simon Cox found them and alerted him. The watchman brought Lord Witt. I stumbled upon the scene on my way home from St. George's Hospital, where I'd been conducting a late-night lecture."

Witt held his wife's hand and looked at Eden and Devlin. "The night watch said Simon was on horseback and headed toward the docks."

"The use of these darts throws suspicion on the Africans," Langford said. "Poisoned darts. It would be in their arsenal of weapons."

"Devlin," Victoria said softly, "there were darts and blowguns on display at the Legend Seekers Club."

"Kane and his partner are mixed up in this," Eden said. "Let's go! We're wasting time."

"I'll stay here with the countess." Langford walked over to where Witt stood. "Go with them. You have two Bow Street men outside."

"My mother, Madeline, and her mother are coming over. They should be here shortly to take charge," Devlin said.

"My Lady Snoop?" Witt said.

"Go, Jonathon. Devlin and Lord Eden will need all the help they can get. And God only knows what Simon has gotten himself into."

Simon tracked the coach to the West India Dock in the Poplar area. He knew the others would be coming, and he didn't want to do anything but keep an eye on what the brutes planned to do with Lady Mercy. He prayed that the Countess Witt and poor Lazarus were going to be all right and thanked God that he'd followed his gut instinct to follow the coach back to Berkeley Square. The devils had picked the footmen off the coach faster than he could eat a piece of pie. The driver was the last to be plucked. All had been drugged with darts and hidden behind shrubbery, while others took their places. Very clever.

"Son of a gun," whispered Simon as he followed the coach to a nearby dock where a vast clipper ship had maneuvered into the Thames. "They're leaving port now, with Lady Mercy on board."

Eden cursed their luck when a street riot broke out ahead of them. "Can we get around them?"

"Perhaps," Witt said, "but it doesn't look good. It's another protest against the regent. Let's stay to the far left and move as fast as we can without putting the horses in danger."

"Come on." Devlin reined his gelding in tight as broken bottles and knives glinted in the moonlight.

The tide of men who entered the streets pushed against them, carrying them in the opposite direction they needed to go. Horses and riders were trapped by a wall of humanity that had other plans, and all the men could do was try to keep from harm and stay mounted.

When they finally reached the docks near the West India Trading Company on the Isle of Dogs, the only thing they heard was the shifting and creaking of the ships bobbing at anchor and the lapping of water against the pier. "We don't even know where on the docks they could be, if in fact they're still here. The docks spread out a good four miles on either side," Eden said.

"There's no sign of Simon or anyone from Bow Street. But if Simon followed them, he's here somewhere. Let's ride east for a while," Devlin said. "If it was Kane and he was fool enough to leave tonight, he'd be headed into the North Sea."

"If it was the Africans," Witt said, "they may have to steal a ship or hide on another vessel to escape. Where are we going to start?"

"Let's ride east till we get more information," Devlin said again. The three stayed close to the banks of the Thames, watching, listening. Up ahead the One-Eyed Whale, a pub favored by sailors, filled the night with rowdy laughter, bawdy jokes, and multiple loud and raucous toasts by its patrons to themselves, each other, and the women there whom they propositioned and fought over.

"I thought you'd never get here." Simon slipped off a chair and hurried to them. "Tell me the countess and Lazarus are going to be well?"

"Thanks to you," Witt said. "Tell us what happened. Did you see anything?"

"I wouldn't be sitting here if I didn't know what happened. Problem is I couldn't do anything."

Eden placed his hands on Simon's shoulders. "Did you see Mercy? Is she all right?"

"It's Kane. I had no way of stopping him and the ship, but I did watch, and they do have Mercy."

"How long ago did they sail?" Devlin asked. "My sister's life is at stake. We need to follow as soon as possible."

"Two hours. The ship was ready to sail when he arrived with your sister. I think John Marks, his partner, organized the readying of the ship. He seemed to know what he was doing."

"I want this man, Simon," Witt said. "Did you notice anything else?"

"I don't know how much it will help, but I've got the coach he left behind. I knew you'd follow me to the docks, but I didn't know if I should wait or return. Knowing you'd head toward the sea to search, I took my chances."

"Show us where the coach is and where they entered the Thames. Let's go," Eden said, hitting the door so hard with his hand that it came off one hinge.

They scoured the coach like ants at a picnic. "Nothing!" Vincent raged. "We don't know their course. How are we supposed to find them?" He scrubbed his face with his hands and tried to calm himself enough to think clearly.

The boy guarding the coach per Simon's request watched them curiously.

"What's your name, boy?" Vincent asked.

"Jack, yer lordship."

"I don't suppose you saw anything unusual this evening. Did you?"

"Not 'ere. Wat's usual 'ere is mostly unusual, yer lordships."

"What do you mean, Jack?" Simon asked.

"From all the jabber 'em black men be makin' whiles creep'n' up the sides o' that ship it's 'ard to know wat's usual, if'n ye take me meanin'."

Simon took the boy by the lapels of his jacket and shook him so hard his hat fell to the ground. "Do you mean to tell me that you saw the Africans steal upon a ship I told you about, and you didn't tell me?"

"Ye didn't ask."

Vincent spun the boy toward him. "I'll give you this half crown—" He held up the silver coin. "—if you tell us every detail about what you saw and heard here tonight. And leave nothing out."

"Gore! 'alf a crown?" Jack said, nearly foaming at the mouth.

Vincent nodded while the others gathered around the boy. "Go on. It's important."

"I was 'ungry and look'n' for food. I heard men comin' and was gonna ask 'em for somethin' ta eat, but I got scared. They was big black men. Painted up faces too. One man looked more white 'en black with a big nose, wide like, and he led 'em past where I 'id say'n' they was goin' ta 'omey. They looked round and then slipped into the Thames like a bunch o' snakes, and hauled 'emselves over the side of the ship, they did."

Devlin let out his breath. "They're going to Dahomey, Africa. But I don't think Kane knows they're on the ship, from what the boy says."

"At least now we know what direction they took," Eden said, handing the boy the half crown.

"What happened after that?" Witt asked and knelt down, giving the boy another half crown.

His brown eyes widened. "Gore! It's me lucky night." He took a deep breath and continued. "I 'eard a coach comin', so I runs and 'id behind them barrels." He pointed toward a wall. "They 'ad a woman tied up and gagged, but she was kickin' and makin' noise good."

"What did they do with her?" Devlin asked.

The boy looked up at him expectantly, and Devlin couldn't help but smile. Then he arched a brow. "What did they do with her, Jack?"

He looked disappointed, but then he smiled back and said, "They put 'er in a boat and rowed 'er out ta the ship."

"Did she appear to be hurt?" Vincent asked.

Jack shook his head. "No, yer lordship." He grinned, showing a row of crooked teeth. "Just madder than a wasp that's been stepped on."

"What do we do now?" Simon asked.

Vincent picked up a stone and threw it into the Thames, since there was nothing around he could hit. "Go after them."

"What do you think you're doing?" Mercy spat out when Kane removed the gag from her mouth in the cabin where she'd been tossed the night before. "What did you do to my sister and the dog? I swear I'll see you hang if—"

"They'll live. It was only a secret recipe to knock them out. I couldn't have them get in the way of our future together, now, could I?"

Grateful that God had protected Victoria and Lazarus, her anger toward Kane erupted. "You are deluded if you think you have a future. My family will not rest until they find us."

"Ah, but they won't find us. We've a good head start, and they have no idea where we are going. So you see there is nothing to concern yourself about." He put his hand behind her head and pulled her close for a quick kiss. "Nothing to worry about."

She hid her revulsion and knew she had to keep her wits about her. "Why did you take me?" She wanted answers, and she wanted to find a way to keep him in the cabin until she could think of a way to gain more freedom aboard the ship.

Kane grinned. "I've been following you since I first saw you in Scotland. I believe you were at the theater with your aunt. I knew then that you would be my wife."

"Your wife? I never saw you in Scotland. It was a man named John Marks who discovered my secret and stalked me. He attended my classes at the university."

"Marks was my rather reluctant partner. I rescued him from a slave ship and taught him how to make money. He's in my debt. I asked him to keep an eye on you, and that's when he discovered you were disguising yourself as a man to study medicine."

"But he was attending lectures from the very beginning. He couldn't have known, and neither could you."

"That was fate. He wanted to learn more of medicine to take back information that might help his missionary parents. They reject vodun healing, and his father is not well."

"His parents are missionaries? But you said he was aboard a slave ship. I don't understand." She pushed against the wall, trying to untie the knots that bound her hands.

"The sun is hot in Africa, and John Marks was quite dark there. However, his skin color eventually faded in the climate of Scotland, which allowed him to attend medical school. He grew up with the Africans and even looked like one. That's why he was on board the slave ship. His ability to communicate with the Africans who searched for their healer was convenient for a while. Unfortunately I had to leave them behind, but I have their treasures in the cargo hold of this ship. Those items will make us rich after the journey I have planned, but you can rest assured we will not be going to Africa. Perhaps the Canary Islands for a while and then on to America."

"But I never even saw you until the night of the Legend Seekers Club lecture." Mercy fought the panic that gripped her.

"That evening almost worked. But it was your sister and not you who entered the basement with Lord Eden. He wants you, but he's not going to have you. I tried to keep you in Scotland. The night you fled to the ship, Agbe threw you overboard to protect you from me. He believes he has magical powers over the sea, and I wondered if he doesn't after you made it to the coast of England. By all rights you should be dead."

"That was you? On the ship? I thought it was John Marks. Why? Why do you want me to marry you?"

"Because I'm a treasure hunter, my dear, and when I choose a particular treasure that I want to go after, I always get it. Always."

"Not this time."

Mercy watched as John Marks raised a pistol to Kane's head. "It's time to go up on deck."

Kane turned a vicious glare on Marks. "What's the meaning of this? Where did you come from?"

"You should have searched the ship before you set sail with your crew, Kane. Now, as I said, it's time to go on deck. You too, Lady Mercy. I'm sorry."

Two of the Africans took Kane by the arms. Two others pulled her to her feet but didn't bother to untie her hands. She recognized one of them as Fox, the one who first approached her when he thought she was a boy after Lord Eden had cut her hair and disguised her.

On deck the wind whipped over her and the sea splashed its spittle in her face. "What are you going to do?"

The African with the giant serpent around his neck stepped from behind the others with the sakpata, his brother, by his side. There must have been twenty of them. The serpent turned its head toward her and hissed. Agbe said something to her in a language she could not understand.

She looked at John Marks and asked again, "What are you going to do?"

He came to her and turned her shoulders out toward the sea. "They are here for you. We must go. Tell them not to follow. Kane must face tribal justice."

She looked at Marks and then Kane's terror-struck face. Suddenly the ropes around her hands were cut, Agbe raised his face toward the men holding her, and she knew she was about to be tossed overboard, again. But Kane broke loose and rammed into her, knocking the breath from her. Both splashed into the sea.

CHAPTER 28

That their hearts might be comforted, being
knit together in love, and unto all riches
of the full assurance of understanding, to
the acknowledgement of the mystery of
God, and of the Father, and of Christ.
—COLOSSIANS 2:2

EDEN AND THE others broke onto the North Sea in pursuit of Kane's ship at the break of dawn the next morning. The ship the regent had given to Eden had just been completed at Blackwall, near the north end of the docks. She was a beauty, and she was fast!

When Eden had sent a message to the regent telling him what had happened, the regent gave him the use of the sailors he would need. These were men experienced at naval combat and skilled in pursuing an enemy at sea.

Standing on the starboard bow with full sails above them and a beautiful sea in front of them, Devlin asked Eden, "How far ahead of us do you think they are?"

"It's hard to know. The wind was at their back last night. It's slowed a bit today, but I believe our ship to be superior to what I've heard of Kane's ship, the *Voyager*, which is good. The fact that the Africans are onboard is in our favor, as well—until Kane discovers he's been tricked. Then there is no way to know what lengths he may go to or what irrational decisions he may choose in the heat of anger and powerlessness."

Hours later they heard the shout from the crow's nest: "Ship ho!"

"Is it the *Voyager*?" Eden shouted. "Captain Mahan, is it Kane?"

Mahan directed his spyglass toward the ship. "Aye, it is. Have a look."

"Bear down on that vessel, Captain Mahan."

"Aye, Lord Eden."

Within half an hour they were alongside Kane's *Voyager* but far enough away to avoid colliding. "You'd better take a look at this, Lord Eden," the captain said, handing Vincent his spyglass.

When Vincent focused the glass on the other ship, his gut clenched. He dropped the spyglass, ran to the edge of the ship's bow, and dove overboard.

The sea, cold and choppy all around him, did not prevent him from swimming his fastest. Fear propelled him forward. Where was she?

He went under again, feeling his way through the water, hoping and praying to grasp hold of her. Surfacing, he screamed, "Mercy!"

Nothing. He couldn't see her. Couldn't find her. "Please, God, please help me!"

Then Kane surfaced with Mercy fighting in his arms. "You can't have her, Eden. She's mine!"

Mercy looked at Eden and then turned in Kane's arms and bit his cheek.

"You witch!" He let go and slapped her.

In the next moment he disappeared under the waves when a dart hit him in the neck.

Vincent glanced up at the Africans. Fox had just lowered a blowgun.

Mercy reached out to Eden, and he pulled her into his arms and kissed her. “You will marry me.” He kissed her again.

“Yes, I will.” She smiled and kissed him back.

Epilogue

St. George's Church, July 17, 1819

Mercy looked into Vincent's eyes, those two dancing, different-colored eyes, and almost laughed with happiness. She wasn't nervous like some silly brides, nor was she afraid of the wedding night to come. *I am my beloved's, and my beloved is mine...*

"Dearly beloved," began the priest, "we are gathered together here in the sight of God, and in the face of this congregation, to join together this Man and this Woman in holy Matrimony; which is an honourable estate, instituted of God in the time of man's innocency, signifying unto us the mystical union that is betwixt Christ and His Church; which holy estate Christ adorned and beautified with His presence, and first miracle that He wrought, in Cana of Galilee; and is commended of Saint Paul to be honourable among all men: and therefore is not by any to be enterprised, nor taken in hand, unadvisedly, lightly, or wantonly, to satisfy men's carnal lusts and appetites, like brute beasts that have no understanding; but reverently, discreetly, advisedly, soberly, and in the fear of God; duly considering the causes for which Matrimony was ordained."

Mercy and Vincent's marriage vows echoed through St.

George's Church. "I love you, Countess Eden," Vincent whispered into her ear after the brief ceremony. "I will always love you."

Devlin and Madeline, Jonathon and Victoria, Dr. Langford, the dowager Countess Ravensmoore, and the dowager Countess Richfield encircled the couple and hugged and blessed them with hopes and prayers for a wonderful future.

"I still can't believe the regent and Princess Sophia are honoring us with our wedding breakfast at Carlton House," Mercy said. "It's an incredible gesture of goodwill."

Vincent grabbed her hand and pulled her toward the front of the church. "Well, let's not keep them waiting. I'm starving." He laughed and kissed his bride again.

Bright sunshine and the shouts from well-wishers greeted them outside the church. "It's wonderful," Mercy said, smiling. Her wedding gown of pearl silk and lace shimmered. The hat of matching silk and a short veil served to cover her still short hair that she'd come to enjoy. But the necklace was her favorite—her mother's emerald necklace that she'd used to pay off her blackmailer in Scotland. That blackmailer had been Kane. Now the emeralds were a wedding gift from Vincent. He'd refused to tell her how he'd recovered them. "A treasure hunter's secret," he grinned. That was all he'd reveal.

Her husband threw coins into the crowd, and everyone scrambled to claim them, especially the children. "Good morning, Countess Eden, Lord Eden," Mac said from atop the coach.

"Good morning, Mac."

Mercy could see a number of coaches lined up to get everyone to Carlton House. It would be a day of happiness she would never forget. A footman lowered the steps, and Vincent assisted Mercy into the coach.

They were made so welcome at Carlton House that Mercy felt like royalty herself. The Blue Room was decorated with bouquets of exotic flowers. A group of musicians playing the pianoforte and stringed instruments greeted them with beautiful strains from Mozart. Ham and chicken and pastries covered the breakfast tables, along with fresh strawberries, and coffee, tea, and chocolate to drink. Warm bread, eggs and bacon, and white soup surrounded a wedding cake with white icing, sugared rose petals, and a bouquet of roses decorating the top.

The regent and Princess Sophia entered the room, wishing them well. "We want this to be very special for you, so please enjoy yourselves," the regent said in a rare show of graciousness.

"Thank you for this wonderful wedding breakfast, Your Majesty, Your Royal Highness," Vincent said, and he bowed deeply while Mercy curtsied, holding onto her husband's hand.

Mercy smiled. "It is more than gracious of you. Everything is so lovely."

"You only get one wedding if you're fortunate, and it should be spectacular. Now go enjoy your wedding day, and we will talk with you later."

"I'd love to dance with you, Countess Eden," Devlin said and then looked to Vincent. "That is permissible this day, brother?" He smiled and whisked her away before getting a response.

"You are lovely, Mercy. I'm going to miss you."

"And you are still ornery, my big brother. I'm not living that far from Yorkshire."

"I hope you haven't forgotten what an adventurer you've married. He's not likely to give up his need to wander, at least not for a while, I would think."

"Well, we leave for a long wedding adventure tomorrow, as you know. But we won't stay away forever."

"I've never been to Egypt. I imagine you will come back with many stories for us. You know we are always here for you, my little sister."

Tears filled her eyes, and the knowledge that she was going to miss her family terribly filled her heart. "I will miss all of you. More than you know."

"I'm sorry you didn't get your medical degree. I know how much you wanted it. I really do."

"Well, if anyone knows that desire, it is you, Dev. But God has a plan. I wish He'd let me know what it is, but I'll try to be patient. I can't believe He's put this yearning in my heart just to sweep it away."

Now Vincent interrupted. "Pardon me, brother. I'd like to dance with my wife." He took Mercy in his arms and twirled her about the room.

"Aren't you handsome," she said.

"If there weren't so many people I'd kiss you again right now."

She smiled up into his mysteriously colored eyes. "We could dance out onto the terrace for a moment."

He whisked her through the door, where a footman stood, and stopped to kiss her. "Did I tell you I love you?"

"Yes, you did, but I'm not tired of hearing it." She looked at the footman and tilted her head back toward the Blue Room. "We'd better return."

"If you insist."

Everyone was dancing when they went back. Even her mother was dancing with Dr. Langford. Madeline looked perfect in Devlin's arms, and Victoria simply glowed as she waltzed with Jonathon. Madeline's mother was dancing with the regent, while his sister looked on with delight.

When the waltz ended, everyone headed to the tables to eat, while the orchestra played a softer more romantic piece. And then to Mercy's surprise, the regent approached her and took her hand. "I need you for a moment, Countess Eden."

"Of course," she said, setting her teacup on the table.

He walked her out onto the floor and asked the orchestra to stop playing with a mere nod of his head. "I have an announcement."

The room immediately fell silent.

"I have been in deep conversation with my sister, Princess Sophia. And as a wedding gift, if you choose to accept it, I have decided to grant you permission to practice medicine in New South Wales, Australia, Lady Eden. I will help you establish your practice if you so desire."

Looking at her family, Mercy didn't know how to react. Her heart leaped for a moment and then she smothered the thought. "I don't understand, Your Majesty."

"It's simple. After your wedding journey is over, you and your adventurer husband can begin a new adventure. He can explore a new land and you can practice medicine. If you are bold enough, you can practice all you wish on the prisoners of Botany Bay. The families making homes there might welcome you. The politics of the Exclusives and Emancipists will keep you engaged with the problems of society, and you may find you like it there."

Devlin jumped to his feet. "No! Botany Bay is a penal colony. It's too dangerous."

"But life is changing there, Lord Ravensmoore," the regent said. "It would give both the countess and earl an opportunity and adventure. It's up to them." He turned his attention to Mercy and Vincent. "Will you consider it?"

Mercy said, "My husband and I will consider it while we are away on our wedding trip." She whispered to Vincent and he nodded. "We will return from Egypt to England to visit our families, and then we will announce our decision."

"We appreciate your thoughtfulness," Vincent said to the regent, "but a decision of that significance deserves much thought, as my wife has stated. We also must consider the distance from those we love."

"But what of your dream to become a doctor?" Princess Sophia asked.

"I'll not give it up," Mercy said. "I know God has called me to practice medicine. I will have to be patient and see where my calling leads. If England will not have me practice here, then I think we will have to journey to New South Wales if the regent is giving us his blessing."

"The offer is there for you to accept or reject as you see fit, Countess and Lord Eden. Now let us continue with the celebration at hand."

The following morning Mercy and Vincent stood on the deck of *Mercy's Way* and waved good-bye to her family. Later, as they broke onto the North Sea and looked out onto the ocean and their new lives together, Vincent wrapped his arms around her.

Shivers of joy and the promise of God's fulfillment for her life overwhelmed her. Still holding her, Vincent turned her to face him. "I will always love you," he said. He kissed her on the forehead and then pressed his lips to hers for all eternity.

Note From the Author

Dear Reader,

I hope you have enjoyed *Mystery of the Heart*. I appreciate that you spent your valuable time escaping into the past with me to explore the world of Regency England and the characters I populated it with who struggle with their own flaws and challenges, much as we do today.

In a world where many things can so easily become idols that distract and pull us away from spending time with God, I hope this story creates a hunger in you, as it did in Lord Eden, to get to know God better.

I've always been interested in the study of archeology. While I was visiting my local library one day I came across a video about the Spear of Destiny from Brad Meltzer's *Decoded* program on The History Channel. I wanted to learn more, and that sparked the flame for this story. I then read the book by the same name written by Trevor Ravenscroft. Later I saw an episode of *The Librarian* with Noah Wyle called "Quest for the Spear." I really didn't know what to make of all this, so I decided to write my own story.

I had also never studied West African vodun, nor do I claim to be an expert on the subject even after the extensive research I conducted. Be aware there are different spellings and different practices within the vodun culture. Magic is utilized for good and evil. In America we know this religious practice as voodoo.

Mercy pursued the passion of her heart. I pray each of you will do the same and seek God's wisdom as you follow your dreams. May God richly bless you and give you the courage to ask Him for direction as in James 1:5: "If any of you lack wisdom, let him ask of God, that giveth to all men liberally, and upbraideth not; and it shall be given him."

This book concludes The Ravensmoore Chronicles at least for now. I don't know if I will return to write more stories about this very special family or not, but I know they will stay with me for a long time. And I hope their adventures will remain alive in your mind for a while to come as well.

GRATEFULLY,
JILLIAN KENT